Focus on Love

by Candee Fick

Bling!
Romance
Lighthouse Publishing of the Carolinas

FOCUS ON LOVE BY CANDEE FICK
Published by Bling! Romance
an imprint of Lighthouse Publishing of the Carolinas
2333 Barton Oaks Dr., Raleigh, NC, 27614

ISBN: 978-1-946016-41-6
Copyright © 2018 by Candee Fick
Cover design by Elaina Lee
Interior design by AtriTeX Technologies P Ltd

Available in print from your local bookstore, online, or from the publisher at: ShopLPC.com

For more information on this book or its author, visit: https://www.candeefick.com.

All rights reserved. Noncommercial interests may reproduce portions of this book without the express written permission of Lighthouse Publishing of the Carolinas, provided the text does not exceed 500 words. When reproducing text from this book, include the following credit line: "*Focus on Love* by Candee Fick, published by Lighthouse Publishing of the Carolinas. Used by permission."

Commercial interests: No part of this publication may be reproduced in any form, stored in a retrieval system, or transmitted in any form by any means—electronic, photocopy, recording, or otherwise—without prior written permission of the publisher, except as provided by the United States of America copyright law.

This is a work of fiction. Names, characters, and incidents are all products of the author's imagination or are used for fictional purposes. Any mentioned brand names, places, and trademarks remain the property of their respective owners, bear no association with the author or the publisher, and are used for fictional purposes only.

Scripture quotations are taken from the HOLY BIBLE NEW INTERNATIONAL VERSION ®. NIV® Copyright © 1973, 1978, 1984 by International Bible Society. Used by permission of Zondervan Publishing House. All rights reserved.

Scripture quotations from The Authorized (King James) Version. Rights in the Authorized Version in the United Kingdom are vested in the Crown. Reproduced by permission of the Crown's patentee, Cambridge University Press.

Brought to you by the creative team at Lighthouse Publishing of the Carolinas:
Marisa Deshaies, Managing Editor
Connie Troyer, General Editor
Brian Cross, Judah Raine, and Jennifer Leo, Proofreaders

Library of Congress Cataloging-in-Publication Data
Fick, Candee
Focus on Love / Candee Fick 1st ed.

Printed in the United States of America.

PRAISE FOR *FOCUS ON LOVE*

What a perfectly titled story! Candee Fick gives her fans more than the sweet romance they've grown to expect from her by crafting a story of love in all its aspects. Readers will rejoice as they watch the heroine discover the true meaning of love—the love a family shares, the love friends provide, the love between a man and a woman, and—most of all—the love that God offers us, if only we'll accept it. If you enjoy Christian romance, you won't want to miss *Focus on Love*.

~Amanda Cabot, CBA and ECPA bestselling author

Candee Fick continues to tug at our hearts as we return to the Wardrobe Dinner Theatre in her contemporary romance *Focus on Love*. This beautifully crafted story offers the reader a glimpse into photography's creative passion, a sustaining gift that helps overcome rejection and betrayal with faith, hope, and most definitely, love. Through the snapshots of her past and the brilliant photography of her present, Liz finds that God's love never left her—He's offering her more than she ever dreamed.

~Audra Harders
Bestselling author of *Second Chance Ranch*

A beautiful story of chasing dreams and taking chances. I couldn't stop turning pages! With relatable characters you can't help but root for, *Focus on Love* is a novel with so much heart.

~Brandy Bruce
Author of *The Last Summer*

In *Focus on Love*, Candee Fick takes readers on a journey of love, faith, and self-discovery. With a love of God woven throughout the story, Fick invites us to join Liz and Ryan as they learn lessons about forgiveness, love, and life. You won't be disappointed. 5 stars!

~Jane Choate
Author of *Shattered Secrets*

A picture-perfect romance that is completely in focus. I couldn't put this book down! I had to keep reading. I fell in love with Ryan and Liz and I wanted them to achieve their goals. This is a book for romance lovers to devour as they flip through the pages.

~Laura V. Hilton
Author of *Love by the Numbers*

Acknowledgments

Once again, this dream did not become reality without the support of a team.

I'd first like to thank my husband, Clint, and my family as a whole for allowing me to pursue my dream of writing. Thanks for putting up with a dusty house and simple meals while I spent hours daydreaming, writing, rewriting, and wrestling through edits in addition to marketing, social media, and other business-y things.

To my longtime critique partner, Laura Hilton, thanks for pushing me to be a better writer and showing me how through your stories. Thanks also to the members of my launch team and other readers—your "can't wait to read your next book" has been the perfect incentive to plant myself in front of my computer and talk to imaginary people day after day.

To Marisa Deshaies, thank you for leading the Bling! team so well and allowing me the opportunity to share this story with the world. Thanks also to Connie Troyer for your amazing insight during the editing process as you and Marisa helped make this story sparkle and shine. Thanks to the rest of the Bling! team for the finishing touches.

And to the crowning jewel, the giver of gifts and imparter of dreams. I thank God every day for the gift of stories and His unending faithfulness to supply all that I need.

Dedication

*To Sandie Bricker, my first fiction editor, for opening the door.
I know you are dancing in heaven with the
One who gave you hope and a future.*

The Lord your God is with you, he is mighty to save.
He will take great delight in you,
he will quiet you with his love,
he will rejoice over you with singing.

~Zephaniah 3:17

Prologue

Elizabeth Foster ripped the Christmas wrapping paper from the box on her lap. It wasn't heavy enough to be the camera she'd asked for, but when she lifted the lid, she grinned regardless.

"These are great." She ran her hand over the FOSTER'S FOTOS design on the front pocket of the royal-blue shirts inside. Not the first color she would have chosen as a redhead, but she'd wear anything if it meant stepping into the family business as the third generation of photographers—to finally build on the foundation Grandpa O'Neill began when her mother was a child. To be who Liz was meant to be. "And you even used my logo design."

"Your design? No, Jerry came up with that." Dad rocked back on his heels from his position near the fireplace. "Isn't it great? Thanks to your recommendation, he's been quite a talented addition to the company."

Liz's eyes darted to Jerry on the other end of the couch—and his smug expression. Merely an hour ago, she'd awkwardly endured his monotone proposition, er, proposal: *"Let's merge our talents. I can do even more professionally if you're behind me."* He'd claimed it was an offer she couldn't refuse. Except she had refused ... and now this. Fueled by her ideas—the creative brainstorming she'd shared via e-mail and Skype calls this semester—her long-distance boyfriend had ambitiously climbed the ladder from intern to more.

Dad chuckled. "Told you she'd be speechless. Bet this will change her mind about a wedding, son."

Liz's face heated. "Son? No, he's a thief. I showed him this very logo idea a month ago." While she'd been off at college, he had apparently been stealing her family's affection too. How could she have been so blind?

"Now, now, dear. You're just confused. The stress of your classes must be getting to you." Jerry had the gall to reach over and pat her arm as if she were a toddler in need of comforting. He glanced at her dad. "I showed her an early sketch back in October."

Liz pulled away from Jerry's hand and took a deep breath, and then another, to calm herself. It would be unforgivable to cause a scene before the elaborate holiday dinner her mother had fixed. She'd already caught a glimpse of her grandmother's wedding china on the dining room table ... four place settings' worth.

Another deep breath in through her nose and slowly released...

At least she'd finally seen Jerry's true colors. But was it too late to fight for her place? If she needed to stay, completing her degree would have to wait.

She squared her shoulders and faced her dad. "Logo designer aside, do these shirts mean I can finally start working with you? Because I'd love to see us expand into new areas and revamp our website."

Dad waved a hand dismissively. "Jerry's full of ideas for doing all that. What we really need is office support."

More of Jerry's words came flooding back to her. *You don't need a business degree to answer the phones and stuff envelopes.* Liz's stomach clenched along with her fists.

Better to know the truth than to cling to hope. "Are you ever going to give me a chance to step behind the camera?"

"That's ridiculous. You can't handle this kind of job on your own. It's a shame your grandparents encouraged those foolish dreams." Dad shook his head. "Besides, a woman's place is in the home, or at least supporting her husband in practical matters."

With "those" dreams shattering into a thousand pieces around her, Liz tossed the box of shirts onto the coffee table and stood. "What I can't handle is *this* right now." She headed toward the doorway to the kitchen. Hopefully Mom wouldn't be too upset if she—

"Just where do you think you're going? We are not finished discussing this."

Tears flooded her eyes as she turned back to face her frowning father. "Why can't you understand? I just want to use the talents God gave me—to see the beauty in the world and share my joy with others. To do more than take pictures of snotty-nosed kids."

"Those school pictures pay the bills, and it's about time you grew up and started contributing around here."

Rage at the injustice dried her tears. "That's what I've been trying to do, except that you would rather listen to the lies of an outsider than the truth from your own daughter. He probably stole the rest of—"

"Enough!" Dad's bellowing voice punctuated the vicious slice of his hand through the air. "This is my house, and you will not speak poorly of our guest and my new business partner. Submit to my authority and apologize, or else you are no longer welcome here."

A gasp behind her echoed the stabbing wound in her chest while Jerry smirked from his relaxed position on the couch. Liz spun on her heel, then rushed past wide-eyed Mom and up the stairs toward her bedroom, chased by Dad's final diatribe about rebellion being like witchcraft and God reserving a place in hell for the devil worshippers.

Liz slammed her bedroom door. No way could she spend another minute around the man—men—who had betrayed her, let alone another night under this roof. Even if it was Christmas, she'd head back to campus and stay at a friend's apartment for a few days until the dorms opened up again. *Sorry, Mom.*

Upending the laundry basket, she dumped her clothes onto the heap still sitting in the suitcase she'd left on the floor. With most of her belongings already at college, what else did she need?

On the bookshelf nearby, Liz spotted the camera Grandpa O'Neill had given her on her twelfth birthday—back when he'd talked about her taking his place in the studio. Back before a fatal stroke turned the running of the business over to his son-in-law, her father, with the slow transition to packages of school pictures. She shoved the camera and case into the bottom of her backpack along with a few books of her photographs.

Sorry, Grandpa. Dad killed the dream. From now on, it's just a hobby.

She glanced around the room, her eyes skipping over the Confirmation Bible sitting on the nightstand as her stomach churned. What kind of God would let this happen?

Grandma's framed painting on the wall above her bed soon found a home in the cradle of clothing inside her suitcase, a precious memento from Liz's fourteenth birthday before a heart attack reunited her grandparents in heaven. She paused to run a finger over the image of a young dancer swirling in joy in the middle of a gorgeous park, which had been divided into quarters on the canvas to show the beauty of the seasons. Grandma had said the girl reminded her of Liz and her spontaneity, but the scenery inspired other creativity, as Liz taught herself to see life through a camera lens.

Only two things had ever given her that sense of deep joy and freedom: dance classes with Grandma and photography with Grandpa. She paused a moment in thought. If she couldn't take photography into her future, perhaps she could recapture the joy of the stage instead, to fill the gigantic hole she felt.

Liz gathered a few stray items before zipping the suitcase shut as she pondered the possibilities. What if she dusted off her dancing shoes and auditioned for the theater department's spring production? Nothing said she couldn't also change her major and hide her broken heart behind the mask of a fictional character.

Liz nodded as she shouldered her backpack and picked up her purse.

It was time to pursue a new dream.

Chapter One

Almost three years later

Liz grabbed the potential offer like the lifeline it was. "Yes, Mr. Sheridan. I'll do it."

"You haven't even heard the details." The Wardrobe Dinner Theatre's director smiled, and his green eyes twinkled. "But I assume your enthusiasm means that you don't have any employment plans after Sunday, when *42nd Street* ends?"

"No, sir. I still haven't been able to find another job." And not for a lack of trying.

"Well, Liz, it just so happens that we're in need of another actress for *White Christmas* and would like to extend your current contract through December. We can take it from there later."

She cleared her throat. "Thank you." Liz leaned against the front of the stage, vaguely aware of other cast and band members mingling around the lower level of the auditorium, as her boss spoke about getting her a script and scheduling a few extra rehearsals before the new show opened the day after Thanksgiving.

Instead of the usual three weeks of rehearsals, she'd have just over a week to learn the show before opening night ... but at least the other girls could help her back at their shared apartment. And any job involving the theater was worth the extra effort.

Actually, any job at all.

"Still think you can handle it?" Mr. Sheridan broke into her musing.

"I'll do my best."

"That's all I can ask." He reached out to shake her hand. "Glad to have you back on board." He checked his watch. "If you'll excuse me, I have some things to check on before our pre-put-in review in a half hour." In addition to preparing for the next show, the sudden loss of an actress also meant blocking adjustments for the current production.

As he walked away, Liz moved on shaky legs to claim a seat at a nearby table before sucking in several deep breaths. To be rescued only four days away from unemployment meant she didn't have to slink home after all. The thought left her lightheaded with relief. It was an answer to prayer even if she hadn't been the one doing the asking.

A burst of giggles pulled her attention to the right just in time to catch her former boyfriend whispering into the ear of his future costar before pulling her close for a lingering kiss.

Liz stood and headed for the stairs.

The only good thing about leaving at the end of *42nd Street*'s run had been not having to watch Trent the Traitor's defection in person.

While Jerry the Jerk had used her to open the door to a business opportunity, Trent had only wanted the convenience of a girlfriend inside the theater company. The moment Liz's name had been missing from the *White Christmas* cast list, he'd started looking for a new flame.

Liz felt so foolish for being used by another loser. She held back her redheaded impulse to punch something and squared her shoulders instead.

Why waste her energy on what might have been when she'd just been handed a second chance?

On the second level, Liz passed a cluster of actors who were eagerly dissecting the past hour's juicy revelations that there had been a thief among them ... and claiming to have always known something was not quite right about their coworker. Just yesterday, the same people had targeted Liz's roommate, Dani, with their rumors and accusations. Yet today's sudden eviction of the thief from the company was the very reason Liz now had a contract extension.

Liz half jogged toward the exit, desperately craving a breath of fresh air outside the circle of egos jockeying for position like politicians on a campaign trail. She could do without the backstage "show biz" drama for a few minutes.

Pushing through the auditorium doors into the lobby, Liz glanced around. To her left, her roommate hugged various members of the Sheridan family while their trumpet-playing, orchestra-leader son watched. Liz's heart clenched as Alex's eyes never left Dani. While she could rejoice with Dani that her boyfriend was back in town, when would her own turn come? Would a guy ever see her heart and talents and love her for herself? Or desire to give her the world instead of taking her dreams away?

Liz rolled her eyes and turned from the sentimental scene. Better to focus on the blessings in her life, especially the miracle of having a job to pay the bills and keep her in Colorado.

The outside door opened then, and a tall man in a flannel shirt and blue jeans entered. He removed his tan cowboy hat as he strode toward the empty box office. Since another quick glance to her left confirmed that Mrs.

Sheridan was still occupied with her family, Liz detoured to the right to greet the visitor.

"Hello, and welcome to the Wardrobe. What can I do for you?"

The stranger ran a hand through his dark hair, ruffling the imprint of the hat band, as he glanced around the room with equally dark eyes. "I didn't think there would be so many people here today."

"It's true that we don't have a show tonight, since it's a Wednesday, but the cast still has rehearsals." Rehearsals she was officially part of again.

"You look happy." The man's intense gaze swept over her face, and she resisted the urge to squirm when he nodded as if he had her figured out.

"I just got a miracle. Didn't think God did those anymore, at least for me." She really needed to thank Dani for praying.

The man smiled, and the serious expression on his face transformed into a look of one who enjoyed life. Laugh lines emerged beside his eyes, along with a deep dimple to the right of a crooked smile reminiscent of Grandpa O'Neill. "I believe He's got a few more miracles up His sleeve. At least I hope so. Actually, that's why I'm here."

"Are you an actor?" With this handsome man around, the theater could get interesting.

His eyes widened in surprise and then shifted toward the ticket window with its display of show posters. "No."

"Oh, right. Never mind." If she hadn't been so distracted by his smile, she'd have remembered where they stood. "If you're looking for tickets to opening night of *White Christmas* next Friday, you're in luck. We still have a few seats available if you're not too picky about where you sit."

"Not that. I'm setting up a business in town…"

"Business?" Liz eyed his worn Wranglers and green flannel shirt open over a white T-shirt. The charmer with the amazing smile couldn't be that much older than her, maybe in his late twenties. "I'm not sure the theater needs a cowboy for anything, unless you really are an actor looking for a part in *Seven Brides for Seven Brothers*. That show starts in January."

"Cowboy? What?" He frowned for a moment as if confused.

She pointed to the hat he gripped in one hand and gestured toward the rest of his attire with a raised eyebrow.

He glanced all the way down to his scuffed boots and then laughed, a deep heartfelt sound that stirred a sense of longing within her heart. "Nope, nothing like that, although I was raised on a ranch in Montana, and it seems to have rubbed off more than I intended." He raised his eyes to hers. "Let's start over, shall we?"

"That might be a good idea." Liz gave her best impression of a regal nod with a slight tilt to the right. "Welcome to the Wardrobe Dinner Theatre. I'm

Liz. How may I help you today?"

He extended a large hand. "I'm Ryan Callahan."

Of course he'd get the Irish name while she was stuck with the red hair.

"Nice to meet you." She placed her hand in his for a quick shake but found it securely trapped.

"The pleasure is all mine."

Warmth from his words mixed with the tingles racing up her arm as she found herself captured by the intensity of his gaze and a peaceful sensation settling around her heart. Was he feeling the same connection?

She cleared her throat. "Um, you were saying something about a business?"

"Yes." He blinked and released her hand. "Well, I normally do a lot of freelance work that takes me around the country and beyond. But when my brother-in-law was deployed last month, I put my contracts on hold for a bit and moved here to help my sister with her kids. I'm trying to drum up some income ... although if nothing comes through soon, I'll either be babysitting while my sister goes back to work or end up becoming a waiter."

"Good luck finding something in this college town." She should know, after spending the past three weeks filling out countless applications "just in case" something opened up. Thankfully, she'd gotten an extended contract instead.

"All that to say, this morning I had a crazy idea."

Liz grinned. "I've been known to have a few of those myself."

"That's a story I'd love to hear someday." His dimple flashed again, along with his sense of humor. "But, actually, I'm a photographer."

"Oh." She fought to keep a smile on her face and the memories in the past.

"Have you ever been on a cruise?"

"What? No." Talk about a random subject change.

"On cruises, they often have photographers roaming around, taking pictures at dinner and other places. Then guests can buy professional photos of their families that are already printed out, often with a promotional logo or date in the corner."

"They do that at Disneyland too." Usually with a cheesy pose and a rip-off price to take advantage of gullible tourists.

"Exactly. I wondered if the owners here might be interested in having someone take pictures of couples and families, especially before your Christmas show. With the right packaging, it would make a wonderful Christmas card photo."

He looked so hopeful that she almost hated to burst his bubble. But if anyone was going to take pictures at the theater, it should be her. "Um, I'm not sure."

"Are they around to talk to?"

She glanced across the lobby to where the Sheridan family was still talking with Dani. Liz shifted her attention back to the hopeful photographer. "They're busy right now."

"That's okay." Ryan pulled out his wallet and thumbed through the contents before drawing out a business card. "Would you pass along my information and maybe even tell them about my idea?"

"Sure." She took his card and glanced at it long enough to notice the "Freelance Photographer" title and a website. Did he really make a living taking pictures, or was this a glorified hobby? Was he even any good with a camera?

"Thanks."

"But no promises."

"Of course." He took one of the Wardrobe's season brochures from the stack on the small ledge at the box-office window and turned it over long enough to nod at the phone number on the back. "Just tell them I'll call tomorrow."

"Okay." He certainly was persistent.

Ryan settled his hat back on his head. "It was nice to meet you, Liz, and thanks for your time." He turned for the door with a rolling gait likely earned from time in the saddle.

Too bad he was a photographer. Even if she'd once dreamed of being the same.

She flicked his card with her fingers and shoved it into the back pocket of her jeans. Today she was an actress, and if she didn't hustle to grab a change of clothes from her car, she'd be dancing in denim during their emergency rehearsal.

And making her boss question the contract extension before Liz even had a script.

Hours later, Liz tossed her new script and rehearsal bag onto the passenger seat before sliding behind the wheel of her bright yellow Beetle. Finishing a successful rehearsal was such a rush of emotion. And she'd get to do it again tomorrow—first with the full cast of *42nd Street* to finish making adjustments for the show, followed by her first rehearsal for *White Christmas*, and ending with the evening performance of the former.

Busy? Yes. But *busy* beat *bored* every day.

Across the parking lot, Her Majesty and her minions piled into Gloria's silver Lexus and pulled out, heading west toward their shared apartment—one of several apartments the theater rented for single, out-of-town cast members. The place Liz could continue to call home for at least another month.

God? I know I haven't spoken to you in a very long time, but I still recognize a miracle when I see one. So, thanks.

A tendril of peace wound around her heart and brought a smile to her face.

She needed to celebrate and then recharge her energy for a long evening studying the new script. Except that her assigned shelf in the shared pantry was nearly bare. First stop was the grocery store, now that she had another four weeks of guaranteed income. Perhaps she'd even reward herself with an artery-clogging trip to a drive-thru for a cheeseburger and fries and call it "brain food."

Almost an hour later, Liz juggled an assortment of bags and a sloshing drink as she trudged up the steps to the second-floor apartment. She set the heaviest grocery bags outside the door and fumbled for her key. Once inside, she headed straight for the kitchen, bypassing the living room where Gloria, Marie, and Renee watched a movie. A half-empty pizza box sat on the coffee table next to Gloria's foot, and a giant bag of ice rested on the knee she'd recently had surgically repaired.

"Did you hurt it again?" Liz raised her voice to be heard over the movie as she piled her burdens onto the kitchen counters.

"No." Gloria's denial seemed a bit forced, as if she was trying to convince herself too. "It's just a little sore because I haven't danced in a while, so I'm being careful."

"That's wise." Liz fished in the junk drawer for a Sharpie to label her groceries before stowing them in the pantry and refrigerator. A few minutes later, she settled in to eat her cooling meal at the dining room table and pulled out her script.

Marie was the first to notice the script, and soon Liz was surrounded and bombarded with advice from both Marie and Renee about which scenes to focus on first. They were also dancers in the group numbers.

"You know, it would really help if you could watch the dance numbers on video and replay them as often as needed." Marie tapped a finger on the scene list where Liz had starred the sections she needed to learn.

Renee snapped her fingers. "Hey. Gloria could film those for you since her character as the general's housekeeper isn't in those scenes."

Gloria bristled from her position on the couch. "Why don't you let me do my own volunteering? I'm not an invalid."

"I never said you were." Renee rolled her eyes.

Gloria stuck out her bottom lip. "Why don't you get me some more ice for my knee?"

"Why can't you get it yourself?" Renee swiveled to face off with the diva. "I don't mind pitching in to help those who need it—like when you fell and had surgery, or now, when Liz has to learn an entire play in a week—but as you've just pointed out, you're not an invalid, so why should you get the royal treatment?"

Liz shot a quick glance to Marie, who gaped at Renee with wide eyes, as if waiting for a lightning bolt to strike through the ceiling.

Renee sucked in a quick breath herself, as if she couldn't believe she'd actually said that—even if it were true—and then braced herself for the backlash they'd all come to expect.

Gloria's face reddened, and she opened her mouth several times as if to say something. A tension-laden minute ticked by before Gloria hoisted herself to her feet and stalked to the kitchen with a slight limp.

Then she silently refilled her ice bag without a word.

What had just happened? A second miracle in one day? Liz exchanged shocked glances with Marie and Renee. It seemed the minions had successfully staged a mutiny.

Gloria pulled out a chair at the table, glared at Renee, and then sat down next to Liz, propping her fresh ice bag on her knee. "She's right about one thing. I could film the dancing scenes for you."

"Um, t–thanks." So Gloria could be helpful after all? Then again, she wasn't threatened by Liz's underwhelmingly ordinary talent ... unlike when Gloria's understudy, Dani, had needed help.

Speaking of whom… "Where's Dani?"

"She stopped by about fifteen minutes before you did and left with a big book. Said something about spending the evening at the Sheridans'." Marie elbowed Renee, and the two burst into giggles.

The topic around the table shifted from speculation about Dani's love life to Gloria's hope of snagging Evan's attention once more.

Liz polished off the last of her fries and balled up the cheeseburger wrapper as she stood. "This has been fun, but I really should attack this script with my highlighter." She threw away her trash and retreated to her room. The dancing might have to wait until the group rehearsals and video, but at least the words were something she could get ahead on now.

Chapter Two

Two hours later, Liz rose to pace the room and dislodge the cramps from her stiff muscles. If only she could do the same for her overloaded brain. She'd wanted this, right?

She spied the framed painting hanging over her bed and nodded. Holding on to this dream would require work not only this weekend, but hopefully all month. The week after Thanksgiving would herald the *Seven Brides for Seven Brothers* cast list drawn from among those with multi-show contracts, followed by more rehearsals throughout December. Thanks to today's casting change, she had a chance to be among the lucky ones ... assuming she successfully learned *White Christmas*.

Which was turning out to be harder than she'd thought.

Since her role as part of the group leaned more toward dance numbers than lines to memorize, she'd tried to reduce the effect of missing three weeks of rehearsals by watching scenes through YouTube videos on her phone—but the choreography differences left her more confused than anything else.

During Liz's fifth circle around the tiny room, Dani returned with a glowing smile.

"Have a good evening?"

"The best." Dani sighed.

"Catch up on the kisses you missed while Alex was out of town?"

A blush flooded her roommate's face. "A few. Can you keep a secret?"

Liz grinned as she plopped onto her bed and scooted back against the wall. "Yes."

"He asked me to marry him."

A high-pitched squeal erupted before Liz could slap a hand over her mouth. It couldn't have happened to a sweeter friend.

"We're only keeping it a secret for a little bit until other things settle down—because not only are we getting married, but I also found my baby brother."

Liz soon hugged a pillow to her chest, trying to squelch her longing for a close family relationship that stirred as Dani spilled out the details of her separation and then happy reunion with her brother on top of a wonderfully romantic proposal.

Dani collapsed onto her bed. "I've prayed for so long about finding my brother again. It's a dream come true."

"Do you really think God gave you that dream?"

"Absolutely. Even though it took a while, I remember the verse in Jeremiah where God said, 'I know the plans I have for you ... to give you hope and a future.'"

Could Dani be right? Did God have plans for her too?

"God is so good to me."

"But of course God blesses you. You follow the rules." Liz frowned over the top of her pillow.

"No, any blessing I have is because of grace. When I accepted God's adoption invitation, I got a loving relationship with a generous heavenly Father instead of a list of rules I could never hope to keep."

"Really? Because most of what I've heard is 'Do this' and 'Don't do that.'" Mostly from her father. And the frowning pastor at the church they'd started attending after her grandparents died.

Dani bit her lip. "There are some rules, but I think of them more like an owner's manual of best-operating instructions." She glanced around the room. "What about your camera with all the complicated settings? Things like taking off the lens cap or changing the shutter speed for a darkroom could be considered rules."

"Or common sense." Liz rolled her eyes.

"Right. To get the best results, do this and don't do that."

"Hmm." Dani had a point, but what did that mean in real life?

"I've seen some of your pictures. When you use a camera within those 'rules'"—Dani paused to add an air quote with her fingers—"you unlock a creative burst of possibilities. The way I see it, the guidelines in the Bible are put there to keep us from wrecking our own lives by getting off track from God's perfect plan for how He made us. There's a lot of freedom inside the boundaries."

Freedom was enticing, but what if those operating instructions sent her home to answer phones in an office? Liz cleared her throat. "Yeah, well, I'll keep an open mind."

Dani must have seen her discomfort. "Enough about that. I heard you have a part in *White Christmas* now."

"I've been cramming all night." She held up the script. "But, seriously, I need to thank you for praying for my miracle even when I couldn't."

"You could." Dani shrugged.

"Well, God and I haven't exactly been on speaking terms for a few years." Liz tossed her pillow aside and clambered off the bed to unpack her rehearsal bag. She'd need to repack it with fresh clothes and plenty of snacks for tomorrow.

"All it takes is a single prayer."

Something she'd actually tried earlier today. Liz shook the wrinkles from her jeans and spotted the corner of a business card in the back pocket. "Oh, no. I totally forgot earlier in the chaos of the pre-put-in rehearsal..."

"Forgot what?"

"This guy stopped by the theater after the cast meeting and wanted to talk to Mr. Sheridan."

"Then why didn't he? Oh, we were having our big family reunion in the lobby."

"Exactly. You all were busy, so I took his card and told him I'd pass along the message."

"What message?" Dani reached around her for the card and eyed the photo on the front. "Cute guy."

Liz snatched the card back. "Watch out, or I'll tell Alex you said that." She eyed the picture herself and remembered the man's broad shoulders and the sculpted legs in his jeans. The crinkle of humor around his eyes. The sense of stability that made her want to...

"Earth to Liz." Dani snapped her fingers in front of Liz's nose. "What message?"

Liz blinked. "Funny you should be talking about cameras a minute ago. He's a photographer and wants to talk about taking group shots of the guests for Christmas cards or something."

"Hmm. Well, if you ask me, if anyone takes pictures at the Wardrobe, it should be you."

A sense of joy flickered near Liz's heart. "That's what I thought."

"So why aren't you?"

"Because I gave up photography for acting." And permanently alienated herself from her family in the process.

"Why can't you have both?"

The spark of hope grew in her chest, and she tapped the business card against her hand. "I never thought it was a possibility."

"So is this guy any good, or does he just have a business card?"

Liz reached under the bed for her laptop and turned it on. "He has a website listed, so he might have a portfolio online. We'd better check him out and save Mr. Sheridan the hassle."

"Sure." Dani whacked her with a pillow. "Check *him* out or check out his work?"

Heat rose in her face. Curse her pale complexion. "Both?" Except, after Jerry the Jerk, the last thing she needed was to date another photographer.

The website loaded and she turned the screen so Dani could see as she scrolled through a series of rugged outdoor scenery and nature shots.

"See? He doesn't even have any pictures of people." Dani snorted.

"But he certainly has a knack for lighting and composition." As Dani lost interest and moved away to get ready for bed, Liz scrolled through a few more that showed a silhouette of an old cowboy against a sunset and the rough lines of a wood fence contrasting the vibrant colors. A few images later she spotted a saddled horse standing alone against a similarly stark background, and her heart tugged with the implication of loss. She cleared the emotion from her throat.

Why would he want to take posed pictures of people?

Liz clicked over to the biography page with a list of awards and prestigious publications before studying the picture of the handsome photographer standing atop a pile of rugged boulders, his camera propped against his hip.

Ryan was far too talented to choose the Wardrobe voluntarily. What was his real story?

"That's a wrap for now." Mr. Sheridan's booming voice echoed across the stage. "Great work, Gloria, especially so soon after your surgery. I'd say you're ready to step back into the ensemble and help polish off our last weekend of *42nd Street*." He paused as a ripple of applause swept through the assembled cast. "If you're in *White Christmas*, please be ready to run through certain scenes from the top in a half hour. The rest of you are free to go until tonight's performance."

Liz jogged down the stairs to the table where she'd tossed her rehearsal bag that morning, pulling out her water bottle for a long drink once she reached it. The next rehearsal was for her benefit, to give her a crash course—including video—of what to study in the little free time she had over the coming weekend.

Dani stopped beside her. "Have you talked to Mr. Sheridan about the photographer yet?"

"No. When I got here this morning, he was on the phone with a reporter. I guess news of the robbery got out, and he was doing damage control."

Dani bit her lip and her forehead crinkled in concern. "I had hoped they could avoid the negative press."

"I did hear him trying to shift attention to the opening of the new show, but I'm not sure he'd be interested in talking to another stranger, even if it's about some photography scheme."

"It might be the perfect distraction. In fact, I'll go with you." Dani linked arms with Liz and tugged her toward the front of the stage, where Mr. Sheridan stood talking to Gloria.

"Hold your horses." Liz laughed. "I need to get the cowboy's card out of my bag."

"Cowboy and horses..." Dani rolled her eyes. "Glad to see your sense of humor has returned."

Liz fished Ryan's card out of the side pocket of her bag with a grin. Yesterday's miracle seemed to have affected more than her job status; her attitude had changed as well. Or maybe her prayer and Dani's verse about God's good plans had put her in a different frame of mind today. Then again, she felt a little awkward around the boss since she'd just been given a reprieve.

"Mr. Sheridan?" Dani left Liz behind and hurried to catch up with the director, who had finished talking to Gloria and now headed toward the lobby. "Can Liz and I talk to you for a couple of minutes?"

"Sure." He glanced over his shoulder to include Liz in his reply. "Why don't we meet in my office while I switch out my notebooks?"

"That works for me." Liz followed them up the stairs, into the lobby, and across the floor to the offices.

She settled onto a chair facing the cluttered desk, while their boss stuffed one large binder of notes into a slot in his bookshelf and moved a different one to the corner of his desk. The colored photo of the *White Christmas* movie poster graced that cover, leaving no doubt about what information was inside. Dani had stopped in the doorway and soon entered, with Mrs. Sheridan behind her.

"So, Dani, what's this about?"

Liz cleared her throat. "Actually, it's something I needed to tell you yesterday."

"Don't tell me you can't—"

"Oh no, nothing like that." Liz smiled at the obvious relief washing across his face. "I'm definitely here for the remainder of the year."

"Whew."

Focus on Love

She held out Ryan's business card. "After the cast meeting yesterday, this guy stopped by the theater. He's a photographer, and he wants to take pictures of our guests in front of a holiday background like they do on cruise ships."

Mr. Sheridan took the card and studied the information. "What did you tell him?"

"That I'd pass along his card ... except that I stuck it in my pocket and then we got busy with another rehearsal and, basically, I forgot until late last night."

Mr. Sheridan looked at his wife. "What do you think?"

"Our guests might like a holiday photo since they are often dressed up already and coming as families to create memories. But before we talk prices and logistics, is this guy any good?"

Liz nodded. "Based on his online portfolio, he's won quite a few awards and is very good at scenery and animals." In fact, if he ended up hanging around for a few weeks, she might be tempted to pick his brain about a few composition techniques.

"But Liz is the one with a knack for capturing people." Dani rested a hand on her shoulder.

Mr. Sheridan raised an eyebrow.

"It's a hobby," Liz deflected.

Dani snorted. "I've seen your camera. You're a professional."

"Whatever. I once thought about doing it full time, but now I'm an actress and I just take pictures for fun." Even if her fingers suddenly itched to trigger the shutter.

Mr. Sheridan pulled over his desk phone, pushed the speaker button, and punched in the phone number listed on the card. "Well, let's see what this Ryan Callahan has to say."

After a few minutes of discussing the idea, Mr. Sheridan cleared his throat. "I'm open to your idea, but it would need to be quality. Nothing cheesy or chintzy about it."

"Of course, sir." Ryan's deep voice oozed respect. "What if I got a ticket to Friday night's show and took some sample pictures? We could meet Saturday morning to look over my work and make a final decision. If we proceed, I'll need a little time to work out the logistics."

Mr. Sheridan glanced at Dani and Liz. "Have you taken pictures of people before?"

"Well, sir, it's been a while." Liz bit her lip at the hesitancy in Ryan's voice but had to admire his honesty. "But I'm grateful for the opportunity."

Mr. Sheridan glanced at Dani and then winked at Liz. "I know of another photographer who specializes in people, so maybe we'll use her as a comparison."

"I appreciate the heads-up." Ryan's voice sounded strained. But surely a man with his credentials would be able to get a job anywhere.

She suddenly recalled his mention of looking for a miracle. Maybe there was more to his story, and now she was unintentionally intruding on his opportunity, even if the thought of picking up her camera set her pulse racing.

Mr. Sheridan ended the call and raised an eyebrow. "Of course, you'll be busy in the play itself, Liz, but I imagine you'll get some interesting shots backstage." He glanced at his wife. "It could be a good opportunity to upgrade our headshots for the next program."

His wife smiled. "What a wonderful idea."

Dani gave Liz a high five. "That's my roommate!"

That evening, Liz staggered into her shared room back at the apartment and dropped her rehearsal bag on the floor beside her bed. After a day packed with rehearsals and a performance, every cell of her body screamed for rest. But she reached for her alarm clock first—tomorrow's plan included hours in the upper rehearsal rooms with her new video recordings.

Muffled voices in the kitchen caught her attention, followed by a clattering—like ice being dumped out—and then Gloria's voice above the noise. "I hate to admit that Mr. Sheridan was right to cast me with less dancing in *White Christmas*. But you just wait and see, I'll be totally ready for *Seven Brides* this spring."

Liz rolled her neck, trying to get the kinks out, then glanced through the doorway in time to spot Marie and Renee walking past. "Hey, you two, can you do me a favor?"

"What do you need?" Marie stuck her head into the room before sidestepping to allow Dani to enter, who was carrying a glass of water.

"Could you meet me upstairs at the theater tomorrow afternoon to go over the dance numbers?"

"Sure." Marie smiled. "Just so long as I don't get too sweaty. I won't have time to clean up before needing to report for my serving shift, otherwise."

"Deal." Liz breathed a sigh of relief that she didn't have to wait tables again until Saturday's matinee show. That frantic pace was partially to blame for her aching back ... and brain.

"Good night. Sleep tight." Renee poked her head around Marie's shoulder and then tugged her roommate out of sight.

"You too." Dani flopped back onto her bed, then groaned. "I'm almost too tired to go brush my teeth. This has been the longest week ever, starting with that bad-news letter on Monday."

"And then the robbery discovered on Tuesday, with a dramatic firing yesterday."

"Don't forget that I was previously accused of said robbery."

"But yesterday ended well, even after the extra rehearsal." Liz toed off her shoes and kicked them under the edge of her bed, where one ricocheted off her camera bag.

Her camera.

"I got a fiancé, and you got a new contract." Dani chuckled as she stood. "And we survived today. Tomorrow has to be better." She headed toward the doorway.

"It will be." A burst of excitement brought a smile to Liz's face as she pulled out the camera bag and set it atop her comforter. She unzipped the top and quickly inventoried the contents. An extra memory card and a spare battery should be plenty for tomorrow night's assignment.

Then again, just to be safe, she plugged in the battery charger and set the open bag beside her rehearsal things so she wouldn't forget it in the morning.

After a quick trip to the bathroom to brush her teeth once Dani was finished, she quietly changed into a large sleep shirt and fell into bed, her mind buzzing with ideas about the shots she would take. One thing was for sure—she would avoid the posed cardboard shots others might expect and strive for spontaneous candids instead, like the ones she uploaded to her favorite online site and had printed into the books stacked on her shelf.

Along the way, maybe she could recapture more of the good memories associated with photography.

Her head sank into the softness of her pillow. What kind of pictures would Ryan take? He didn't have as much experience with people. Even with his knack for lighting, this was one tryout she just might win.

But would he hate her when he learned that she was the other photographer?

Chapter Three

Liz sidestepped a collection of props for the upcoming show and adjusted the zoom on her camera. After a shift to the right, Gloria's face filled the frame, with the hint of a smile flirting around the corners of her glossy lips and an unusual warmth in the blonde woman's eyes.

Liz captured a few shots as Gloria's smile grew and then slowly zoomed out to include Evan's handsome face. Such a romantic pose would be perfect on the cover of a novel. Assuming she could ever get them to sign a permission form to sell the image. But just in case, she took several more pictures, the shutter on her camera clicking away.

Gloria turned at the continual sound and frowned. "Just what do you think you're doing? Spying on us?"

Liz swallowed hard. "No way. Mr. Sheridan said I could take some backstage pictures tonight since he's thinking about updating the cast photos." She tilted her head toward the auditorium, where she'd spotted a well-dressed Ryan mingling among the tables with his camera earlier. "There's another photographer out there angling for a different job, but I'm the only one with access back here."

"Are you any good?" Gloria quirked a finely plucked eyebrow.

Was she? Could photography ever be more than a hobby? She wouldn't know unless she took the risk and tried.

"Come and see." Liz switched her camera to the review mode and scrolled back to the first shots she'd taken in the kitchen. She angled the screen toward Gloria and showed her how to advance the images, then held her breath as Gloria pursed her lips.

Evan reached around Gloria's shoulder to tap the screen. "I love how you captured the light glistening off the lettuce."

"It's just salad." Gloria frowned and then continued scrolling.

Evan shrugged. "It makes the food look fresh. Slap a couple of those onto the website and folks won't wonder about the quality of the menu."

Liz found a smile. That was exactly what she'd been thinking when she captured the food preparation while shaking off the rust in her quick-focus skills.

Gloria's rapid scrolling slowed and a tiny smile flickered across her face again. She must have reached the shots of her.

Liz bit her lip and looked at Evan, who was studying the screen over Gloria's shoulder. His raised eyebrows and low whistle boosted her confidence.

"I've got one hot girlfriend."

"Really?" Gloria glanced over her shoulder and almost bumped noses with him. "So I'm forgiven?"

Her on-again, off-again boyfriend dropped a quick kiss onto her lips and rested his hands on her shoulders. "Absolutely."

Gloria smiled and turned back to the camera. "We do look good together."

"I love how you've got us focused with it all blurry in the background. You're really good at this." Evan lifted his eyes to Liz's. "Could I get one of these printed?"

"Me too," Gloria inserted. "Maybe even framed?"

"Sure." Butterflies danced in Liz's stomach. She'd known it was a good shot ... but she really needed to get her camera back to take more before the show started.

"Are you done?" She reached for her camera, but Evan took it from Gloria's hands before she could touch it.

"Hey, guys, come check this out."

Soon they were surrounded by other actors and actresses, some in costume and others just arriving backstage. As Liz again explained the task their director had given her, Trent arrived.

He took his turn looking through the images. "Not bad."

Certainly not the gushing praise of the others that boosted her confidence, but definitely a more favorable response than Jerry or her dad had ever given her.

Trent handed her camera back. "But I think you need more than just these two lovebirds. What do you say, gang? Think we could help Liz?"

Within minutes, she had almost tripled the number of pictures on her memory card with a variety of solo and group shots. One of the actors suggested they silently sneak onto the stage itself since the curtain was down and the audience was making plenty of noise while eating their dinners. Soon she had close to live-action images, taken with the large props and backdrop, to add to her collection.

The buzz of energy grew each time the shutter clicked as Liz sank deeper into a creative zone. How was it possible to have such laser-targeted focus on her subjects that her camera almost became a natural extension of her imagination?

She hadn't felt such freedom in years.

A movement in the wings to her right caught her attention, and she quickly shifted her focus toward a different gathering of actors watching the onstage fun. The shadows from the curtains created an interesting visual element. As the shutter whirred, she could almost imagine some of the shots in black and white or with a sepia filter.

Then the backstage speaker crackled to life with the typical warning call to preshow. With just fifteen minutes until the curtain rose, her photographic subjects scattered to finish getting ready for the opening number.

Liz trailed behind them to the dressing room, pensive. What had happened back there?

"I know the plans I have for you."

Was it a sign that God wanted her behind the camera? Or had she instead felt the energy of the stage?

She turned off the camera to preserve the remaining battery and zipped it away in its padded bag. Turning toward the wall of mirrors to check her costume and makeup, her mind drifted to the photographer out among the audience.

What kind of shots had the cowboy been able to take in the dimly lit auditorium? Or was he focusing his photographic audition on the production itself? Would he enjoy the show?

But more importantly, would his pictures be better than hers?

Her stomach fluttered at the memory of some of the candid shots she'd taken, especially between Gloria and Evan—and the ones of Dani and her secret fiancé, Alex, before he slipped under the stage to lead the band.

Love was such a powerful emotion to capture ... almost as invigorating as the hope and longing she'd caught on the face of Trent's new costar, Anna.

A similar longing tugged at her heart. Someday it would be her turn to be the focus of someone's undivided attention.

Speaking of focus, she wondered whether Ryan would take a picture of her during the show. A shiver of anticipation ran up her spine and brought a smile to her face. She'd know when they met in the morning.

Just minutes before ten, Liz slammed her car door shut and jogged across the mostly empty parking lot toward the doors.

If only the cast didn't have to park so far away on show days, she could have walked like a sedate, normal person. Then again, she would have arrived earlier if she hadn't spent so much time this morning choosing and editing just the right photos and loading them onto the flash drive in her pocket.

Some things were worth rushing for.

About a hundred feet from the front doors, she spotted the tall cowboy exiting a large truck parked nearby, and her stomach whirred like her fast-action shutter.

Of course, it had to be nerves about showing her pictures to the Sheridans in front of the professional photographer—nothing to do with how handsome he was.

Ryan grinned as his long stride brought him quickly to her side. "Fancy meeting you here this morning. Liz, right?"

Liz tipped her head in a semi-curtsy. "I'm looking forward to seeing your pictures."

His eyebrows rose. "Pictures? Does that mean you're the other photographer?"

Uh-oh. "I thought you knew that." Liz slapped a hand against her forehead. "Of course not. Mr. Sheridan didn't mention my name."

"Well, if you're as talented with a camera as you are on the stage, then this might be a wasted trip." The laugh lines around his eyes deepened along with his smile, stirring her heart in unexpectedly delicious ways until heat rose in her face.

Perfect. Now her complexion might match her hair color.

"Don't make me wonder whether you need your eyes examined. I'm not star material." Liz shook her head. "Not to mention, I've seen your website."

"Really? Checking me out?" He reached the front door and held it open for her.

"Curiosity." She cleared her throat and gestured toward the area where they were to meet. "But I'm still not sure why you would give up professional gigs for this."

Mr. Sheridan appeared in the doorway of his office. "You're right on time." He stepped forward to shake Ryan's hand. "I can't wait to see what the two of you have come up with."

Liz preceded Ryan into the office and felt the warmth of his large hand on her back as he guided her to the closest chair. Such a gentleman. His mother must be so proud of him.

"So who's going to go first?" Mr. Sheridan swiveled his office chair as he looked from one to the other.

Her stomach clenched with a sudden wave of nerves. "The professional."

"No, ladies first." Ryan settled back in his chair with folded arms.

"Okay." She took a deep breath for courage before handing over her flash drive. As Mr. Sheridan plugged it into his computer, she whispered a prayer of sorts that God would help her boss to like the pictures ... or at least not hate them. That would be humiliating.

Mr. Sheridan turned the monitor so all three could see the screen, and once the program loaded, he began to scroll.

She clasped her hands in her lap, squeezing them between her knees. "I thought it might be good for the website to have some pictures of the kitchen and food." She bit her lip to stop the flood of nervous chattering building inside.

Mr. Sheridan nodded, then pushed a button on his phone. "Theresa? Can you come here for a few minutes?"

She peeked at Ryan. He seemed serious yet not concerned as he observed her work. Then again, as Gloria had pointed out last night, there was nothing impressive about salad. Ryan's expression suddenly changed, and she glanced back to spot the first of her images of Gloria and Evan on the monitor.

Mr. Sheridan whistled. "Dani was right."

"Dani?" Ryan leaned forward and propped his chin on a hand as he studied the screen.

"My roommate is the one who told him I—"

"These are amazing pictures." Mr. Sheridan clicked the mouse to enlarge one shot of several laughing actors gathered around the onstage piano.

Mrs. Sheridan entered and stopped just inside the door. "Wow. Mr. Callahan, you really are a professional."

Ryan chuckled. "Thank you, ma'am, but Liz took these." He winked in her direction. "She certainly has talent."

Liz's heart leaped suddenly in her throat, and she squeaked out a thank-you. Praise from an award-winning professional? She must be dreaming, because the last photographer to praise her talent had been her own grandpa.

Or maybe Ryan was simply teasing her with a backhanded compliment. He didn't seem at all threatened by the competition.

Mrs. Sheridan crossed to her husband's side. He adjusted the display to view rows of thumbnails at once, and the Sheridans began a whispered conversation, punctuated by a few fingers pointed at the monitor.

"Where did you learn?" Ryan's question eased some of Liz's tension.

"I mostly taught myself with online YouTube videos in the years after I got my first camera for Christmas. My grandpa started a photography business back in Kansas, but my dad runs it now."

"He must be very proud of you."

"Not exactly." She frowned. Why had she brought *him* into the conversation?

He raised an eyebrow. "Has he seen your work?"

"Not lately." And before that, not voluntarily.

"So, Mr. Callahan..." Mr. Sheridan's interruption came at the perfect time.

"Ryan, please." He shifted his intense gaze to the Sheridans.

"Let's see what you've got for us."

He handed over his own flash drive, and soon the monitor displayed a variety of colorful images of happy families enjoying their meals. Then came the shot of a single tabletop candle juxtaposed against the bright lights of the stage in the background, followed by a series of scenes from the play itself. A close-up of each cast member—including her—completed Ryan's bid—and they were every bit as realistic as her own compositions.

"How did you get such clarity without a flash? The auditorium lighting—"

"Was a challenge." He shifted in his chair to face her as the Sheridans resumed their whispered conversation. "I've invested in a Leica Noctilux lens that can practically see in the dark."

Her jaw dropped. "That's an expensive lens."

"I was able to write it off as a business expense." He gestured toward the screen. "And it just happened to come in handy here."

Here. Where any hopes she had of winning this job had been obliterated by ridiculously expensive camera equipment. If she had a lens like that, well, she'd be afraid of dropping it.

Still, the whole experience had been good for her ego and forced her to pick up her camera again.

"Liz?"

"No worries. Ryan's the pro and his pictures will—"

"We'd like to pay you for a few of these kitchen shots for the website as well as individual cast pictures for the next program."

"Really?" She discreetly pinched her arm.

A low chuckle from Ryan revealed that it hadn't been as discreet as she'd have liked.

"Absolutely. Now Ryan can probably help us figure out what a fair rate would be."

"But I'm sure he'd rather—"

"I can do that." The photographer rubbed his hands on his jean-clad legs.

"Especially since we'd also like to buy several of Ryan's shots for our website and brochure."

"Thank you, sir." Ryan nodded. "But what do you think about my other idea?"

Mr. Sheridan waved a hand at the screen. "You've obviously got the talent to deliver a quality product, and I think the added value of a holiday family photo would make many of our customers happy, assuming the price isn't unreasonable. Just what did you have in mind?"

As Ryan and Mr. Sheridan discussed the logistics of creating a backdrop in the lobby for interested groups to have their picture taken—for free, with the opportunity to buy a print or digital version after the show—Liz relaxed against her chair.

Last night's magic with her camera had translated into a paycheck today. Of course, she didn't really know how much yet since Ryan's quoted price per photo would probably get negotiated down because of her amateur status, but still ... she'd earned her first actual money as a photographer.

What would her father say now?

As if she'd ever be brave enough to tell him.

But in the meantime, the extra earnings would pad her savings account, and if she could work up enough courage to charge Gloria and Evan a bit more than merely reimbursing her printing costs, well, that would totally make her day.

She glanced at the clock behind Mr. Sheridan's desk. Good news like this deserved another cheeseburger as a reward, and she should have plenty of time to indulge before reporting back to serve the matinee show. Then, with the photography distraction behind her, she could resume her crunch-time studying for the *White Christmas* dance scenes.

Mr. Sheridan soon typed up a document on his computer as Ryan dictated a brief contract for the freelance pictures and a percentage of the profits from the holiday shots. Liz did a little math and realized just how many pictures Ryan would need to take and sell each weekend to make a decent hourly wage.

Once again, the nagging question rose to her mind: what had brought the award-winning photographer with the expensive equipment to the point where he was happy to take family photos for barely minimum wage?

Then again, if he was doing something he loved, the wage wasn't as important.

A few handshakes, file transfers, and signatures later, Liz and Ryan walked out to wait near the box office while Mrs. Sheridan wrote their checks.

"I'm sorry we had to split the money."

She laughed. "I'm just thrilled to get paid something, and thanks to you, it was a whole lot more than I ever dreamed." She sobered. "But if you're willing to take pictures on spec, you must really need the money. And in that case, I'm the one who's sorry for cutting in on your opportunity."

"No question about it, the money's important." He ran a hand through his hair as if missing his cowboy hat. "Like I said before, my brother-in-law recently deployed and his income took a big hit. I'm trying to help my sister bridge the gap in their budget. But God will provide, and this sure beats waiting tables."

"I sometimes wait tables here—and off the record, I'd much rather be taking pictures than refilling water glasses."

"Hmm. Say, I don't know what your schedule is like, but I've got a paying gig lined up for Tuesday."

"I wasn't fishing for an invitation."

"Still, I could use an extra camera."

"More posed family shots like you're planning here?" She grimaced.

"Not if I can help it." He grinned at her expression. "It's a pre-Thanksgiving charitable benefit. They want a bunch of photos for their website and future promotions in addition to gifts for the guests."

"What do you get for something like that?"

"It's a flat-fee job in exchange for a disk of licensed images, but I'm a little worried about delivering what they want single-handedly. With two cameras flashing, they'd get more than enough pictures ... and based on what I just saw of your work, I know you'd do a great job capturing the emotions."

"So how much? Or does that sound greedy?"

He laughed, and the lines around his eyes emerged again. "Sounds like a smart business practice. I'd pay you $100 for three hours of your time."

She blew out a low whistle. "And obviously you're keeping more than half since you lined it all up."

"True."

"So with jobs like that, why stoop to taking posed shots here?" She gestured at the lobby. "You can't be doing this just for the income."

Ryan's smile faded. "It's because my mom loved going to the theater and *White Christmas* was one of her favorites. When Dad died, she kept herself going by singing that song about counting blessings instead of sheep."

"Some things are worth more than money." The intensity of his gaze pulled her in until Mrs. Sheridan interrupted them with their checks. As the business manager walked away, Liz stashed her check in her purse along with her flash drive before clearing her throat. "But speaking of money, I'm very grateful for this ... and your offer for more on Tuesday night. If you are serious about needing help, I accept. Just tell me when and where."

His smile reemerged. "What if I pick you up here at five o'clock and we ride together? Dress up."

"Black tie or semiformal?"

"Church clothes should fit in nicely."

She fought to mask her internal cringe at the mention of "church clothes" and extended her hand. "Deal."

Their warm handshake sent sparks up her arm.

"I look forward to working with you, Liz."

He turned to leave and she bit her lip to control her smile. Acting on the stage this weekend, the dress rehearsal for the new show on Monday morning, and a photography job on Tuesday night...

Maybe she really could have two dreams at the same time.

Chapter Four

Liz waited until she reached her car to dance a happy jig. After she slid into the driver's seat, she pulled the check out of her purse and blinked back tears as she stared at the amount.

While the money was nice, the validation was priceless. Here was proof that someone liked her photography enough to pay her. Not to mention, Evan and Gloria wanted reprints. And super-pro Ryan had not only called her talented, but he wanted *her* help with a photo shoot.

Her heart swelled. *God, I don't deserve this, but thanks!*

She replaced the check in her purse and pulled out her keys instead. Time to get that reward cheeseburger before turning her attention back to her main job at the theater.

A few blocks away from "restaurant row," her phone rang. She fished the device out of her purse and quickly glanced at the screen.

Her breath caught in her throat. Mom only called about once a month and usually on a Sunday night while Dad was at a church board meeting—likely because she hid most of their conversations from her husband. In the years since her own parents had died, Mom had faded into a shell of her former self.

Liz swiped the screen to connect. "Hi, Mom."

"Hello, Elizabeth." Her mom paused to clear her throat, and in the background Liz could make out her father's gruff voice. If Dad was in the room, this couldn't be good.

Liz eased off the road into the closest parking lot and braced herself. "What's up?"

"Your father wants to know when we can expect you to arrive. He needs to finalize next week's schedule—"

"Arrive?" Why did Mom think she was coming home? "Oh. You mean for Thanksgiving? I wasn't planning—"

"No, for good. Doesn't your little show end this weekend?"

"My little..." Liz took a deep breath and forced it out between clenched teeth.

"Did I get the dates wrong?" Her mother's voice wavered with doubt.

Why had she ever told Mom about her job search because of the expiring contract? "No. The current show ends this weekend. But I got good news a few days ago and—"

"Good." Mom's relief flowed through the receiver. "So we can expect you on Monday? You'll probably need a day to travel and then get settled in—"

"Mom, listen to me. I can't come home, not even for a visit. I'm—"

"You're not coming? Whyever not? It's been three years, and I'd hoped that after college—"

"I got another contract." Liz finally smiled at the memory. "I'll be busy with rehearsals since the new show starts the day after Thanksgiving and runs through Christmas."

"And how long... Wait a minute. Your father wants to speak with you."

Liz took another deep breath for courage as a mixture of whispers and shuffling echoed in her ear. Telephone conversations with Mom were one thing, but she hadn't truly spoken to Dad since loading her car on Christmas Day all those years ago. If he had something to say, he had Mom call.

"What's this about not coming home? Don't you realize that your mother—"

"Hi, Dad. I have a job."

"Your job is over. And your rebellious tantrum should have ended years ago. You've wasted enough time on this frivolousness, and it's time to grow up and honor your commitments."

So much for the hope that things would get better given time. "That's what I'm doing—honoring my commitments to my boss and my coworkers."

"But your mother said that your contract was ending."

"It would have, after tomorrow's matinee. But just this week I was offered a new contract through the end of the year."

"This week? That's convenient." Skepticism dripped through the phone line.

"Yes, on Wednesday. One of the other actresses had to leave unexpectedly, and the director asked if I was available to fill in."

"But you're not available."

Liz blinked back a few untimely tears. Why couldn't Dad ever listen to her heart? "Yes, I *am* available. I live here, and I already know the rest of the staff."

"So it sounds like you think life is going well for you."

"It is."

"Like maybe even God is blessing you?"

"Yes." The faint reminder of peace lifted her spirits, along with the memory of a check in her purse ... except that wasn't anything she would dare share in her father's current mood.

"But how can you expect God to bless you when you refuse to honor your father and mother?"

"That's not fair. I honor—"

"It's what God commanded: obey your father and mother, that it may go well with you in the land. And if you stay in Colorado, that's not obedience. I prayed you would come to your senses by now."

"My senses?" Liz clenched her fist around the steering wheel.

"I need your help."

"Oh." Her flash of Irish temper receded in the face of possibilities. "Help? Does that mean Jerry left and you need my camera skills?"

"What? Of course not. Jerry's still here and part of the family. He recently expanded to doing senior pictures too; that's why I need your help with booking team photos and processing the orders."

Her heart sank. Dad might want her to come home, but only on his terms. After all this time, he still didn't believe in her abilities. Not while Jerry was there, the son he never had … the boyfriend he apparently hadn't forgiven her for leaving behind.

"Dad, we've been over this. There isn't a place there to use my gifts." Not as a photographer and certainly not in developing their business plan.

"You don't need to be *gifted* to answer phone calls."

"Exactly. I just want to use the talents God gave me."

"God? You've rejected Him just like you've rejected your family."

"That's not true. I never rejected—"

"Then why did you leave?"

"You gave my dream job to Jerry, and I don't want to be stuck in the office instead."

"Jerry? He'd probably still marry you."

"No, thanks." Liz shuddered, then noticed the clock on her dashboard. "I need to go."

"You need to pray and ask God to tell you where you're supposed to be. Because it sure isn't there."

"What makes you so positive of that?"

"Because God knows I need you here."

"This conversation isn't getting us anywhere." Liz sighed. "I have a job here through the end of the year, and I'm not quitting. Tell Mom I'll talk to her another time."

"Don't bother calling either of us unless it's to apologize. And don't expect me to be waiting with open arms when you finally decide to come crawling home."

Liz blinked back fresh tears as a muffled argument took place on the other end of the line. Then the call disconnected.

She held the phone for another minute just in case her mom called back, but nothing happened except for an empty feeling growing in her stomach and heart.

Still cut off from her family until she buckled under the pressure? Her dad obviously wanted her to slide into his confining plans, but what if God also told her to give up acting?

She was afraid to ask in case the answer was yes.

If only she hadn't opened up that line of communication by thanking God for her miracle reprieve.

She slid the silent phone back into her purse—the same purse that held a photography paycheck.

And yet it seemed God had answered other prayers beyond a theater job, especially since doors were opening for her to do photography again.

Why did the future have to be so confusing?

Her stomach growled. She'd find time to sort it all out later, but in the meantime, she needed to get lunch.

Better make that cheeseburger a double and maybe even add bacon.

Liz adjusted her zoom lens and captured the expression on Dani's face as she and Anna started their "Sisters" routine. Monday's dress rehearsal for *White Christmas* was the perfect opportunity to capture action shots in the new costumes in case the Sheridans were willing to post more pictures on the website.

Especially if they paid for them.

But even without pay, she'd still thank them for the opportunity.

She moved farther to the right on the second level of the auditorium and captured Evan and Trent in the frame as their characters watched the duo perform. Either Trent's acting ability had improved or his feelings for Anna went deeper than they'd ever been when he had dated Liz.

A twinge of rejection pricked her heart, but she brushed it away. She wanted more than a lighthearted distraction the next time she was blessed with a relationship.

She snapped a few more pictures of the scene and then lowered her camera.

"Fancy meeting you here." The deep voice rumbled to her left, and she turned to face Ryan.

"I could say the same for you."

His eyes trailed over her costume from her first scene. "Is this what photographers wear these days?" His dimple deepened as his crooked smile grew.

She glanced at his standard Wranglers and red-plaid flannel shirt in confusion until remembering her feathered headband. "I'm sure it looks ridiculous out of context, but I just finished a group number and wanted to get a few shots of the leads in action before I get ready for my next scene." As a member of the ensemble, she had seven big dance scenes, and most of them were before the intermission.

They turned toward the stage, where the four leads had gathered around a table for a period of dialogue. Liz lifted her camera and captured some of the interactions before turning back to Ryan. "You never said what brought you here today."

He pulled out a chair, turned it backward, and then sat, resting his forearms on the top. "I wanted to talk to the Sheridans about where to take the guests' pictures in the lobby. The ideal place needs to be visible yet not block the flow of traffic."

"And it needs to be festive." Liz rested her chin in the palm of her hand. "If we were at my grandpa's studio—"

"Your grandpa has a studio? No wonder you're a pro."

She flinched. How could she be tactful? "He *had* a studio. My dad runs it now, but I've learned a few things." She cleared her throat. "Anyway, if this were a studio, I'd say you could use a green screen with either a wintry outdoor background or a formal living-room setting complete with wainscoting backdrop ... with a few real props or a decorated tree, of course."

"Of course. But a green screen?" Ryan's eyebrows rose. "Like what a weather forecaster uses if he's not outside?"

"Tricks of the trade. But they're expensive, on top of the software piece."

"And one would make the lobby look hokey." He winced. "Sorry. That sounded like a slam on green screens or your dad."

She shrugged. "I prefer the real thing myself." A glance at the stage had her trying to capture a few more shots of Trent and Anna, who were flirting as they danced.

"They make a nice couple."

"The dancers?" Her eyes widened.

"Them too." He waved a hand at Evan leaning in toward Dani. "I was thinking of how their coloring complements each other."

Liz snorted. "Appearances can be deceiving. That's Dani, my roommate, who's very seriously dating the trumpet-playing bandleader, who happens to be the Sheridans' son."

"Oh." He cleared his throat.

She smiled at Ryan's discomfort. "And the guy next to her is Evan. He's a narcissist who has been wrapped around the pinky finger of the cast's diva while sharing her spotlight." Except that after his attempt to discredit Dani for the theft had failed, he was more focused on schmoozing the director than truly making up with Gloria.

"The diva being the dancer girl?"

"No, the dancing couple is my ex-boyfriend and his flavor of the month." She bit her lip. "That came out wrong."

Ryan's warm smile sent a wave of tingles toward her heart. "No worries. Broken hearts are tricky things."

She shook her head. "It wasn't so much broken as bruised. And that was mostly my pride, before realizing that we were just passing the time while being sucked into the proximity factor of the cast. I guess part of me is actually glad it ended, because it wasn't going anywhere."

"So which one is the diva?"

She welcomed the change of subject. "You saw her picture on Saturday. She's the blonde who'll be playing the part of the general's housekeeper in a few more scenes."

"That's not a diva role."

Liz grinned at Ryan's insight. "Believe me, she's let everyone know it too. But she fell and messed up her knee back in October and had to have surgery. Mr. Sheridan's trying to ease her back into work while letting her knee rest as much as possible."

"And before the injury, she was the star?"

"Nailed it."

"Must make for interesting backstage dynamics."

"And at home." She grimaced, recalling a few issues, including the most recent one when Renee told Gloria to fetch her own ice.

"Home?"

"Dani's my roommate, but we share a company-leased apartment with the diva and two other girls."

The lighting changed onstage as the scene shifted, and Liz picked up her camera once more.

"So then I saw you in the last show. What part are you playing in this one?"

"I actually didn't have a part at all until the day you stopped by the theater."

"Oh." He gestured toward her costume with a raised eyebrow. "So this is your miracle?"

She swatted away his hand with a giggle. "Don't knock it. It pays the bills and keeps a roof over my head."

Ryan watched the dress rehearsal beside her for a moment before sighing. "This obviously isn't a good time to talk to the owners about a backdrop."

"We've got about another hour and a half before Mr. Sheridan will be free during our lunch break. You can either enjoy the free show now or come back in a bit and hope to catch him before our afternoon rehearsal."

"This is kind of interesting." He glanced at her hair. "I especially want to see where that getup fits into the script."

She laughed, then snapped another few pictures. "This one is already past, but there are a few more outfits coming up. Speaking of which, I need to head backstage soon to get ready."

"If you trust me with your camera, I can cover the scenes when you're onstage."

She glanced sideways at him. "I don't have your fancy Leica lens."

"I can manage."

"All right, then. Oh, I meant to tell you earlier, Mrs. Sheridan mentioned setting up a few Christmas trees in the lobby just for decoration, but if you replaced one of the framed pictures with a wreath or stockings and moved a tree nearby—"

"Then the classic chair-rail-and-textured-wall backdrop could resemble a family living room of sorts without spending a ton of money."

"Right. You'd still need to do something about the lighting, even with your fancy camera."

"I have a couple of portable diffusers."

"You could test the lighting tomorrow night before we go since it'll be mostly dark outside. Then if you need to have a plan B, you've got time before Friday night's opening."

He tapped a finger against his chin. "I was thinking to leave here at five, but an extra half hour beforehand should be plenty of time."

"I can be ready." Liz snapped a few more shots of Trent and Anna dancing. So how many hours was that again before she got to see him dressed up? Scratch that. Ryan might be cute—well, more than cute. And he might have helped reignite her love for photography in a roundabout way, but if she didn't focus on *White Christmas* and show Mr. Sheridan she could do the job he'd hired her to do... Well, if she hoped to find her name on the upcoming cast list for January's show, she had to head backstage and make it clear that she'd learned the moves for this new production.

Liz stood and stretched. "I need to get ready for the train-ride scene that's coming up."

Ryan reached out a large hand with tapered fingers, and she placed her camera in his grasp. "I'll get shots of the rest of the show for you."

"Thanks. We can split the fee if—"

"Nope. This is a favor for a friend."

Her heart skipped a beat and her smile grew. "Well then, friend, thank you. And in return, I'll help you decorate a prop tree later."

He held out his other hand, and they shook on it before she made her way down the stairs and detoured through the kitchen doors to the backstage area, the memory of the warmth of his hand on hers still sending delicious tingles up her arm.

She reached the dressing room, ducked inside, and changed into her next costume.

"Weren't you out there taking pictures? Where's your camera?" Renee applied another layer of lipstick in front of a mirror.

Liz stepped toward the adjacent mirror to check her hair. "I left my camera with a friend who'll finish up the rest of the show for me." And probably do a much better job with some of the shots.

"Must be some friend, to put that smile on your face." Marie's teasing was punctuated with an elbow to Liz's ribs.

"That's for me to know—"

"And us to find out." Renee looped an elbow through Liz's and tugged her toward the door.

Marie linked up on the other side. "Except you're moving out tonight and won't have time to interrogate her."

"Moving out?"

Renee shrugged. "With the cast downsizing and then our thief getting fired, well, that left only two girls in the other apartment while we have five in ours. So I asked Mrs. Sheridan if I could switch."

"Wish I'd have thought of that." Yet then she'd have been sharing an apartment with Trent's new girlfriend, and that proximity would have been awkward and a half.

"Me too." Marie playfully shoved Renee's shoulder. "She says it's because I snore, but I say Gloria—"

"Will miss me too." Renee tilted her head toward the wings, where Gloria awaited her entrance into the current scene. At least Renee was smart enough to avoid further antagonizing the former star.

Then again, maybe Gloria should have been the one to switch apartments, leaving the rest of them in peace.

The trio huddled behind the side curtains and monitored the onstage action for another few minutes while going over last-minute instructions and reminders about the upcoming scene.

The timely input helped Liz focus on her positioning and the necessary steps, as she made it through without too many missteps and they swept on toward the next dance number she had to remember.

Once the dress rehearsal was over, she'd have time for a quick lunch before the cast returned to go over her dancing scenes specifically this afternoon. Gloria's video recording had helped her mentally prepare for her scenes, but for muscle memory, she'd need every repetition she could get before Friday night's opening.

If only she weren't so aware of a certain someone on the second level and her promise to help him later.

Chapter Five

"So what can you tell me about this event?" Liz straightened her skirt to prevent wrinkles and then fastened her seat belt. Climbing into Ryan's truck in a dress had already been an adventure.

"It's the semiannual celebration gala for a community foundation here in Northern Colorado. Their mission is to honor the well-rounded achievements of local youth from the area and encourage rising stars from underprivileged and underserved communities. In addition to the dinner and presenting awards to the monthly honorees over dessert, they usually have a really funny show."

"And how do you know so much about them?" Liz nudged her camera bag out of the way of her feet and swiveled to face Ryan during the drive.

Of course, from this angle she could easily admire the muscles in his forearms below the rolled-up sleeves of his dress shirt as he steered into traffic. A suit jacket hung on a hook behind his seat.

"My mom served on the foundation's board for several years."

"Wait a minute... I didn't think you were from around here."

"I'm not." He glanced over with a grin. "I grew up on a ranch in Montana."

"But your mom was here because…"

He cleared his throat. "When Dad died, Mom decided the ranch was too much for her to handle on her own. And, honestly, while I loved the rugged outdoors, I never wanted to take over the day-to-day operations of the ranch."

"Did your dad know your dream was different than his?"

The faint lines around Ryan's eyes deepened with his smile. "He used to drive me to my uncle Roy's shop—Callahan's Cameras—so I could sweep the floors and wash windows to earn the money to buy a camera of my own. Then I must have carried that camera with me everywhere I went and took more pictures in a day than he had cattle."

"It must have been nice to have his support."

"It sounds like you haven't had that, yourself."

"That's a long story for a different day." Liz waved her hand. "So your mom sold the ranch and ended up here?"

"My sister and her husband had already moved here to Fort Collins and started a family, so Mom bought a small house and spent her time spoiling the grandkids and volunteering anywhere that needed help."

"She sounds like an amazing lady. Will she be there tonight?"

A vein throbbed in Ryan's jaw. "Actually, no. She had a heart attack in July and graduated to heaven a few days later."

"Oh. I'm so sorry to bring it up."

"You couldn't know." Ryan turned right into the parking lot of a large hotel. "Anyway, she always loved this event, so when I came to town to help my sister and needed to drum up a little business, it jumped to the top of my contact list."

Right. They were here on business. Time to get professional. "Remind me what shots you want me to take." Because the only reason he had for being so nice to her was the fact that he needed her help, even if she wasn't nearly as accomplished behind the lens as he was.

He pulled into a parking spot, turned off the engine, and rolled down the sleeves of his shirt. "We'll start with the mingling of guests as everyone arrives. Candid shots of groupings and tables. In general, anything that strikes your fancy to capture the mood of the evening—including the awkwardness of dressed-up teenagers."

"Ouch. That's a bit harsh."

"But true." He grinned. "I only say that because I know exactly how they feel in this monkey suit. Give me my Wranglers and boots any day."

She smiled in response, retrieved her camera bag, and followed Ryan toward the entrance before she brought the conversation back to tonight's job. "Candids over dinner. Got it. Then I assume we regroup for the award presentations."

"Yep. More formal and posed shots there, to document the recipients. Then more candids during the entertainment portion of the evening."

"I can do that."

They entered the front doors of the hotel and followed the signs to the Rocky Mountain ballroom. Liz hung back a bit as Ryan greeted a silver-haired woman with a clipboard. He waved her forward and introduced her as his assistant before asking where they should leave their camera bags so they wouldn't have to carry them around.

Inside the ballroom she eyed the typical banquet decor, taking in the centerpieces comprised of floating candles in fishbowls with scattered confetti on white linen tablecloths. Accordion-pleated napkins topped a printed program.

It reminded her of the Dinner Theatre, especially since Ryan had mentioned a show later.

A high-pitched squeal brought her head around in time to see a stunning blonde wrap her arms around Ryan. Her tiny black dress fit like a designer gown.

Of course, the handsome photographer hugged her back and pressed a quick kiss to her cheek.

A twinge of jealousy pinched Liz's heart. Who was she to hope that Ryan might ever be interested in her just because they both liked to take pictures?

Ryan released the goddess and turned her way. "Liz? I'd like you to meet my sister Cheryl."

Sister? Relief made her weak in the knees, but somehow she stammered through a semi-coherent reply while searching their faces for a similarity or two and finding it in the color of their eyes and the shape of their noses.

Cheryl led them to a table near the back where place cards designated seats for the chairing committee. "I'm sorry there's only one seat reserved here. I didn't get Ryan's message about bringing *a friend* until it was too late to change the seating chart."

"Don't worry." Time to deflect the woman's curiosity with the reminder that Liz was only there to work. If a tiny part of her wanted to get to know Ryan better personally, then that was her secret to keep. "I'll be mingling and taking pictures during most of dinner anyway."

"*We'll* be taking pictures." Ryan nodded. "And Liz can eat the meal."

"No, we can share it ... as long as I get the dessert."

His sister laughed. "I'll keep my eye on the guest list to see if there's an unclaimed plate." She turned to Ryan. "I'm so glad you're here to take pictures. Mom would be so proud."

"Wait a minute—if we're both here, who's watching the kids tonight?"

"I got my neighbor to help out in exchange for Matt's shoveling her driveway after the next two storms. I love bartering."

"Especially since you'd have had him do the shoveling anyway."

"True. But this way Mrs. Stewart thinks she's doing me a favor."

"But she is."

Cheryl shrugged and then laughed, a happy sound that made clear the keen sense of humor running in the family. She glanced around the room. "Oh, there's Mary Ellen. We need to go over the program one last time."

Ryan grinned as his sister scurried off and then pulled his camera out of his bag, switching over into professional mode. With each competent gesture—the flick of the wrist, strap around his neck, and click of the battery—focus appeared on his face.

Time to get to work.

Liz scrambled to catch up with his rapid and practiced preparations. Thankfully, she'd remembered to recharge her battery last night. She draped her camera strap around her neck and freed her shoulder-length hair. The lens cap went into the bag, and the bag slid under the chair. "Ready when you are."

Ryan nodded. "Circle back here by the time the food starts to appear. In the meantime, try to be discreet and blend in, if possible."

She raised an eyebrow. "Discretion is my middle name. Or at least it could be."

He winked. "Even if you're too beautiful to blend in."

"W–what?" Her response came too late, for he had already walked away.

He thought her beautiful? *And* he was among the first to like her pictures since Grandpa died?

She restrained her sudden urge to do a victory dance, in the name of that discretion she'd claimed.

A rising hum of voices signaled the arrival of the guests. Ryan's sister and the older woman with the clipboard met the attendees at the door, while Ryan snapped away from an ideal angle.

Liz pivoted to capture the essence of the decor, the dessert table, and the cascading fountain of punch in the corner. She then moved to get a shot of the tabletop filled with shiny plaques glistening in the candlelight. A pivot later, she seated herself on the top step to the stage and began to zoom in on the faces of the guests.

A teenage girl with braces gazed up in awe at a slender young man with glasses, while a slightly overweight boy with an acne problem cracked jokes with them both. Three shots later, Liz adjusted her focus to a couple of businessmen in suits holding punch cups while animatedly discussing something as riveting as whether the Broncos could win another Super Bowl.

Two elderly women sipped their punch to the right of the stage, and Liz zoomed in to capture their secretive expressions—as if they were engaged in sharing the juiciest gossip of the year. A whir of the shutter followed by a quick shift in zoom… She depressed the shutter-release button and heard a *beep* instead of a *click*. A red light came on in the corner of the viewfinder.

The memory card was full.

Her stomach sank to her knees.

How could that be? She hadn't taken that many shots yet tonight, and yesterday's dress rehearsal didn't add up to much … unless Ryan had filled the card while she was onstage.

After a busy day rehearsing the dance scenes and a few hours of pleasant distraction decorating a Christmas tree or two for the lobby, the last thing on her mind had been reviewing the pictures on her memory card and moving them to a flash drive.

And she'd left her spare card at home since it still held the pictures from *42nd Stree*t.

Why hadn't she thought to check the available memory or bring along an extra card when she'd been checking on the battery?

Too late now. But how could she fix it?

She'd have to do a quick review of the images with a manual delete of the unusable photos—a process that would consume precious time while she missed new photo opportunities.

Or she'd have to admit to being an amateur and ask whether Ryan had an extra card she could use for the remainder of the evening. And if she chose that uncomfortable option, there was no way on earth she could accept money for tonight's work. She never should have come.

If only she could disappear to the ladies' restroom. Or call a cab to take her home. Except she'd still see Ryan several times every weekend while he took pictures at the theater where she worked.

Her stomach churned. There could be no escape tonight.

She rose on shaking legs and skirted the crowded ballroom toward their rendezvous point. She caught a glimpse of him across the room as he headed that way as well. "Hey, are you okay? You don't look so good."

She took a deep breath and pushed a hand against her stomach before looking up at Ryan. "I do feel sick, but it's with stupidity." She lifted the camera slightly. "I didn't realize how full my memory card was after the dress rehearsal yesterday. I just maxed out."

"No problem. I've got a couple of spares in the outside pocket of my bag."

She raised an eyebrow. "Just like that? No lecture?"

He shrugged. "Why? It doesn't fix anything, and besides, I have a feeling that I'm the real reason you didn't know how full the card was."

"It's not your fault."

"No." He rested a hand on her shoulder and leaned in with a mischievous twinkle in his eyes. "I suppose it really is your fault. I was having so much fun yesterday watching you and the rest of the cast that I just kept taking picture after picture."

Her face bloomed with heat. "It's a wonder you didn't break my camera."

He chuckled, a deep sound that sparked warmth in her chest. "We can debate that later. For now, just grab another memory card and get back to work."

"Aye, aye, boss."

He reached out and tapped her nose. "And don't you forget it."

She watched him stride away, as confident in a suit as he seemed in jeans, and tried to picture him on a horse at his family's ranch.

He was certainly unforgettable.

She turned away before the heat in her face matched her hair and hurried to find his camera case. Even with permission, it still felt like an invasion of privacy to unfasten the front pocket. Inside were three memory cards, one still in the packaging.

While he'd told her to take a card, what if one of them already had pictures on it? Then she'd be in the same situation as now.

After a moment's hesitation, she took the unopened one just to be safe. A minute later, she secured her full card in her camera bag and slipped the new card into its slot in the camera, fastening the door. Time to make her temporary boss happy he'd rescued her.

She again skirted the perimeter of the room, this time with an eye on the growing crowd. Spotting a proud father with an arm around his daughter, she lifted her camera.

She'd finish tonight's job and stick to the theater in the future. Acting like she had her life together came easier on the stage.

Chapter Six

"How did you feel about tonight?"

Liz zipped the top shut on her camera bag and glanced at Ryan. "You mean before or after I messed up the assignment by not being prepared?"

He frowned. "Why are you so tough on yourself?"

She blew out a frustrated breath and eyed the hotel staff clearing the tablecloths as the event coordinators packed up their things. "Why don't you ask a hard question for a change?"

"Seriously." Ryan looped his bag over his shoulder and gestured for her to take the lead toward the exit. "We're human, so we make mistakes."

"Humans should also find the thing they're good at." Tears stung her eyes. "What if I'll never be good enough? I'm not a star-quality actress, and I'm obviously not a smart photographer—"

"Hey." He stopped her progress with a warm hand on her arm.

"I just wish I could find my sweet spot." Or find a way to make her father proud for a change.

"If you ask me, I think you already have."

She rolled her eyes and continued out the ballroom door.

He caught up with her in the lobby. "Let me ask you this. What exactly is a sweet spot, and what does it feel like?"

She bit her lip while she thought before answering. "I think it's when you're doing the thing you were designed to do. When everything is—"

"If you believe you were *designed* for something, don't you think the Designer might help you figure it out if you asked? 'For I know the plans I have for you, declares the Lord.'"

What was it about her friends lately? First Dani and now Ryan with their easy answers about God working in her life had her longing for something more. And yet...

"What if God wants me to do something I don't want to do?"

"Like go to Africa?" He jostled her shoulder as if punctuating his joke.

A joke that wasn't remotely funny. Strangers in Africa were interesting. Facing Dad in Wichita was another story.

Ryan paused near the door leading out into the frigid night air. "While I believe God gave each of us unique gifts to use for His purposes, I also know that He is infinitely good and wants the best for us."

"I might agree to the first part of that."

"But the second part takes faith." He sighed. "I know." He turned up the collar of his coat and gestured toward the door.

She hugged her coat tightly to her body and ducked her head against the wind as they made their way across the snow-glazed parking lot toward Ryan's truck.

A minute later they piled inside the cab, happy to be out of the icy weather. Ryan turned the key in the ignition, twisted the heater knob to full blast, and then rubbed his hands together. "Did I ever tell you about the time I … oh, probably not."

"About the time you what?" She held her chilled fingers in front of the blower.

"The time I accidentally erased a full memory card of pictures."

"What? How is that even possible? They're small but durable."

He offered half a smile. "I guess I'm talented that way."

She eyed the dimple beside his adorably crooked smile. "So what happened?"

"Well, I was in Florida on assignment, taking pictures in the Everglades. Alligators and herons and tortoises galore, from sunrise to sunset. I even got a picture of the endangered Florida panther. With a full card and a heap of satisfaction, I sat back to enjoy the airboat ride to my guide's car." He placed his hands behind his head as if to demonstrate his posture. "So we're skimming along, just inches above the water, and kicking up a refreshing mist."

"And then?"

"Patience." He grinned to take the sting out of his words. "There I was, celebrating the joy of a good day's work, and I decided to pull out my camera to review some of the new shots." He pantomimed the motion.

"Go on."

"The boat pilot swerved to avoid an alligator ahead, and my camera and I flew overboard."

"No!" she gasped in horror.

"My splash scared off the gator, and I quickly climbed back into the boat with the camera strap still looped around my wrist."

"But a powered-up camera and all that water…"

"Yep. Shorted it out." He shrugged. "I tried the bag-of-rice trick on the card that night, but it was a total loss. Had to beg my boss for an extra day, buy a new camera, and hire another guide to take me out again to reshoot as much as I could."

"Bet you lost a lot of money."

He nodded. "But I learned a valuable lesson: never count your shots before they're uploaded, saved, and backed up."

She laughed at the twisted cliché. "Glad to know I'm not the only photographer who's ever bungled a job."

He growled. "You did not bungle this job."

"If you say so."

"In case you missed it, that's what I've been trying to say for the last fifteen minutes."

"Yeah, well, thanks for cheering me up." Because somehow in the middle of his own story, he had actually lifted the guilt from her shoulders.

"Glad it worked." He fastened his seat belt and turned on the headlights, preparing to pull out of the parking lot. "Because I can't wait to see the shots you took tonight."

"Speaking of which"—she leaned down to the bag at her feet—"should I just give you the cards to load onto your computer?"

"Are you up for a cup of coffee?"

She blinked at the change of subject, then glanced at her watch. She'd planned to do more private rehearsals at the theater tomorrow, but she could certainly sleep in. "Sure."

"Good. I've got my laptop stashed behind the seat, so we could upload the pictures tonight."

"Before they accidentally fall into an alligator-infested river? In Colorado? In November?"

"Exactly." His chuckle warmed the cab of the truck faster than the heater had.

Fifteen minutes later, she cradled a cup of hazelnut-mocha coffee between her hands as Ryan plugged her first card into his laptop. The program's icon spun as the images copied into a file.

"So, while we're waiting, what do you think about helping me out with the Christmas pictures at the theater?"

A flash of excitement buzzed through her and then fizzled. "I don't know why you'd ask me. Besides, it was your idea, and you need the money."

"Your excellent work as a photographer is the reason why." He gestured toward the parade of thumbnail images on his screen. "As for the money, maybe you can help me come up with a few more ideas so there's more available to split. If you're roaming around, you can get some of those great candid shots you excel at."

"But I heard you talk to Mr. Sheridan about printing out five-by-sevens of everyone who poses for the family shot whether they end up buying them at the end of the evening or not. You can't afford to print out candids on speculation too."

"Hmm." He stroked his chin. "What if we gave them a glimpse of the preview shot and they placed an order? Maybe even collect the money, print the pictures they paid for, and then deliver them at intermission?"

"That could work." Except for the part where she'd probably be the one handling the cash and photo paper just like Dad had wanted.

"I know your first job is the show itself and possibly waiting tables." He switched out her first memory card for the second one and clicked it to upload as well.

"I could give up a few shifts' worth of tips as a waitress, but intermission is always crazy even if I'm not serving."

"Oh, don't worry about that. I'd do all the printing and delivery myself. Just help take pictures during the preshow meal."

An invisible burden lifted from her shoulders. Miracle of miracles, his invitation to be involved really meant behind the camera instead of behind a desk. And maybe he'd be open to a few of her ideas too.

"How much were you going to charge for the five-by-sevens? You could offer the candids in a four-by-six size for less money."

"Less?" He raised his eyebrows. "How exactly does that make money?"

"First, like you said, printing the candid pictures is guaranteed income because you've taken the orders. Plus, if you use standard-size photo paper, you save on printing costs overall."

He nodded. "Go on."

"If I'm going out to a fancy dinner and show with my family and perhaps already pushing my budget at a time of year when money might be tight thanks to Christmas shopping…"

"Folks might be likely to pose for a family shot and then not buy it at the end of the evening." He frowned as if realizing his business idea might not be as lucrative as he'd hoped.

"Right. But if there's a cheaper alternative that feels more natural—rather than a stiff pose—they can pay for it before ordering extra dessert, drinks, and tacking on a tip…"

He grinned. "More sales overall and less financial risk for me."

"Exactly. Maybe you could even offer a discount deal if they purchase the larger posed shot too." She sat back in her chair and took a long sip of her drink while eyeing Ryan over the top of her cup.

A lot had happened in the last week. Instead of unemployment forcing her home, here she sat with a handsome man, trying to juggle her acting duties with photography while talking business practices. And feeling remarkably alive in the process.

Almost as if she'd found her sweet spot.

She was so tempted to jump in and spend more time with Ryan since she could probably learn a lot from someone with his freelance experience, but could she take a risk with another photographer? What if he was only interested in her help and not her heart?

She took another long sip of her coffee and watched as Ryan switched out the memory cards again since both of hers had finished loading. Soon the pictures he'd taken filtered onto the screen.

"I know you'll need to delete the dinner theater pictures you uploaded from my first card, but do you think you've got enough good ones from tonight to make them happy?"

"Um, *we've* got a wonderful collection." He leaned back and took a swig of his own coffee before resting the cup on his stomach. "I know I'm paying you, but I'm truly thankful for your help."

"And I'm thankful for the chance to do some real photography work again. I haven't taken this many pictures in years."

"Probably since you were at your dad's studio, right?"

Her stomach cramped as the formerly delicious drink soured.

"Hey, I just thought of something. With the new show opening on Friday, you're not going home for Thanksgiving, are you?"

"Nope." And the thought brought a wave of relief instead of the regret it should have.

"Any plans? Like with the rest of the cast?"

She shook her head. "Not really." Dani would be spending the day with Alex and his family, while Gloria would probably be arm-twisting Evan into taking her out to dinner, assuming her globe-trotting parents weren't in town. Her own plans would likely be a microwave turkey dinner after watching the Macy's parade on television.

"What about you?"

"Well, with John deployed in Afghanistan, my sister and I are hoping to distract the kids with a day of sledding at Poudre Canyon."

"That sounds like fun, even if it could get cold."

"That's what a Crock-Pot of chili is for."

"What? No turkey dinner?"

He laughed. "Growing up on a ranch, we were always more likely to eat steak or prime rib than a silly bird, no matter how nicely Mom stuffed him."

She eyed the laugh lines around his eyes, and a sudden longing welled up within her. When was the last time she'd felt such joy at family memories? Probably not since her grandparents had died.

"Say, if you don't have any plans, why don't you join us?"

"Me? No. I'd hate to intrude." Even if the temptation to get to know Ryan better was overwhelming.

"Good. We could use an extra adult along. I'll pick you up at eight."

Chapter Seven

The crisp air filled her lungs and awakened her senses as Liz stepped outside her apartment. Ryan had called for her address and said he would be there within ten minutes. But with a grumpy Gloria inside complaining that her parents had canceled their plans at the last minute to fly to the Bahamas instead, well, Liz would rather brave the wintry scene while she waited.

She tugged a green knit hat over her low braids and tucked the matching mittens into the pockets of her parka. As prepared for the snowy weather as she could be, she paced down the concrete hallway toward the stairs, the swishing of her ski pants keeping time with the *thunk* of her snow boots. She reached the outdoor stairwell, then gasped at the view.

An overnight cold front had christened the trees with a glittering glaze. Contrasted against the deep blue Colorado sky, the pristine white frost coating each individual branch and twig sparkled in the rising sun.

The perfection called to something deep within her, and she spun back toward the apartment to retrieve her camera. A few minutes later, with the bag hanging behind her and several dozen images already saved, she squatted in the stairwell and zoomed the focus onto a single frost-covered nub, capturing the crystalline detail. Before her eyes, the warmth from the sun began to transform the sharp angles into a softer sheen. She captured the transition as a droplet formed, grew, and eventually released. With her fast-action shutter, she should have a few stunning shots.

The nerves in her fingertips began to tingle as she switched focus to another tree and moved down a few steps.

By the time she'd reached the sidewalk, the crystalline paint dripped everywhere. If she'd been a few minutes later, she'd have missed the moment when everything changed.

She lowered the viewfinder with a sigh as a truck pulled into an empty spot nearby.

"I should have guessed you'd be out here with a camera."

She turned to face Ryan as he leaned out the open window. "You should have seen it. It was magical. And gorgeous."

"Yes, I see." He eyed her rather than the trees.

A sudden warmth flooded her cheeks as she swung her camera bag around to her side and hurried around to the passenger side of his truck. She'd be wise to remember that while flirting was fun, it was too soon to feel anything more than friendship for Ryan, no matter how tempting.

After climbing in, she scooted to the middle of the bench seat. "Check these out." She scrolled through the pictures and showed Ryan the previews.

His eyebrows rose. "Like you said. Gorgeous."

A different giddy feeling rose in her chest only to war with the knowledge that humility should be the word of the day, considering the company she kept. Ryan's awards were well deserved.

She smiled anyway and stowed the camera in the bag at her feet. "So where are the others?"

"Cheryl and the kids were still Skyping with John this morning, so they'll meet us at the turnoff to the property."

"The property?"

"Nothing we own. A friend of theirs from church has a ranch in the mountains and offered an open invitation to come up to sled and such. She gave me directions, but I'm not sure my GPS will get a signal past the foothills."

"That's why we're meeting them at the turnoff. I get it." Liz settled against the cushioned seat as Ryan backed out of the parking spot. It would be interesting to see him around his family instead of in a professional setting. Did he know how to relax and have fun?

As they turned west, he reached over to adjust the volume on the radio. Haunting lyrics poured from the speakers as a man's voice sang, "I love the Maker and the Maker loves me."

If only that could be true.

Yet based on the expression on Ryan's face as he sang along—off tune, a fact that made her smile—he believed it.

And when they met the rest of his family, she quickly discovered he wasn't the only one with faith in God. Especially when seven-year-old Matt tugged on his uncle's sleeve and told him how they'd prayed with his dad, that God would keep him safe and bring him home soon.

It wasn't that many years ago her faith had been as childlike.

And yet instead of downplaying his nephew's earnest plea, Ryan picked up his five-year-old niece, whose enormous green eyes shone with her uncle's attention, and gathered them all into a circle. With little Hannah on one arm, he wrapped his free arm around Liz and bowed his head.

"Father, on this day set aside for giving thanks, we'd just like to say thank You for listening to us when we pray. Thank You for keeping John and his unit safe. And thanks that we have the chance to spend the day in Your beautiful outdoors together as a family and with our new friend Liz."

Cheryl chimed in from her other side. "Thank You for the gifts You've given us, and thanks in advance for providing a job for me. Thanks for Ryan's willingness to take a hiatus to come help us, and thanks for the opportunities for him to take pictures around here, especially at the dinner theater."

What kind of man put aside his own career and ego and fame in order to help his family? What would it be like to be loved that thoroughly?

Yet she'd already gotten a glimpse of that generosity through his invitation to help with the awards-night photo shoot and candids tomorrow night at the theater, especially since it took money away from his close-knit family.

A warmth that might have originated with his arm around her waist or the emotion he sparked in her spread through her chest and brought a few tears to her eyes.

She had a lot to be thankful for too. *God, thanks for my job. For the chance to take pictures again and even to make money doing it. And thanks for this amazing man who is sharing his family with me today.*

"Will you sled wiff me?" A tiny voice to her right alerted her to the embarrassing fact that their impromptu prayer circle was disbanding. And drew Liz's attention to the missing tooth that was causing the lisp.

She swallowed to clear the emotion from her throat. "I'd love to, sweetie." Hannah's hot-pink stocking cap matched the trim on her coat and highlighted the blonde hair so like her mother's.

"Uncle Ryan and Matt went to get the sleds."

"How long have you known my little brother?" Cheryl knelt in front of her daughter.

"Little?" She glanced over at Ryan's height and the way he easily reached into the truck bed and lifted out several sleds.

"He's still little and annoying when I can get away with teasing him about it."

If only she'd had a brother to deflect the family pressure. Not to mention that Jerry the Jerk wouldn't have weaseled his way into the business quite so easily.

Cheryl tugged Hannah's mittens into place before looking at Liz. "You didn't answer my question."

Liz counted back the days. Had it only been—"A week."

Too soon to be falling in love, even if she couldn't deny her instant attraction or the uncomfortable discovery that Ryan had already awakened in her a dormant desire for photography ... and faith.

"Hmm. I would have thought it was longer, the way you worked together Tuesday night." The gleam in Cheryl's eyes hinted at a possible fishing expedition into her brother's social life.

"Um, he's really easy to get along with." Perhaps she should turn the tables to find answers to her own questions. "Does he have any secret flaws I should know about? Besides not being able to carry a tune?"

Cheryl laughed. "True. He got his singing voice from our dad. Along with being annoyingly talented at what he does. But he's always on the move and never stays in one place for very long. Plus, he drinks all the coffee in the morning."

"Oh ... I guess I should have realized he was staying with you."

"He sure is. Why rent a furnished apartment when I've got an empty guest room? He's great with the kids, which will come in handy once I get a job." Cheryl nodded to where Ryan helped Matt adjust his grip on a sled, nudging Liz's side with her elbow. "He's going to be a great dad someday."

Liz choked at Cheryl's over-the-top hint, and Cheryl laughed. What was it with this family and their bend toward romantic teasing?

Except there was truth hidden beneath the fun.

And she was falling fast. For a photographer, no less.

"All right, who's first down the hill?" The man in question held two sleds under his arm. His gaze shifted from Liz to his sister and then to his niece. "Anyone want a piggyback ride to the top?"

"Me!" Hannah giggled as Ryan swung her onto his back and then started tromping out a path up the hill.

The group's first few slow trips down the hill served to pack the snow into the ideal sledding surface, but then the sleds started to pick up speed. After reaching the bottom again with Hannah, Liz handed the little girl to her mother and retrieved her camera from Ryan's truck.

Using her fast-action shutter, she was able to capture the joy in Matt's face as he and Ryan flew down the hill with a blur of snow flying up behind them. And then the love in Cheryl's protective arm around her daughter. Ryan's strength as he carried all the sleds up the hill, and his gentleness as he cradled Hannah during a crash and dusted snow off her hat. Young Matt's valiant attempts to be a gentleman with his mother, before bursting into childish antics like throwing a snowball at his uncle.

They couldn't fake the love shared within their family circle, and a dormant part of her heart longed to create more memories like these in the future—like the vague memories she had of a happy family life before Grandpa O'Neill died. Before Grandma's suffocating grief and Mom's battle with depression left Dad free to take the business in a different direction, destroying Liz's dreams in the process.

But even back then, her memories were mere shadows of these playful interactions.

She adjusted the camera focus in time to see Ryan toss a handful of snow into his sister's face and then not so helpfully add more and rub it in, under the ploy of brushing it off.

After a brief skirmish, Cheryl escaped her brother's icy exfoliating facial scrub and joined Liz at the foot of the hill. "Did you get any pictures of that?"

"A couple." Liz switched her camera to preview mode and showed Cheryl.

"Nice." She whistled, then toggled the switch to see more.

"Hey, ladies, if you're done chatting, we're thinking to take a break from sledding to build a snowman." Ryan stuck the sleds into a nearby snowbank. "Uncle Ryan—I mean Hannah—can use the rest."

Matt, red-faced and sweaty, pointed a finger at his uncle. "You might need a nap this afternoon."

"No way. That's when the football games are on."

Cheryl groaned. "Of course. No break from that Thanksgiving tradition this year."

By the time Liz had returned her camera to the truck and pulled on her mittens, Ryan and Matt were at work rolling a massive ball of snow for the base while Hannah watched. Cheryl had disappeared into the nearby trees looking for branches and pine cones as decorations.

"Do you want to help me with the middle?" Liz grinned as the little girl nodded like a bobblehead doll. Soon she straddle-walked behind Hannah as they packed the snow tight, then angled their path to intersect where the guys smoothed out the giant base. The activity tugged at memories of the year Grandpa O'Neill had helped her build a snowman and stole Grandma's scarf for a decoration.

"Hannah, that's the best middle I've ever seen." Ryan's praise brought a sweet smile from the precious little girl, filling more of the lonely spots in Liz's heart. "But do you think Liz can lift it up here?"

"You could help, you know." Liz paused to straighten a kink out of her back.

"I could." He waggled his eyebrows, then moved to face her.

With his arms under hers, they lifted the middle section and then sidestepped toward the base. One could imagine they were almost hugging … if not for the icy mass between them.

And only if one were prone to imagining the start of a romance where friendship grew.

Cheryl emerged from the woods with an armload of potential decorations and whistled. "Looking good, you two."

"Yep, looking good." Ryan's teasing wink implied that he wasn't thinking about the snowman.

Liz helped steady the mass of snow while Ryan packed handfuls of snow in and around the gap to seal the connection, his arms frequently brushing against hers. Heat rose in her face as she changed the subject. "What are we going to name him ... or her?"

"I'm thinking he looks like a Herbert." Ryan stepped back and tilted his head to the right, as if in thought. "What do you think, Hannah?"

The little girl giggled, then nodded so hard that her stocking cap slipped down over one eye.

With everyone's help, soon Herbert had a head, arms, face, buttons, and pine-needle hair. Liz retrieved her camera from the truck and directed the Callahan clan to gather around the snowman for a family photo.

"You need to get in a few too." Cheryl left the group and reached for Liz's camera. "Go stand over by Ryan and pretend you like him."

"Pretend?" Ryan huffed as if offended but gestured for Liz to take a spot between him and the snowman.

As if she belonged there with him and the two giggling children at their feet.

Caught somewhere between the wispy dream of a family of her own and the conflicting sense of coming home, it didn't take much, if any, "pretending" to like Ryan.

"Now that Herbert's done, I think you need another turn sledding. Since we packed down the snow, the slope has gotten faster."

She glanced at him, vaguely aware of Cheryl taking pictures. "Are you challenging me to a race?"

"No. We'll go together."

Her nerves tingled, partly from anticipation of being close to Ryan and partly from anticipation of sliding down the slick snow. Kansas didn't have these kinds of hills. "You'll take care of me, right?"

"You're in good hands." He grinned, then snagged her hand and a toboggan sled before leading their charge up the mountain.

They passed the main starting spot and continued another twenty feet up to a place Ryan had used for a few solo runs earlier.

"Are you sure about this?" From up here, the clearing between the trees started to resemble the peak of a roller coaster before it plummeted at top speeds. "I can't get hurt the day before *White Christmas* opens."

"Trust me." Ryan set down the toboggan, then sat on the back end, bracing his feet in the snow. "Climb on."

With Matt and Hannah cheering from the base of the hill, Liz soon found herself surrounded by Ryan's solid strength—behind her, one arm around her waist, and one hand on the sled's rope handle. Almost before she'd gathered her courage, Ryan lifted his feet and wiggled just enough to get them moving.

The sled picked up speed as they tore down the hill, the wind pulling a *whoop* of excitement from her mouth.

How long had it been since she'd felt such freedom?

Ryan tugged on the rope handle, but they veered a bit off course, hitting fresh powder that sprayed into her face.

"Hold on!"

Barreling into an uncharted section of deeper snow, the sled hit something underneath that acted like a brake, and suddenly they went flying through the air.

Liz landed face-first in a snowdrift, then momentum rolled her over until she ended up half-buried underneath Ryan's sprawled body near the tree line. "Can you get up?"

"What if I don't want to?" He groaned, then tried to lift himself up to his knees—except their boots were tangled together. His head bumped into a nearby pine branch, sending a shower of snow on top of them. While his body had blocked the worst from her face, some must have gone down his collar because his eyes widened in surprise.

She couldn't help but laugh. Served him right for asking her to trust his sled-steering skills.

His eyes narrowed as if contemplating revenge. "I think you're just asking for a..."

Would he wash her face in snow as he had Cheryl's earlier?

The flirtatious twinkle in his eyes transformed into something more potent, and his voice lowered to a whisper. "A kiss."

Her relief at the reprieve morphed into anticipation. Her lips started to curve into a smile as he leaned down, their breaths mingling.

And then a snowball exploded against the back of his head. "Break it up, you two."

Chapter Eight

Liz took a deep breath and counted to ten as the large group at tables six through eight debated which of her candids they should buy. How long could it take to make up their minds? At this rate, the servers would be collecting empty plates before she had collected an order, making her question the decision to give up her waitressing shifts.

"I like so many of these. What if I change my mind later and want one of the others too?" The silver-haired matriarch pursed her lips. "Will it be too late to order more?"

More? As in more money? Liz smiled. "That's a great question, and I'll check with the other photographer when I turn in your order. I don't see why we couldn't load the images from tonight onto his website and have them available for a week or so."

A dark-haired woman swiveled in her seat and leaned into the conversation. "If you did that, could we buy a digital image for our Christmas card? Or would you only make additional prints available?"

Liz glanced at her watch. "Tell you what—I'll go find out right now, while you finish the order form." If she hurried, she could get back here to complete this level and then start on the next before the call to preshow.

She pivoted and headed toward the exit, pausing only to sidestep one of the other actors carrying an empty tray ... which was another reminder that she'd better hustle, because once all the meals were delivered, the call to preshow wouldn't be far behind. And every minute counted double, especially on opening night when things tended to go wrong. She still needed to change into her first costume for *White Christmas.*

She pushed through the door to the lobby and caught sight of Ryan bent over a laptop computer at his temporary workstation in the corner.

After yesterday's almost-kiss, she'd been nervous about a repeat encounter. But between Hannah's insistence that she ride along in Ryan's truck, being surrounded by his family during the delicious meal, and now the chaotic opening-night festivities with guests eager to have their pictures taken, they hadn't had much of a chance to talk about the questions that lingered in her mind.

Was it only the heat—er, chill—of the moment, or did Ryan really want to kiss her?

Was their friendship about to cross a line into something more?

But those questions would have to wait because right now she had a job to do. Liz took a deep breath and hurried forward.

"Hey, pretty lady." Ryan looked up from loading his camera's memory card into the computer.

"Quick question or two from a table that wants to know if they can access the unpurchased candid shots later, and if so, can they get a digital file rather than a print?"

He stood and rested warm hands on her shoulders. "Whoa. Slow down there."

She took another deep breath, filling her senses with his spicy cologne, just like yesterday in the snowbank. She blew out a stream of air and felt her blood pressure drop.

"Okay. That's better." His crooked smile emerged. "Now, what do you think we should do?"

She deflected her gaze from his smiling lips in order to maintain her composure. "I think we, or you, could load the images onto a hidden page on your website, keep them there for a week or two, and get a few more orders after the fact. You could price the digital image along with reprints or even create a package deal for additional sales."

"I like the sound of additional sales, but why hide the page?"

"Whether you set up a password for access or only share the URL with certain people, either way, it only makes it available to those who actually purchase candids during the evening. Otherwise people might delay placing an order at all until looking online and then never get around to it."

"Impulse buys are money, right?"

"Right."

"Brilliant. Now how should we do this?"

"We could print up a few sheets of business-card-type thank-you notes—to be delivered with their print orders tonight—that lists a web page expiring in a week or two, to entice them to order soon."

"Done this before?"

She felt heat rise in her face. "Dreamed it, or something like it."

"It's a terrific idea. Where do we start?"

"First, is your website easy to update, or do you need to contact your web guy?"

"I'm the web guy and, yes, it's easy to add a page."

"Good. While the first part of the show is going on tonight, do the printing you need to for orders. Then create a blank page on your website so you know the URL works and print out a few quick quarter-page flyers with the address."

"And what else do I put on that flyer?" He pulled out a blank order sheet and started taking notes.

"For now, thank them for their order, and then put that additional reprints, digital files, and other images from tonight's show will be available for purchase after twenty-four hours. Add the URL after that."

She glanced toward the auditorium doors. "I'll go tell them that we can do both, with details available before they leave this evening."

"So we promise something that isn't ready yet?"

"Yet." She thumped his arm. "If you know how to do a web page, we can slap the images into a gallery with image numbers and, once we figure out the details, then post specific instructions on the page itself for them to e-mail you their picks and mailing addresses. If we can't figure out how to set up an easy shopping cart in the morning, you can just e-mail them a PayPal invoice this weekend."

"What's with all this *we* and *you*?" His eyes took on a gleam that reminded her of yesterday's almost-kiss and sparked her hope for a repeat opportunity that wasn't so spontaneous … or interrupted. Or rushed.

This connection between them was happening so fast and yet felt so right.

"I'll definitely help, but I also have a show to do." She rolled her eyes. "And now I'm behind on accessing a complete level."

He squeezed her shoulder again before glancing around the empty lobby. "Since everyone is now seated, I'll grab my camera and head inside to finish up the candid rounds. Then I'll make up something with a web address to add to their orders."

"Great."

"And … I'm taking you out for dinner or coffee or something after the show tonight because we obviously need to work out the rest of the details. Especially if you come up with any other great ideas between now and then."

"Deal." She stuck out her hand to shake on it.

The tingles from his warm grip lingered as she rushed back into the auditorium, but the warmth of his praise for her business ideas carried her through the opening act.

A week later, Liz exited stage right after the "Let Me Sing and I'm Happy" scene. With just one more scene before intermission, her mind jumped to a daydream about a long drink before changing costumes and maybe even a power nap in the dressing room over the break.

Even after last weekend's learning curve and several days of setting up an online shopping cart on Ryan's website, there were still issues to be clarified. And by the time the stressful preshow camera craze was done, she'd been more than happy to leave her camera and memory card with Ryan to handle the printing and deliveries of all the Christmas-clad family photos.

All that stood between her and a few minutes of rest ... was the growing crowd gathered around a fluttering piece of paper stapled to the wall outside the dressing rooms.

Surely that couldn't be the next cast list right in the middle of a show.

Yet a glance toward the kitchen showed a retreating Mrs. Sheridan slipping through the doorway. And a few muted squeals from the growing crowd around the paper confirmed that the anticipated-but-late cast list had finally been posted. Just in the nick of time since rehearsals were supposed to start on Monday morning, with under a month to go until *Seven Brides for Seven Brothers* opened in January.

While most of the actors on multi-show contracts would simply move from one type of role to another, was she about to discover she'd been cut again—just two and a half weeks after getting her reprieve miracle? Then again, since she'd replaced an actress with a multi-show contract, could she hope for good news?

"Oh, please, Lord." The whispered prayer escaped before she could stop it.

She edged toward the small mob and braced her shoulders. She could do this with the biggest fake smile on her face if necessary. After all, she wasn't an actress for nothing.

"Congratulations, Liz!" Renee's semi-whispered cheer came seconds before Marie wrapped her in a hug.

"For what?" She spit out a chunk of Marie's dark, overly sprayed hair. Surely they weren't this excited about her getting another contract ... unless they saw something else on the cast list.

And congratulations only made sense if...

She pulled out of Marie's arms and stepped toward the sheet, her eyes scanning the list of names.

Adam Pontipee, oldest brother of the clan, played by Greg Schmidt.

Milly, his bride, played by … Elizabeth Foster.

The list continued with the other six brothers and their six girls plus an assortment of previous suitors and other townspeople, but her eyes quickly returned to the top. She blinked several times but her name remained.

"Look at her. She's in shock."

"I remember how I felt the first time I had a lead role."

"Shock" was too mild a word for the surge of emotion that left her light-headed and wobbly-kneed.

Not only was she staying with the company for another show, but for the first time in her acting career, she'd been given the lead female role in a production. What would her dad have to say now?

Well, at least someone believed in her enough to give her the opportunity, and she really needed to say thanks—to more than one person.

She sidestepped away from the list to allow others access, leaned against the wall, and closed her eyes against a rush of tears. *I don't deserve it, but thanks again, God.*

On stage, the "Count Your Blessings" scene drew to a close. Just one more scene until intermission, when the guests would be served dessert. Mr. Sheridan could usually be found near the sound-and-lights board at the back of the auditorium. If she changed back into her photography clothes from earlier, she could slip out and thank him personally. And if anyone asked, she could always pretend she had to check on Ryan and the pictures, which she could probably do anyway even though they'd decided she would stay focused on the play.

Liz pushed away from the wall and exchanged smiles with several of her castmates before slipping into the women's dressing room.

A few minutes later, she eased around the perimeter of the chaotic kitchen just ahead of the dessert rush. By the time the house lights came up, she had a clear path to the sound booth and intercepted the director just as he removed his communication headset.

"Mr. Sheridan? Thank you." Her voice cracked. "I can't believe it. I was just hoping for a crowd part as one of the girls, but this is more than I imagined."

"I wouldn't have given you the part if I didn't think you could do it." He laid his headset beside the control panel and stepped down out of the booth. "But maybe I also needed to thank you for helping out so much lately—not only on the stage by keeping this show from falling apart, but also with the photography. Our website has never looked better."

Liz shifted to the side to allow a few guests room to pass on their way to the exit and the usual parade of those seeking the restrooms. "Again, I should be the one thanking you for that opportunity." Through the open doorway, she spotted Ryan with an armload of pictures in plastic bags. "It looks like he's been extremely busy during the first act."

Mr. Sheridan's gaze shifted toward the lobby and his smile grew. "The whole setup hasn't been much of a hassle at all, and so far all I've heard are positive things from our guests."

Liz grinned. "That's what we like to hear."

He grinned back. "And the extra income is a nice Christmas bonus, especially since I'm not doing any of the work."

"I'm glad it's going well. I won't keep you, but thanks again for—"

He waved her words aside with a smile. "You're a very talented young lady, and it's my pleasure to get to direct you. Now, if you'll excuse me, I do need to check in with my wife and the kitchen numbers."

She watched him weave through the packed tables in the auditorium, soaking in the energy of the crowd as they chattered about the holiday show and got into the festive spirit three weeks before Christmas.

They weren't the only ones because, with the new cast list and her first starring role, it felt as if Liz had unwrapped an early Christmas present of her own.

Chapter Nine

Monday morning found Liz skipping down the auditorium steps toward the stage for their first day of rehearsals for *Seven Brides for Seven Brothers* ... and soon the reality of an increased workload as the star would come crashing down.

But until then, she rode a wave of exhilaration, hoping it wasn't a dream after all.

After a few days of mental fatigue, blisters, and sore muscles, then she'd know for sure that her name really was on the list.

She breathed in the soothing calm before the storm as she set her things on a first-level table. After a quick glance around the auditorium to make sure she was still alone, she bounded onto the stage and strode toward center stage.

What would it be like to stand here in the spotlight, rather than lost in the crowd? Facing a multilayered ring of tables allowing hundreds of pairs of eyes a clear line of sight for the action?

She closed her eyes for a moment as her mind spun through the upcoming scenes. Her character would be whisked into marriage after a speedy courtship, discover that her new home is filled with six additional messy brothers, clean up their act, and help them find girls of their own before later consoling and protecting those kidnapped brides. With the colorful costumes, humor, and active dance sequences, the audience was sure to leave happy.

And she would be right in the middle of transporting their guests to another world.

A throat cleared off to her right. "Just what do you think you're doing?"

Liz flinched at Gloria's accusing tone but stood her ground. "I was trying to picture the new play from here." She eyed her housemate's red face and sweat-dotted T-shirt. "I could ask you the same question."

Gloria used her sleeve to dab her forehead and hairline. "I was using a rehearsal room for some of the rehab exercises my physical therapist gave me. They're harder to do than I thought."

"Does your knee—"

"It's fine." Her rubbing action contradicted her words. "Being on crutches for so long caused the other muscles to get lazy, so I'm still whipping them back into shape." She quirked a finely plucked eyebrow. "But between rehab and rehearsals, I'll be dancing better than ever. In fact, I'll be more than ready to step into your shoes."

Liz blinked at the reminder that Gloria was listed as her understudy for *Seven Brides*. "*If* that time ever comes, at least I'll be more gracious than you ever were."

Gloria sputtered. "What are you talking about?"

"You know." Liz narrowed her eyes at the former star. If Dani hadn't been proactively learning the understudy parts for the female lead in *42nd Street*, the entire show would have been in jeopardy when Gloria got hurt. Not to mention the continuing barrage of barbed accusations Gloria threw at Dani. Liz raised her pitch to imitate Gloria's tone. "I'm glad I'm not an understudy. It's a bunch of wasted time and energy. You'll never fill my shoes."

The reminder hit a nerve and Gloria glanced away, smoothing her shirt over her ample chest with a manicured hand.

Liz sighed. As much as she would love to pay back Gloria's treatment of Dani, she wanted to be a better person than that, at least for her roommate's sake, if not her own. Especially since after filling the lead role for most of two consecutive plays, Dani had graciously accepted a lesser part as one of the six brides for the next.

Then again, maybe Liz would survive Gloria as a cast rival simply because she had established boundaries now. If so, it would go a long way toward peace in the coming months—and hopefully more—that they would spend working together.

The door to the lobby opened as a trio of chattering actors entered, and Gloria hurried off to greet them.

Liz stepped off the stage to retrieve her script notebook. After a short overview orientation about the play, they were scheduled to start with the community dance-and-brawl scene since it involved just about everyone in the cast. Then they would move on to a few other scenes if they had time.

She flipped the pages to the first dance scene and fingered the end of her braid. While she personally may not have much to do in the choreographed chaos, unlike most of the rest of the first act, she still needed to pay attention to the other roles. Experience had already shown that, in twelve weeks of performances, parts could shift around with even the unlikeliest of circumstances.

An hour later, Liz stretched a kink out of her neck as the cast finally got to work on an actual scene. Mr. Sheridan paced the floor in front of the stage, his director's notebook splayed open at waist height on the front edge.

"First up, I need the Pontipee family, including Milly, at stage left."

After a quick swig from her water bottle, Liz left her notebook behind and headed for the stage. Soon she was surrounded by seven young and mostly handsome men who joked around and jostled for position while the director pointed other actors toward their opening places.

But a vague sense of emptiness swirled through Liz. Other than some opening dialogue, she would spend most of the scene as an interested observer. So much for stardom... Then again, maybe boredom was her problem because why else would she feel alone in the middle of a crowd?

This afternoon would be better since she'd be the center of attention as they staged the "Goin' Courtin' " scene.

A sudden vibration in her back pocket had her reaching to muffle the sound. At least her phone was still on silent mode since she'd been absentminded enough to forget to leave it at the table with the rest of her things.

Ten minutes later, she snuck a peek at the screen while Mr. Sheridan blocked the basic outline of the dance sequence.

A quick swipe revealed that the new message came from Ryan:

> I KNOW YOU'RE BUSY WITH REHEARSALS, BUT GIVE ME A CALL WHEN YOU GET A CHANCE. I HAVE A FAVOR TO ASK.

She quickly slipped the phone back into her pocket and glanced around, hoping no one had seen her break the-cell-phone-during-rehearsals rule. Yet an energizing rush of joy remained.

As the dance scene transitioned into a brawl between the brothers and the townsfolk, Liz found her mind wandering toward Ryan.

What would he think of the onstage shenanigans? Would he side with the rowdy ranching brothers or the proper townsfolk? She bit back a smile. He was definitely the rugged outdoors type. Her memory flashed back to that hint of a smile above her in the snowbank right before their almost-kiss—well over a week ago now.

If Ryan were playing the role of her burly husband in the play, she'd definitely find it easy to accept his fictional proposal. So much easier than Greg with his annoying offstage laugh. She glanced around the stage, seeking a distraction to ward off the flush of heat in her face.

Part of her wished Ryan had texted just because he wanted to talk to her and didn't need something. She'd just seen him yesterday while taking pictures at Sunday's matinee show—and was already counting the days until she'd see him again for their third weekend of providing guests with unique holiday photos. They had packed a lot of working together into the last two and a half weeks since he'd first walked into the theater with his crazy idea.

But rather than spend time thinking about Ryan, she needed to focus—to learn a bunch of lines, songs, and dances. She had her job, and he had his.

Two hours later, Mr. Sheridan finally called a break for lunch. Liz staggered toward the stairs and collapsed into a chair near her things. Rehearsals were tiring but in a good sort of way ... especially since her heart was so full. Not only had they made tremendous progress on the scenes themselves, but she'd found herself fitting into her new role and surrounded by a supportive cast ... with more to come this afternoon as they shifted focus to the group scenes with the brothers.

Dani collapsed into a chair across from her. "Do you have time for lunch before your rehearsals this afternoon?"

"I can make time for you." Liz stood with a smile and stretched.

Dani grinned. "Good to know where I rank in your list of priorities."

"Ahem. As if you haven't been spending every free moment during the past few weeks with a certain someone."

Dani practically glowed as she beamed. "Guilty as charged." Her phone buzzed, and she giggled. "Just a minute." Dani's fingers flew over the screen as she texted a message.

Oh yeah. Liz had a call to make herself. She retrieved her phone and swiped the screen to call Ryan while she collected her things into her rehearsal bag.

"Hey, pretty girl."

Her heart skipped a beat at his usual greeting. "Hi, yourself. We're taking a lunch break, so I've got a few minutes. What did you need?"

She heard a whirring sound in the background that sounded suspiciously like a printer. And Ryan's printer was now officially, temporarily, stationed in Mr. Sheridan's office, just a few doors away. "Wait a minute. Are you here at the theater?"

"Give the girl a prize." He chuckled in her ear, and warmth spread around her heart.

Liz swung her bag across her shoulder and caught the knowing grin on Dani's face. "Um..."

"Go ahead. But you have to spill the details later." Dani waggled her eyebrows.

Liz stuck out her tongue and then grinned before turning toward the lobby and taking the steps two at a time. "I'm heading your way now."

"I like the sound of that." His deep voice sent fresh tingles over her skin. This relationship was definitely turning into something more than she'd imagined.

He met her just outside the door of Mr. Sheridan's office. "So how was practice?"

"A bit overwhelming, with how much we have to learn in the next few weeks, but it's really fun at the same time." She peeked through the doorway to the array of papers and photographs inside. "Wow. Looks like you've been busy too."

"Your idea to post the extras for reprints is really paying off. I'm getting orders from both this weekend and the one before."

"With more work for you."

He shrugged his broad shoulders. "It's not like I have that much to do during the day while the kids are at school. Cheryl got a part-time job, so all I'm really needed for is to pick them up, have a few snacks, and put stickers on the chart once they finish their chores."

"Snacks sound like fun."

He laughed. "Extremely fun. Especially when I accidentally load them up on sugar just in time for their mom to get home and expect them to eat a decent supper. Won't be doing that again." He fake-shuddered. "The wrath of Cheryl is a force to be reckoned with."

She grinned but directed the conversation back to the reason he'd contacted her. "So you texted because you need help filling the orders?" She gestured toward the paperwork.

"No way. I've got this covered. Not to mention, I'm getting a few more ideas about how to simplify the shopping cart. Since I'm my own web guy, I'll have to make the necessary tweaks later."

"Better you than me on the website side of things."

"Glad to know I'm still better than you at something." He reached out and tweaked the end of her braid.

"As if, Mr. Award-Winning Photojournalist."

"Turned wedding photographer."

"A wedding?"

"That's the favor. What's your schedule look like next Tuesday?"

"I can guarantee at least a few rehearsals during the day between nine and four, but let me check." She dug into her bag for the rehearsal schedule in the front of her script notebook. "Looks like I'm actually clear after lunch that day." Thanks to several scenes with just the brothers.

"Great. Then would you be open to helping me shoot a late-afternoon wedding and evening reception?"

"How many posed shots would be required?"

"From me, a bunch. From you, not many at all."

"Whew."

"What's your issue with posed shots, anyway?"

"Dad's business now specializes in school IDs and sports teams. Point, smile, *click*, next. Point, smile, *click*, next." She mimed the repetitive action. "Day after day after month after year."

He whistled low. "I would go crazy."

"Why do you think I'm here? I'm avoiding the loony bin." Of course there was more to it than that, but this wasn't the time or place to bring out the family skeletons.

He smiled at her lighthearted attempt to make a joke, but his eyes let her know he'd picked up on something in her tone.

"Why hasn't your dad ever branched out into other areas? I bet you were full of great ideas, like you've been here."

She winced. "He wasn't crazy about my ideas, but then he hired someone else who ended up doing everything I'd suggested. With too many cameras in the family business, I turned to the stage instead."

The perception in his steady gaze grew too uncomfortable, and she quickly changed the subject. "So here I am, about to rehearse a scene where I wrangle six ornery, immature, and mannerless—albeit fictional—slobs into shape for courting."

"I like courting. Unless you mean the kind without a basketball." He frowned as if confused, but the twitching of his very kissable lips gave him away.

"Brat." She slapped his arm. The blasted man from Montana was an expert at the first kind of courting too, if his flirting and ability to read her emotions so easily were any indications.

Yet his knack for making her feel both treasured and appreciated had virtually eliminated her hesitation about dating another photographer. When it came right down to it, she could easily balance her job as an actress with the role of supportive girlfriend who shared a common hobby with her very handsome hunk.

Ryan was definitely prime boyfriend material.

Assuming he ever tried to kiss her again.

Chapter Ten

Liz set her camera bag on the small table in the entryway of the apartment. No matter how hard she squinted, the bulky, black, nylon case would never be the perfect accessory for her sage-green silk dress. Oh well. She wasn't attending this wedding as a guest anyway, and the bag would hopefully keep her mind on the job instead of on the handsome photographer who should be arriving any minute.

She glanced over her shoulders as she swiveled from side to side, checking for unprofessional runners in her nylons below the knee-length skirt.

Across the room, Dani laughed from her lounging sprawl on the couch. "Relax. You look beautiful."

"Are you sure the updo isn't too much?"

"Like I said before, it's casually elegant and will keep your hair out of your face while you work. Not to mention, it draws attention to the fact that your dress matches your eyes."

"You're right." Liz pinched her glossed lips together and remembered that she'd forgotten to add the tube to the side pocket of her camera bag. Halfway down the hall to her bedroom, a brisk knock on the door announced Ryan's arrival.

"I'll get it." Dani jumped off the couch. "I can't wait to officially meet your cowboy."

"He's not my—" Liz sighed and rolled her eyes at her roommate's teasing and went to gather her lip gloss ... and a new box of peppermints. Fresh breath never hurt when interacting with guests at a wedding.

And those had nothing to do with any silly thoughts about...

"Oh, Liz, your date is here." Dani's voice carried through the apartment.

She grabbed her nicest coat on her way out and hurried to rescue Ryan before Gloria or Marie decided to intrude too. Rounding the corner, she stopped short at the sight of Ryan talking to Dani in the entryway.

"Is that a tux?" While she'd seen him dressed up when photographing the foundation event and at the theater, this fitted formal suit emphasized his broad shoulders and impressive height.

And made her feel drab in comparison.

Until he turned toward her with his easygoing grin that quickly transformed into a low whistle and a heated assessment of her from the toes of her black pumps to the loose curls pinned atop her head.

Suddenly his reaction justified every dollar she'd invested in her new dress and the extra minutes spent fussing with her hair.

He cleared his throat. "My sister talked me into going the extra mile, and now I'm really glad I did, even if we'll be there to do a job. Speaking of which…" He reached into the inside pocket of his suit coat.

She laid her own coat on the table beside her bag and slid the lip gloss and mints into her camera bag before accepting the folded check from Ryan. She peeked at the amount. "Wow. That's a lot."

"That's for the first two weekends of picture sales. I'm still catching up on this past weekend's bookkeeping, but I know that a few more orders will trickle in from the website."

"With two more weekends to go before we even open the new show in January."

"Except that it's already mid-December and only one of those weekends falls before Christmas. Folks won't be as interested in our digital Christmas card option."

And just like that, this extra income stream would dry up. But in the meantime… "Thanks for this. Let me just put it in my room and then I'll be ready to go."

"No problem."

Liz turned toward the hall and nearly ran into Gloria. "Excuse me."

"If you're deciding not to go on your date, I'd be happy to go instead." The blonde eyed Ryan as if he were a triple-fudge brownie. À la mode.

"What?" Liz stopped. "I'm not—"

"No way, Gloria. I wouldn't let her miss this." Dani's interruption deflected Gloria's attention.

"That's too bad." Gloria's sultry purr put an extra hustle into Liz's steps.

Unfortunately, by the time Liz returned, Gloria had her manicured claws on Ryan's bicep while Dani bracketed him on the other side, loyally chattering about the weather forecast.

As she reached around the trio for her coat, she caught Ryan's panicked expression. One would think he'd be used to predators, after living in Montana. Or shooting pictures in the Everglades. "Are you ready to go?"

"More than." Ryan dislodged Gloria's hand and helped Liz into her coat before they made their speedy escape.

Minutes later, she was happily settled in the cab of his truck as he adjusted the blowers.

"Is she always like that? Because I never would have pictured the general's housekeeper as a clingy piranha."

Liz swallowed her smile at Ryan's accurate assessment and tried to be kind. "She has this need to be the center of attention."

He glanced her way. "I can see how she'd be threatened around you."

"Me? You should have seen her with Dani a month ago."

"Dani? Isn't she the one who started it all?" Ryan chuckled and then imitated Dani's announcement that Liz's date had arrived.

Liz rolled her eyes. "I'd talk to her about it, except she'd grill me for details instead."

"Details?" His voice deepened a bit with a husky tone.

"She'll be sorely disappointed when all I'll choose to talk about will be the flowers, other decorations, the bridal party's dresses, how the ring bearer refused to walk down the aisle, and how the flower girl twirled her fancy dress so much that she flashed the audience and then fell down dizzy."

He laughed. "That'd serve her right."

"And since she'll be planning a wedding of her own very soon, I can always pretend I thought that's what she wanted to know." Liz grinned at the thought of Dani's disgruntled face and the internal knowledge that she'd probably still tell Dani all the *other* details too, assuming there were any to tell.

She peeked a glance at Ryan and then changed the subject. "Speaking of weddings ... I never asked why this one is at such an odd time of the week. Every wedding I've gone to has been on a weekend, certainly not on a Tuesday evening."

"The bride is a church friend of my sister's. Her fiancé just learned that his deployment has been moved up, and they wanted to get married before he leaves. With such short notice, possible venues only had midweek openings. Same with other services like the florist or me, a photographer."

"True. If it were on a weekend, neither of us would have been able to help out."

"Exactly. And even if it's work, I'm really glad for the chance to see you outside the theater again. Although I'm realizing that, as an actress, your social life is limited to the midweek, off-times also. But I'm sure you find it worth it, to pursue your passion."

"Absolutely. Although when we're in the middle of rehearsals for a new show—like now—then midweek isn't empty either."

The rest of their ride was filled with Ryan's questions about the new show and a discussion of their plan for the wedding shoot itself. Liz relaxed when Ryan repeated that he would handle the more traditional posed shots in addition to a wide collection of more natural candids from them both. Maybe someday she'd be able to take posed pictures without painful reminders of her dad's opinions.

A half hour later, Liz hovered around the edges of the small nursery that had been designated as the bride's dressing area. She captured the laughter of the happy bride and her three bridesmaids as they reminisced about a past adventure while fixing their makeup. Maybe someday in the near future, Dani would be the radiant bride with Liz as one of her giggling bridesmaids, remembering the first night Alex sent Dani flowers.

The bride's mother arrived in time to hurry the women along in getting ready for their pre-wedding posed shots. Liz's lens zoomed in on the wistful expression in the mother's eyes as she attached her daughter's veil to the top of her polished updo and adjusted the folds of the translucent fabric.

A quick shift of the lens to the floor-length mirror and she had a face-by-face comparison of the duo—in time for both expressions to flood with a wealth of memories and silent advice. And an abundance of love.

Would her mother ever look at her that way again? While Liz hoped to someday find a special someone to build a life with, would Mom even be there to adjust her wedding veil?

Her heart clenched with regret. Not if Dad stood by his ultimatum not to talk to her unless she came home on his terms. The way things stood now, he wouldn't be there to walk her down the aisle either.

Except, in a cruel twist of irony, here she stood with a camera in her hand. She could go home again ... just not take the kind of pictures she loved. And unless something changed, she wouldn't be able to stay, either.

But if she'd even consider jumping through the necessary hoops to reconcile with her parents for the sake of a happy wedding, shouldn't she be more focused on building a life with her prospective groom than on who would attend the ceremony?

A flurry of high-pitched giggles pulled her back to the present as the trio of bridesmaids teased their friend about the groom's possible reaction while they all made their way toward the door for the pre-wedding pictures.

Liz trailed in their wake. If she were surrounded by this many adoring friends, the lack of her dysfunctional family wouldn't matter so much. Maybe.

What was it about weddings that made every girl start to dream of the future?

She shook off the melancholy feelings as they entered the sanctuary. For now, she had a job to do, starting by ushering the women down the aisle toward where Ryan waited.

"Hello, ladies. You're right on time." Ryan rubbed his hands together and eyed the group. "Let's start with the bride alone, and then we'll add in the rest of you. Liz?" He tilted his head her direction. "Keep working your magic."

"Sure thing, boss." She found a spot in the front row to his right. While Ryan gave directions to the bride and her mother smoothed out the train of her gown, Liz captured the faces of the three bridesmaids, who were watching with dreamy expressions. As the poses continued, she focused her lens on one face at a time until she had a dozen more pictures to be proud of.

With a half hour to go before the wedding was scheduled to start, Ryan dismissed the bridal party into the care of the church's wedding coordinator and joined Liz in the front pew.

"Do you think that went okay?"

"I believe you got all the posed shots she'll expect." Liz ticked them off on her fingers. "Bride with bouquet. Bride glancing over her shoulder at her humongous train. Bride and Mom. Bride with each bridesmaid. Bride surrounded by her friends."

"Even the bride sticking out her tongue at those teasing friends?"

"You noticed that too?" Liz grinned at the priceless sequence of images she'd captured just moments ago.

"Hope you got it on film, because I have it on good authority that it's her fun personality the groom fell in love with first."

Liz scrolled through her images and then leaned against his solid shoulder to show him. "How's this for fun?" The scent of his cologne stirred her senses as he shifted her direction for a better look.

"Those are perfect." He grinned down at her and then glanced around the empty room, shifting back into work mode. "I was thinking about camera angles and had an idea to help capture the wedding itself. If I huddle around here in my tux, I can get the coming-down-the-aisle pictures and then swivel to get the wedding shots from the audience's perspective."

"So where does that put me?"

He pointed to the balcony that ringed the sanctuary on three sides. "If you'd be open to using my Leica camera—"

"You'd let me use your Leica?" She lifted a fluttering hand to her chest. She'd only dreamed of owning such a quality camera.

"Yes, you can use my Leica." He winked. "With the zoom and shutter speed, you can get amazing shots from further away—"

"And easily change angles without causing a distraction." Her mind raced with the possibilities. If she ditched her shoes, she could quickly change positions.

"You certainly would be a distraction." His eyes warmed and he nudged her shoulder with his, sending heat into her face.

"I accept."

"That you are a distraction? That was quick."

"No, I accept the use of your camera." She elbowed his tuxedo-clad ribs. It remained to be seen whether Ryan or his camera was the bigger distraction.

In the month since meeting him, she'd seen his professional talent, the tender care for his family, his fun sense of humor, and even glimpses of a faith she envied. No matter how often she told herself to slow down, her heart still raced at the sight of him.

By the time the majority of the guests had arrived, Liz was safely stationed upstairs with Ryan's amazing camera on a strap around her neck. Her palms sweated with anticipation as she practiced zooming in and out on Ryan's face near the front row below.

Until he glanced her direction and quirked an eyebrow.

Caught.

She turned the focus toward the audience and a bubble-blowing boy near the middle instead. A few minutes later, the music changed and ushers escorted the immediate family members to their seats in the front row.

After capturing a few of those shots from a different angle than Ryan's, she zoomed farther, through the back door of the sanctuary, spotting a tender moment as the father of the bride rested his hand against his daughter's cheek.

Priceless.

But that was a similar angle to what Ryan would be getting in just a few moments. She hurried around the balcony toward the back of the sanctuary in time to see the groom enter. Pausing, she zoomed in on his face and waited for the moment when he'd see his bride for the first time.

The music shifted again and the rustle of fabric and feet below let her know the guests were rising to their feet. And then it happened.

The groom's face transformed with stunned awe, a teary gaze, intense longing, an elated smile, and finally a fierce pride as the woman he loved made her way down the aisle to join him at the altar.

As the ceremony continued below, she caught expressions of the wedding party and then shifted to capture the faces of the parents in the front row. Ryan must have sensed her movement because he glanced up from his crouched position near the aisle.

He smiled as if he knew what pictures she was taking and approved. And then his smile grew until it mirrored the special look in the groom's eyes from earlier. A shiver of longing ran up her spine.

She'd never felt this intensity with Jerry the Jerk or Trent the Traitor or any of her college dates in between. What was it about Ryan that made her think such impossible things? Or was she simply picking up on their current surroundings with undertones of Dani's secret engagement fueling her imagination?

Liz pulled her attention back toward the bride and groom in time for the pastor's short sermon about how marriage was a partnership with a common purpose. The longing in her soul finally found a name.

No longer content to be part of a fun couple who spent time together, she needed to have a purpose. To be a contributing partner. That was the missing piece in her previous relationships.

She adjusted the camera around her neck and took another picture of the groom's expression toward his bride before moving around the balcony to the other side, capturing the bride's face in perfect detail, including the shimmer of a tear on the edge of her eyelashes.

Ryan's camera made all the difference. No, actually, Ryan was the difference. Their whole relationship already felt more like a partnership than anything else in her life ever had. She supported his dream by helping with the photography, and he supported hers by accommodating her schedule on the stage.

The revelation carried her through the remainder of the wedding and the exit of the happy couple. As the guests made their way toward the reception a few blocks away, Ryan gathered the entire wedding party for another round of formal shots.

She retrieved her shoes and returned to her previous position in the front row. After replacing Ryan's expensive camera in his bag and retrieving her own, she captured several more close-up candid moments to balance out the required but possibly boring shots Ryan continued to take.

While Ryan positioned the large group around the couple, Liz caught the newlyweds in an intimate moment of whispers and a tender kiss.

A kiss that triggered memories of a sledding snowbank and a grinning photographer.

A glance at Ryan found him watching her. Then he shifted his attention toward the direction of her lens. A blush rose in his face, and he raised his voice slightly to get the newlyweds' attention. "All right, you two. Save that for later."

The wedding party laughed, and soon they were finished with the required shots and heading toward Ryan's truck and the reception.

"Save a dance for me?" His flirtatious tone held a hint of seriousness.

"If we get a chance." She shivered in anticipation despite the warmth of his hand on the small of her back as he guided her through the nearly empty parking lot.

There it was again. What was it about weddings that got a girl all starry-eyed? Or was it the company she was keeping?

"I'll make sure we get a chance." His low growl made her almost lightheaded.

"Whatever you say, boss." As if she could focus on the job. They were here as work partners even if a not-so-tiny part of her was falling for the man. Fast. "After we get pictures of the newlyweds' entrance, toast, first dance—"

"And cutting the cake. That seems to be an important one for brides."

"Only if their grooms don't shove the frosting up their noses. I've never understood the point of that messy variation on the tradition."

He opened the passenger door for her and helped her get settled into the front seat before circling around to the driver's side. "I'd never shove cake up your nose."

She sucked in a quick breath. "That's good to know."

"If it weren't a waste of a perfectly good piece of cake, I'd aim for your right ear instead."

Chapter Eleven

Two hours later, they strolled hand in hand down the main street of Old Town in search of a late-night coffee shop.

Liz would be tired in the morning, but a piece of her heart never wanted the evening to end. Except that the memories of dancing in Ryan's strong arms earlier would make for the sweetest of dreams, especially when the music slowed and she'd heard his heartbeat under her ear while nestled against his chest.

Somewhere in the past few hours, their working relationship had shifted into something more. Beyond the confirmation that their attraction was mutual, something deeper began to fill the empty places of her very soul.

The twinkling white lights draping around every tree sparked the lingering sense of romance as the warmth of Ryan's hand on hers wrapped itself all the way up around her heart.

"Here. This should do nicely." Ryan tugged her into a small café, and soon they were seated at a table near the window with a couple of steaming mugs and a small plate of gourmet brownie bites.

"I can't believe you have room for any dessert after the buffet line."

"A man's gotta eat." He shrugged. "Besides, I'm a sucker for cannoli."

"What else makes you line up for seconds?" She blew across the foamy surface of her cinnamon-sprinkled mocha before taking a sip.

"Manicotti, lasagna, and alfredo." He ticked the wedding-reception menu off on his fingers.

"Basically anything Italian with cheese-laden calories? Like everything they served tonight?"

He grinned. "Then again, if they'd served enchiladas instead, I wouldn't have complained."

"Ah. So it's food in general?" Seemed the way to this man's heart really was through his stomach.

"When I'm working, that's probably true." He shrugged his broad shoulders. "But I've always enjoyed trying new foods, especially when I'm traveling."

"Have you been to a lot of places?" Suddenly, she wanted to know everything she could about the man seated across from her.

"Coast to coast in the USA, including the Everglades, the Rocky Mountains, and a riverboat on the Mississippi. Jungles in Belize ... mountains in Peru..."

"Wow. I'd love to hear more sometime, even if I'm a bit jealous. I haven't been in more than a handful of states, let alone any countries."

"So far."

"Perhaps." She took another sip as she remembered the passport she'd gotten on a whim after college, before auditioning for a role at the Wardrobe Dinner Theatre. "Were you taking pictures in all those places?"

"Mostly." He finished off the last bite of brownie and leaned back in his chair, cradling his coffee mug on his chest, as he launched into a story about an assignment regarding the anniversary of the opening of the Panama Canal.

"And you gave all that up to come here to Fort Collins and take pictures at a wedding?" She rested her elbows on the tabletop beside her empty cup.

"Yeah. I love my family. I just wish I could figure out how to balance family responsibilities while still being spontaneous and free with my camera. There's nothing quite like hiking around a gorgeous location few people have seen—except it gets lonely sometimes." He sighed. "I had started to think that maybe it was time to settle down and spend more time with my family, so John's deployment was actually a good chance to try that out for a season. To see if I could figure out why I was losing the joy in my life—that spark I see in you."

"Me? I don't have anything to offer someone like you."

"Yes, you do. I didn't realize it until we met, but I needed to be around someone with the same passion for photography. Someone with an eye for excellence who pushes me to bring my best to every job. Someone to reignite my creativity."

"I did all that?" Meaning she *wasn't* the biggest taker in their relationship.

"You did. So yes, shooting family photos, a wedding, and that foundation banquet have not been what I expected. And to be honest, I definitely feel stifled sometimes, but my family is worth it. They need me, and it's not like it's going to be forever."

She shook off the reminder that he might leave. "And in the meantime, you've got some amazing equipment at your fingertips."

"Liked using my extra camera, did you?"

"You have no idea. I thought my current Canon was a giant leap from the first camera I got as a kid. I actually asked for a Leica for Christmas a few years ago." But she'd gotten something very different instead. She shrugged away the painful memory.

He peered deeply into her eyes, as if he could tell she was holding something back, and then his gaze shifted to sweep over her face and hair ... just like when he had picked her up at the apartment, then in the middle of the wedding, and later, when asking her to dance.

"Tonight I got a glimpse of what I've been missing," Liz finished. And it wasn't just a fancy camera.

"Then I'm glad I thought to share." He set his empty coffee cup on the table, then stood before reaching out a hand. "But I have a feeling you're also missing out on your beauty sleep, so I should see you safely home."

"I don't mind." She stood and accepted his help into her coat before turning to face him. "It's been a wonderful evening."

"It's not quite over yet." His crooked smile warmed her more than the coffee had, especially when he then offered his arm to escort her out of the café.

As they quietly rambled along the sidewalks back toward his truck, she soaked in a heady awareness of his muscled arm beneath her hand along with the strength of his character. The talented and handsome photographer took his responsibilities seriously. He loved his family deeply, and they could depend on him to be there for them.

Just like he steadied her when her feet slipped, before shifting his hold to wrap a strong arm around her back as they continued on through the wintry night.

Snow crystals filtered through the air around them like a snow globe, especially when the abundant Christmas lights set them to sparkling. It was both magical and awe-inspiring to be caught in such a beautiful moment.

Beside her, Ryan sighed. "I'm always amazed that the One who created all this beauty actually loves me and wants to walk through life with me." He squeezed her a bit closer to his side. "Just like I'm walking with you."

She could almost believe in the miracle of God's love right now. Especially with Ryan beside her.

A shiver of emotion rippled up her spine, and he rubbed a hand over her arm as if he thought she was chilled.

Time slowed until she was in tune with everything about him. The puffs of frosty breath in the snow-sparkled air. The texture of his sleeve beneath her fingers. The *swish* of their coats between them as he timed his pace to hers. The scent of his cologne.

She glanced at a storefront window as they passed by.

Were they really the couple she saw in the reflection? The couple they had been while dancing earlier at the wedding reception?

Beyond the glass, she caught a glimpse of several wrapped boxes with festive bows. With Christmas just ten days away, what could she give Ryan to show how much he had come to mean to her?

She turned away from the display to focus on the man gazing down at her and smiled at him. "What do you want for Christmas this year?"

"More time with you." His smile grew mischievous. "Without a snowball down my neck this time."

She sucked in a quick breath at the reminder of their almost-kiss in the snowbank.

He winked at her reaction. "But speaking of Christmas, the theater is closed next weekend on Christmas Eve and Christmas Day. Do you have plans, or would you like to join my family?"

"I don't have plans." A momentary twinge of regret that her family was not only out of state but currently not speaking to her gave way to joy. She now had the perfect excuse to spend more time with Ryan and his family.

"We're planning to go to the Christmas Eve service together and then for a light meal and maybe a Christmas-movie marathon until the kids crash. You'd be welcome to spend the night on the couch—or I'll even give up the guest room—if you want to be there early on Christmas Day when the kids open their presents. I know they would love to have you there. They're still talking about Thanksgiving."

A sense of longing stirred within her again. It wasn't just a desire to spend time with Ryan, but there was a hint of something more, like being around a loving family. Or the living faith he exhibited.

"So what do you say?"

Church might be awkward, but she would put up with anything to spend time with Ryan. Then again, with God's blessings in her life lately, she was already on her way back to the faith her grandparents had shown her.

"I'd love that."

"Church or the whole package?" They stopped beside the passenger side of his truck.

"The whole package." Her eyes roamed over his face.

His slow smile in the streetlight morphed into something more intimate, and he reached out to stroke her cheek. "I like this whole package too."

With the magic of the moment, she wasn't at all surprised when his hand moved behind her neck. "Merry Christmas, Liz." The frosty air between them disappeared as his lips descended to cover hers with a gentle touch, followed by a deeper kiss that laid claim to her heart.

Merry Christmas indeed.

Ryan held her hand as he led her into the church sanctuary and toward a section of open seats in the middle of the room. They slid into a pew, and soon Liz had Hannah snuggled up beside her with Ryan's strong arm around her shoulders.

She glanced at the row of poinsettias along the edge of the stage and the swags of greenery tied with red bows, the latter of which were accented with strings of white lights reminiscent of their late-night walk downtown last week.

There had been a hint of the same magic on their ride tonight. Then Ryan had turned up the radio as they listened to the song from weeks ago about loving the Maker and the Maker loving her.

Could it be that simple?

Okay, God. I'm here. And I'm hoping You're really more like what Ryan and his family say. What Dani says You're like. That you have a future for me. That You gave me these dreams.

A burst of laughter on one side of the room competed with a crying baby on the other. Liz eyed the sanctuary as it rapidly filled with families, the older generations easily mixing with a multitude of children ... all gathered to celebrate Christmas.

Her dad would have a fit if he were here. Between the chatter, the coffee cups, and the casual clothes of many attendees, he would be making a list of complaints. But the children being both present and vocal would have topped his list. Yet wasn't there a verse in the Bible where Jesus told His disciples to let the children come to Him?

A remarkable peace settled over her heart with the truth. God really did love everybody, including all the children. Including her. This could be the rebirth of something wonderful in her life.

Soon, the service began with familiar carols sung with a mixture of exuberant voices. Hannah actually stood on the seat beside Liz so she could see the band on the platform, singing very loudly, "Joy to the world, and let's have fun; let earth receive her keys."

Liz smiled at the little girl's reinterpretation of the familiar lyrics. Then she had a sense that God was smiling too, to see all His kids gathered for Jesus' birthday party. *Let's have fun; the Lord has come. Let earth receive her King.*

A few songs later, the pastor walked to the pulpit. His welcoming words and smile were as comforting as the red sweater he wore with a pair of dark slacks. Casual but respectful—and she found herself anticipating whatever he had to say.

The pastor first read the familiar Christmas story about Mary and Joseph and the angels, shepherds, and wise men. There had been quite a collection of people and even animals there. All had traveled a distance to be there, some farther than others, and most were probably surprised at the change in accommodations. A pregnant woman—who had already overcome the whole virgin-gets-pregnant scandal—and her husband had come quite far and then gave birth surrounded by strangers. The outcast shepherds on the hillsides got a personalized singing telegram and headed to town in time to find a treasure born on the wrong side of the tracks. Wise men used to silks and spices offered their expensive gifts … while kneeling in a stable.

The Christmas story was full of surprises because all sorts of things didn't turn out as expected.

It looked like chaos, but God had a plan. He had orchestrated every piece to get them there at that moment, and each guest to the party had exercised faith in order to be there. Then, in return, the guests found that the infant they saw had actually traveled the farthest and experienced the greatest change in circumstances.

Liz scrambled backward through her former Sunday school lessons to connect the dots, fascinated by the storyteller on the stage.

The pastor smiled as if he held a secret and turned the pages in his Bible to read from the Gospel of John about the Word of God becoming flesh. Then he flipped to another familiar verse a few chapters later about God loving the world so much that He gave His only Son. Another flip over to Philippians told about the Jesus who did not hold on to His position but gave it all up to come to earth.

"Jesus limited Himself into a human shell, even all the way to becoming a baby dependent on the care and feeding—and, yes, diaper changes—of his mother. Why? Because He loved us. Not because we deserved it, but because He loved us just the way we were."

Liz's heart ached at the thought. Oh, to be loved for who she was, including her quirks, her eye for photography, and her business ideas.

"And because of that love, He wanted so much more for our futures."

Wasn't that what Dani said? That God had plans for her to have hope and a future? Well, she had a future at the theater with a starring role in a show to begin the new year, and that reality certainly gave her hope.

"That's why He came—to live among us. To really know what life as a human was like. Then to grow up to teach us how to serve God in return before personally paying the price for our failures in the perfect mixture of justice and mercy—so that our future would be an eternity spent in relationship with the Creator of the universe."

The pastor closed his Bible. "So this Christmas, let us remember a chaotic, not-so-silent night when Love came down from heaven just for us."

Love came down for her.

The thought lingered through the next minutes as the ushers passed out small candles, the lights dimmed, and wicks were lit in the darkness.

From the front of the sanctuary, the worship leader started an acapella version of "Silent Night." Tears trickled down her cheeks as the holiness of the moment wrapped loving arms around her spirit.

The peace she had longed for was found in the amazing love of Christmas.

The Maker loved her. How could she help but love Him back?

Chapter Twelve

Hours later, Liz tossed and turned on Cheryl's couch, unable to fall back to sleep. It wasn't the stiff cushions, lumpy pillow, or the fact that she'd declined Ryan's offer of the guest bedroom that kept her from getting comfortable. It wasn't even a heady awareness that such an amazing man slept down the hall.

Since she had gotten some rest, now her brain simply refused to slow down. Giving up on going back to sleep, Liz sat up and wrapped a blanket around her shoulders.

Last night's life-changing decision while singing "Silent Night" had been followed by the joyful chaos of a meal here at his sister's house and then watching both *Rudolph* and *The Little Drummer Boy* on video. Of course, before the kids were even remotely ready for bed, their dad had texted, and soon the happy family had clustered around a laptop for a video call.

After helping to wear out and corral two giggling children into bed, she'd joined Ryan in the kitchen for a mug of hot chocolate while trying to ignore the continued conversation from the living room as a military wife whispered words of love to her husband overseas.

And now—in that same living room—she saw more evidence of love all around, from the abundance of framed family photos to the mound of gifts underneath the lit tree and the worn Bible on the coffee table nearby.

More faded memories of her grandparents flooded back to replace the pain of that Christmas Day three years ago. Every visit to their home across town had been what she was supposed to feel at Christmas. Grandpa O'Neill had started each meal with a heartfelt prayer, which led to laughing conversations while Grandma lavished them with equal parts hugs and baked goods.

Both then and now, love was such a wonderful thing to fill a home with.

"Good morning, beautiful."

She glanced over to find Ryan wearing rumpled sweats just like her and leaning against the doorjamb with a mug in his hand. "Is it morning? And if so, please tell me you have coffee to go in that mug."

"It's about five, so the morning part is relative, but with two kids in the house, it will get chaotic before you know it. That's why we adults need extra fortification." He lifted the mug. "Want some?"

"Absolutely." She tossed aside the blanket and stood. "But if the day is about to start, I need to do something about the way I look."

"I wouldn't change a thing." His eyes swept over her, and her face grew warm.

"Well, I should still find the little girls' room and maybe brush my teeth." She grabbed her overnight bag on her way toward Ryan.

"That might be a good idea." The crinkled lines around his eyes deepened as his gaze centered on her mouth. "I'll meet you back here with coffee." He stepped aside far enough for her to pass him in the archway.

She resisted the urge to hug him on her way by. "Make it a big mug."

His chuckle followed her down the hall.

Ten minutes later, she returned to the living room in new clothes, with clean teeth and freshly brushed hair left loose around her shoulders. Ryan had moved her pillow and blanket out of the way and now sat on the couch with his Bible open on his lap. His coffee rested on a coaster near the lamp on the end table, but no other mugs were in sight.

She dropped her bag beside the wall and crossed over to the couch. "I don't see any coffee for me."

He looked up with a smile. "I wasn't sure how long you'd be, so I left yours in the pot so it didn't get cold." He set the open Book on the arm of the couch and stood.

"You don't have to get up. I can find my way there."

"No way. You're my guest, and I always keep my promises." He gently nudged her until she took his spot on the couch, before picking up his empty mug. "I'll be right back. Just save me a seat."

"Deal." She wiggled into the cushions to find a more comfortable spot and caught his Bible just before it fell to the floor. As she smoothed the pages, an underlined section caught her attention.

"Surely goodness and love will follow me all the days of my life, and I will dwell in the house of the Lord forever."

Goodness and love for all her life? Wasn't the verse supposed to say *mercy*?

"Here you go." Ryan set a giant travel mug on the end table beside her elbow and then settled in beside her, his own refilled cup propped on his knee.

"Thanks." She left the Bible open across her lap and reached for her coffee. "You certainly found one big enough."

"You asked for it." He pointed to the Bible. "That's one of my favorite verses. I just love the Psalms and the idea of dwelling in God's house forever. That's a relationship I want."

When it came to relationships, she really wanted one with Ryan. But now it seemed like she was starting one with God too. She took a sip of the hot coffee as the truth sank in.

"The 'goodness and love' parts sound good, but after spending time at my parents' church, God's house became the last place I wanted to be. I mean, the pastor—and my dad—always seemed to be focused on a list of rules so we could be good enough to make God accept us."

"I've met a lot of people who think like that. Maybe it comes from growing up in the wide-open spaces of Montana, but I always held awe for the Creator. I even thought His house must be more like the great outdoors and not full of stained-glass windows. So when my dad told me that God wanted to be my friend and walk through life with me, I said sign me up. I mean, who doesn't want a friend like that?"

"I certainly do. But what about all the rules in this Book? Aren't they important too?" Was it okay to forget about the rules and just be friends with God?

He shrugged his broad shoulders. "There are definitely rules about how to live an optimal life, but I signed up for a Person, not a list of obligations. Jesus told His disciples to follow Him. He never told them to follow the rules."

"But he must have said it somewhere ... somehow." Or else Dad was wrong.

"Sure. He said that if we loved Him, we should keep His commandments."

"There you go. Rules to follow."

"True, except that the religious leaders made it too complicated. Jesus quoted the Old Testament all the time, but He also simplified all those laws into two big categories: love God with everything you've got, and love people like you love yourself."

"That sounds so simple. Just love." There couldn't be that much freedom, could there? Yet her heart warmed with more than the coffee she'd been sipping.

"And it's a lot more fun than collecting check marks on a list like the stickers on Matt and Hannah's chore chart, just hoping to earn God's favor and avoid His anger. I think a lot of people hang onto their list of rules because they can see them and measure how they are doing. Trusting in God's grace takes a whole lot more faith."

"His grace." Liz blinked as the reality of her second chance began to grow.

"Grace's 'get blessings I don't deserve' piece goes hand in hand with mercy's 'don't get what I do deserve.' Thanks to God's unfailing love, I've been offered both. It's like a gift. But it's up to me to accept the gift and open it."

"A gift." Like the one she'd received last night at church. She smiled. "I wish I'd grown up hearing more about God's love than about His judgment."

Ryan shifted on the couch, his dark eyes staring deep into hers. "I think a lot of the world's problems would be solved if we just understood God's love better. After all, it's why we're even here. God is love and love needs something—or somebody—to receive and then return that love. Of course, it's not really love unless it's freely given, so God lets us choose. When many rejected His love and suffered the natural consequences of their choices, God—because of love—limited Himself to come to earth as a baby, and Jesus—out of love—sacrificed Himself to set us free."

"So then the Christmas story—the whole Bible, even—is actually all about love." Her heart yearned to start turning the pages of Ryan's Bible and read the old stories again through the lens of love.

"Right. God loved us so much that He gave His Son. And when I walk through life with Jesus as my friend, my life becomes about love too—about loving God and loving people enough to show them a better way to live."

"Wow." So much truth there to unpack later. Maybe part of the stability that attracted her to Ryan was really God's love being lived out toward her.

"Sorry. Sometimes I get a little carried away. My sister says I could have been a preacher."

"I could see that." Liz took another sip of her coffee. "But then you wouldn't be using your other gifts, like photography."

"I've been known to do both when I meet new people." He turned his head toward the doorway. "But speaking of gifts, I think I hear a couple of hooligans who will be lookin' to tear into those presents before breakfast."

A round of giggles echoed down the hall followed by the quieter tones of Cheryl's voice and the tromping of running feet before the children burst into the room and headed straight for the tree.

Cheryl poked her head into the room. "You can sort them out, but nobody opens anything until I get my coffee." She eyed Ryan and Liz. "Assuming somebody left me some."

Ryan raised his mug. "Already started a second pot, so you should be good."

Under the tree, Hannah and Matt searched the tags and squealed whenever they spotted their names. The room sparkled with the unparalleled joy of Christmas morning she'd only seen in movies. Knowing this family, these presents had been carefully chosen for each person with love and then wrapped with anticipation, with the giver hardly being able to wait to see the recipient's face when they opened their package.

Gifts the way they were meant to be given, since these gifts came with the kind of unconditional love the pastor had talked about last night—and the love Ryan had just explained. She frowned at the sudden memory of a box of business shirts. In her experience, not all presents came without strings.

"What's that frown about?" Ryan nudged her side with his elbow. "Afraid there's nothing there for you?"

"Just remembering Christmas at home."

"You must miss your family."

"Yes, but..." She swallowed the lump in her throat. "It wasn't always joy-filled like this. Maybe if it had been, things would have turned out differently."

"Perhaps you can tell me about that sometime."

"Someday I will." She gazed up into the warmth of his eyes, then chose to leave the past in the past and move into her future—a future filled with the theater and possibly even more time with Ryan or behind the camera.

"I'll hold you to that." He patted her knee. "But in order to erase that frown, I happen to know that there *is* a package under the tree with your name on it."

"There's one for you too." She thought about the framed picture of them beside the snowman. Cheryl had captured a moment of shared laughter with Liz staring up into his eyes, and it was a perfect reminder of their growing relationship. A duplicate picture already sat on her bedside table.

"Then I suppose I'd better help the elves sort out the presents so we can get this party started."

While Ryan and the kids delivered gifts to their scattered spots around the room, Cheryl returned with another large travel mug and claimed the recliner. Liz stowed Ryan's Bible out of the way and continued to sip her own coffee. She'd have to find time later to read a few more psalms and find promises about God's love since the new warmth of that truth was as soothing and as energizing as the caffeine seeping into her veins.

Soon the ripping of paper began, followed by a few squeals of delight and numerous shouted thank-yous. After watching the chaos for a few minutes, Liz reached for Ryan's gift and opened the card first.

> I'VE BEEN BLESSED TO GET TO KNOW YOU AND HAVE ENJOYED WORKING BESIDE YOU THIS PAST MONTH. WITH ONLY ONE MORE WEEKEND TOGETHER AT THE THEATER, I CAN'T WAIT TO INVENT NEW EXCUSES TO SEE YOU. I KNOW THAT GOD HAS GIVEN YOU A SPECIAL EYE FOR PHOTOGRAPHY AND I WANTED TO HELP YOU CONTINUE TO USE THAT AMAZING GIFT AS YOU BRING OTHERS JOY. (THIS MIGHT NOT BE A LEICA OF YOUR OWN, BUT I'M HOPING THE THOUGHT TRULY COUNTS CONSIDERING MY BUDGET RIGHT NOW.)

Tears sprang to her eyes at the mention of a Leica under the tree. "Thank you."

"You haven't even opened it yet." Ryan stopped ripping the paper from another package.

"The thought truly does count."

"Hmm. Well, then I guess I can keep this." He reached for the small box on her lap.

"Oh, no, you don't." She swiveled away from him and opened it to find a trio of brand-new memory cards with another note attached.

> Here's wishing you hours of joy from behind the lens while you use your gifts to pursue your dreams.

Her dreams. While she needed the money from her job in the spotlight on stage, she felt equally enticed by the thought of cameras and Ryan's compliments.

And Ryan himself.

If given the choice, what dream would develop?

Chapter Thirteen

On the first Monday in January, Liz rolled over in bed and groaned. A full weekend of shows and waiting tables always took a toll on her body. As part of the dancing ensemble in *White Christmas*, she'd only been in a few scenes—with even fewer lines to memorize—giving her extra time backstage to change costumes and think about the next part of the production. Or better yet, to think about Ryan sitting out there somewhere in the lobby, printing and packaging pictures.

She yawned. But since she'd occupied the female lead's role in *Seven Brides for Seven Brothers*, it was extra exhausting. While she'd spent weeks memorizing the pages of dialogue and rehearsing her songs and dances, the compressed pace of the show required intense focus and concentration—especially on opening weekend. Not to mention, the few scenes she wasn't onstage were spent ducking in and out of the dressing room rather than catching her breath or grasping for mental sanity.

It was probably a good thing that their picture-taking project had ended at Christmas because she hadn't had a spare moment to even think about Ryan, let alone juggle any camera responsibilities during the weekend's shows.

She eyed the painting over her bed. *Grandma, I wish you could see me now.*

Still, being the star wasn't all she had hoped it would be, but the steady income was invaluable to her savings account. Not to mention, she was practically guaranteed another contract.

A glance at the clock revealed that she'd actually slept in for a change, but her body still ached and her mind swam in a fog. Hopefully she wasn't coming down with a cold.

She'd been invited to tag along as Ryan entertained the kids on their last day before going back to school, but she'd begged off, claiming exhaustion. And it was a good thing too because after loading up on some extra vitamin C with breakfast, her plans for the day would involve curling up on the couch with a book or the classic movie channel.

With that in mind, she threw back the covers and swung her feet out of bed. Perched on the edge of the mattress, she rolled the kinks out of her neck and stretched her arms over her head before reaching down to touch her toes.

"Hey, Sleeping Beauty. It's about time you woke up."

Liz sat up in time to see Dani set a half-empty glass of orange juice on top of the dresser. "You know I won't really wake up until after my second cup of coffee." She fought a jaw-breaking yawn and changed the subject. "What are you up to today?"

"Touring wedding venues."

"Oh, look at that sappy smile."

"Guilty as charged." Dani admired the sparkling ring on the wiggling fingers of her left hand. "Now that we're officially engaged, we need to price enough things to put a budget together. Mr. Sheridan offered to help pay for the wedding, but Alex and I want to do it ourselves. However, in addition to a budget, we mostly need to get some reservations made ASAP for a wedding in early June."

Liz grinned and sang one of Dani's lines from the play. "They say when you marry in June, you're a bride all your life."

"Very funny." Dani stuck out her tongue. "That's not why. Alex graduates in May, but this way we can squeeze in a traditional wedding weekend with the Sheridans during that rare off-weekend before the summer show starts."

"What about a honeymoon?" Liz waggled her eyebrows as Dani's face turned a bright pink.

"We'll have a weekend away together before the dress rehearsal, at least. With *Annie* and all the kids acting this summer, there will be fewer adult roles. I'm actually thinking to voluntarily skip a show or be an understudy while waiting tables so I can spend more time with Alex."

"But won't he be playing in the band?"

"True. Guess we need to talk about that too." Dani glanced at her watch and then gasped. "Alex will be here any minute and I'm not ready."

While Dani rushed around the room, Liz stumbled down the hall to the bathroom. By the time she returned to their room, Dani was gone. Craving caffeine, Liz headed for the kitchen.

Gloria sat at the dining room table, scrolling through something on her phone while balancing an ice pack on her knee, with a half-eaten cup of yogurt in front of her. She looked up from her phone in time to raise an eyebrow at Liz's tattered college sweatshirt and yoga pants.

Liz bypassed her housemate and headed straight for her can of coffee in the cupboard above the empty coffeepot while fighting another yawn. Clothes were the least of her worries right now, because at this point, she might have to settle for a cup of the horrid instant coffee in her emergency stash just to bridge the gap while the real stuff brewed.

"How's our *star* this morning?" Sarcasm dripped like the melting bag of ice on Gloria's knee.

"Better than you, it appears." It had been a couple of months since Gloria's surgery, but obviously she couldn't handle the extra dancing.

"Oh, well, this is nothing."

"Doesn't look like nothing to me. Does Mr. Sheridan know that your knee still hurts?" Liz finished filling the coffeepot with water and flipped the switch to start it brewing.

"Don't you dare tell him." Gloria's threat chilled the room. "It's already bad enough that I had to endure a month as a housekeeper, and now I'm stuck in a crowd of giggling girls. I need to get a good part like yours again or else…"

Liz propped a hip against the counter and faced the diva. "Well, I have to admit that being the star, as you put it, is harder than I thought. I'm so busy rushing from one scene to the next that I can hardly enjoy the moment."

"True. But that's the price I'm willing to pay."

"Can I ask you why? Why is being the star so important? It's not like you get paid more than the rest of the cast—or at least I'm not." Behind her, the trickle of coffee dripping into the pot turned into a stream.

"I need to be the star so I can earn a bigger stage with a bigger marquee." Gloria fingered her new diamond-studded watch, which the other girls had drooled over after Christmas. "Then my dad might finally come see me in person—for the first time in my life—instead of working all the time or sending little gifts through the mail. Well, his personal assistant probably does the shopping for him, but he does sign the card." Gloria's nonchalant shrug couldn't hide the flash of pain in her eyes.

"At least he's thinking of you and sends gifts. All my dad gives lately are ultimatums." Liz grimaced. The only positive thing about that negative revelation was her discovery that God wasn't like her earthly father.

"Ultimatums?" Gloria scraped the bottom of her yogurt cup before moving into the kitchen to throw away her trash and empty the melted ice bag.

"He offered me a menial job in his business with no room for advancement. Obviously I wasn't a good enough photographer to—"

"What? I've seen your pictures. You're very talented."

Unsolicited praise from Gloria? Someone circle the date on the calendar.

"I don't know. Maybe I was too good or too different and he felt threatened." Liz shrugged and reached for her largest mug. "Either way, I wasn't willing to cram myself into his confining mold for my future. I had to be myself, and he didn't like it. So when he said it would be his way or the highway, I left."

"Wow. You're braver than me."

Was she really brave to forge her own path in life as Gloria suggested or merely rebellious, as her dad accused?

Gloria rummaged around in the refrigerator as if looking for something else to eat. "I might still be trying to get my dad to really see me for me, but at least we get along."

"Then you are blessed, even without a starring role right now."

"Maybe." Gloria pointed to her knee. "Or maybe not."

"Something to think about." Liz poured coffee into her cup and headed back to her bedroom.

If only she could talk to her dad. Or at least her mom.

She'd tried calling her mom on Christmas Day, but the call kept getting disconnected as if her phone number was blocked. When she'd finally gotten through using Ryan's phone, her mom had gasped and then said, "Sorry, I can't talk right now," before hanging up.

After setting her coffee mug on the nightstand beside the framed picture of her and Ryan with the snowman, Liz reached for her new Bible. Thanks to her talk with Ryan, she'd been reading a lot in her spare time and highlighting every verse she found that mentioned God's love.

It turned out there were a bunch of them listed in the back of her Bible. On days like this, when she needed the reminder of His unconditional love, that list was a good thing indeed.

She propped herself against the pillows and flipped through the pages while sipping her coffee. What was it Ryan had said? Something about love limiting itself for others and sacrificing to set them free.

Just as Ryan had done for his family—limiting his freelancer contracts and sacrificing his freedom to stay in his sister's guest room and babysit her kids while she was at work. And to think, he had volunteered to do that. Cheryl might have asked whether he could help out a little between jobs, but he certainly had not caved to perpetual begging or even emotional blackmail.

That was the key. Helping was Ryan's choice.

If Liz had been asked to help with the family business rather than have a trivial role dictated to her, would she have stayed? If things had been different, perhaps she could have eventually talked her dad into letting her branch out into another direction ... but once Jerry the Jerk weaseled in and stole her place, she just couldn't handle the risk of being forever stifled.

Neither man seemed to love her enough to let her use her talents with a camera.

Neither seemed to love her enough to even listen to her feelings.

She might have sacrificed her personal dreams—at least temporarily—for her dad, but for Jerry, never, especially after his businesslike proposal and the discovery that he considered their romance a distracting inconvenience on the road to his personal goals.

God, thanks for saving me from making a huge mistake. I could never have been happily married to Jerry even if my dad approved. I'm not sure he ever would have sacrificed anything for me, and therefore he probably didn't even love me.

Unlike Ryan. Ryan had already sacrificed some of his earnings by allowing her to help with the photography jobs. And she'd do the same for him. Did that mean she loved Ryan?

An incredible warmth spread around her heart until it triggered memories of their first delicious kiss in the falling snow. Oh, she had it bad. But the fact remained, the more she learned about loving God, the more she wanted to love others that way, including Ryan.

Liz fanned her face and blamed the heat on the coffee steaming under her nose.

Better to think about her need to model God's love toward her dad and try to patch their relationship enough that they could talk again. Or even exchange presents.

She thought about the Christmas holiday that had come and gone without acknowledgment after the latest ultimatum right before Thanksgiving. But what could she give her dad—her parents—now to make up for her part of the silence? To show love as a peace offering?

Her eyes drifted around the room seeking inspiration and eventually fell on the small stack of books filled with pictures she had taken. The photography itself should appeal to her dad. She reached for the most recent book and thumbed through the pages of her photos of the melting snow crystals, the sledding outing, and even some from the theater, including one of her that Ryan had taken. Dad might appreciate the artistic craft in the pages, but her mom would enjoy the glimpses into Liz's life here in Colorado.

She could always jump online to order another copy for herself and send this one today.

With the gift selected, she just needed to write a letter to go with it. To let her dad know that she still loved him even if she'd never return to work alongside Jerry. After finding a piece of blank paper in the back of a rehearsal notebook, she clicked open her favorite pen and began to write.

Dear Dad (and Mom),

Please don't rip this to shreds without at least reading it.

> First, I wanted to say that I'm sorry our relationship has fallen apart to the point that we can't even wish each other Merry Christmas. I know you've accused me of turning my back on God and my family. Well, thanks to my roommate here at the theater company and a special guy in town, I'm back in church and reading the Bible with fresh eyes.

She eyed the Bible on the nightstand, feeling—and then squelching—the urge to quote a few verses about God's love. Her dad might take the truth as an accusation and twist it somehow. Better to keep the focus on herself.

> As for turning my back on our family, I might have changed majors and stayed away from home, but you were never forgotten. I'm sorry that I did not see the invitation to join your business for what it was—a gift. Honestly, now that I look back on it, the biggest reason I left was because of Jerry. I couldn't bear to spend any more time around him after we broke up, yet he'd become an integral part of your business, and it was obvious that he was weaving himself into the family as well. I suppose I was afraid that if I asked you to choose between us that I'd lose, so I left to make it easier. Except it hasn't been easy at all.

Liz wiped unexpected tears from her cheeks.

> Anyway, I might have left home and the official business behind, but I couldn't give up the creative magic of photography. Even through my last two and a half years of college and while here in Colorado, I've continued to use my camera to capture the world around me. Since pictures still give me joy, I'm enclosing a book of some of my recent ones so you can see what I've been up to lately. The ones in the snow reminded me of that one year we got a huge snow right before Christmas, and Grandpa O'Neill helped me build the giant snowman in our front yard.
>
> In addition to taking pictures for fun, I've actually gotten paid by the theater for taking new headshots

OF THE CAST. I'VE ALSO BEEN HELPING OUT A LOCAL PHOTOGRAPHER WITH SOME OF HIS JOBS, INCLUDING SHOOTING A WEDDING. DO YOU REMEMBER HOW I WANTED TO DO THAT? WE EVEN TOOK PICTURES OF THE DINNER GUESTS AT THE THEATER LIKE HOW THEY DO ON CRUISE SHIPS. I SUPPOSE MY IDEAS COULD HAVE BEEN A BIT TOO FAR OUTSIDE YOUR COMFORT ZONE OR BUSINESS MODEL, BUT I THOUGHT YOU MIGHT LIKE TO KNOW THAT THE PHOTOGRAPHY GENE IS ALIVE AND WELL.

She took a deep breath and asked God for the courage to continue.

SO WHERE DO WE GO FROM HERE? I AM SO SORRY FOR MY IMMATURE HANDLING OF AN UNCOMFORTABLE SITUATION AND AM ASKING FOR YOUR FORGIVENESS. WHILE I'M GRATEFUL FOR THE PREVIOUS OFFER TO WORK AT FOSTER'S FOTOS, PLEASE ACCEPT THAT I'VE BUILT A NEW LIFE HERE IN COLORADO. IN FACT, AFTER I GOT THE CONTRACT EXTENSION FOR THE CHRISTMAS SHOW, I WAS THEN HONORED TO RECEIVE A LEAD ROLE IN OUR CURRENT PRODUCTION THAT RUNS THROUGH MOST OF MARCH, AND I EXPECT TO CONTINUE HERE AFTER THAT. SO, IF YOU HAVEN'T ALREADY, PLEASE GO AHEAD AND HIRE WHATEVER ADDITIONAL HELP YOU MIGHT NEED AND LET ME SIMPLY CONTINUE TO BE YOUR DAUGHTER.

I'M HOPING WE—OR AT LEAST MOM AND I—CAN TALK FROM TIME TO TIME.

THE MORE I'M DISCOVERING ABOUT GOD'S LOVE, THE MORE I REALIZE THAT I'VE NEVER STOPPED LOVING YOU BOTH, EVEN WHEN WE DISAGREED. SO LET ME SAY IT AGAIN. I LOVE YOU AND WANTED TO WISH YOU A BELATED MERRY CHRISTMAS FROM COLORADO.

YOUR DAUGHTER,
LIZ

After closing her pen, she sat back as a wave of peace washed over her. She'd done what she could to mend the fences, and the rest was out of her hands. Well, that wasn't quite true … yet.

Liz scooted off her bed, twisted her hair into a messy bun, and was soon out the door toward the post office. The sooner the package was in the mail, the sooner they could be reconciled. And then she could ask her mom for advice about Ryan. Who knew? Maybe they'd be picking Dani's brain for wisdom about wedding planning in a few months. Fifteen minutes later, Liz left the post office feeling at least ten pounds lighter and having a fresh burst of energy. She took a deep breath of the crisp winter air.

God? Please help this letter and gift move our family past the pain into a better future.

There was no better way to start the new year than getting her relationships with God and her family back in order. But speaking of relationships, how was Ryan handling his babysitting duties today?

Halfway to her car, her phone rang and Ryan's face appeared on her screen.

"Hi, handsome. I was just thinking about you."

"Can you meet me at the emergency room?"

Chapter Fourteen

After a lengthy conversation with the emergency room's triage nurse, Liz was finally allowed past the waiting room. She rounded the corner into a cubicle and found a pale-faced Matt sitting on the bed, cradling his right arm on a pillow.

Ryan stood beside him, holding a teary Hannah in his arms. "Thanks for coming so quickly."

"What happened?" She dropped her purse into a chair and crossed over to the hospital bed.

"An epic sledding jump that would have had an epic landing—except that he flew so far, he hit a tree, and now he can't move his right arm." Ryan groaned. "It's all my fault."

Liz rested a hand on his arm. "It sounds like an accident."

Matt's high-pitched voice chimed in. "I went off the jump before, no problem. I just started higher up the hill this time. But the path was packed down harder, so I went a lot faster."

Ryan blew out a breath as if he was starting to accept the truth with a bit of relief. But tension lingered in the firm set of his jaw.

Time to get practical. "Has the doctor been in yet?"

"Once. We're waiting for someone to wheel our adventurer down to X-ray." He shifted Hannah in his arms as the little girl nestled her head underneath her uncle's chin. It must have been scary to see her brother get hurt and then be in such pain.

Ryan cleared his throat. "The doc hinted at a broken bone and maybe even needing—" He glanced at Matt. "A screw."

That could only mean one thing: the possibility of surgery ... and Ryan obviously didn't want to scare Matt any more than the doctor already had. They could always hope it just needed a cast. But the look on the boy's face made it obvious that something was seriously wrong, and he probably wished his mom was nearby.

Speaking of which. "Where is Cheryl?"

"She's on standby. She wanted to leave work right away, but I told her to wait until we knew something for sure. If there's a ... screw ... needed, then she should be here. If he just needs a cast, then I can help Matt pick out a cool color, and she can save her flex time for later." Ryan's eyes swept over her face. "Thanks for coming. I knew you had the day off ... but even though you planned to rest today, I couldn't quite face this alone."

"I'm happy to be here." Even if a sterile hospital room would never rank as a romantic spot, anywhere with Ryan beat sitting home alone.

A middle-aged woman rolled a wheelchair into the already-crowded space. "I'm here to take our sledder down to X-ray." She set the brakes on the chair and then helped Matt transfer from his position on the bed.

Ryan set Hannah down in order to help hold Matt's stabilizing pillow in place. "Can I tag along?"

Matt whispered, "Please," and the X-ray technician quickly agreed.

Liz took Hannah's small hand in hers and shifted them out of the way. "We'll be right here when you get back."

As the minutes ticked by, Liz tried to make them comfortable on the chairs while they waited, but Hannah developed a case of the wiggles. First she wanted to watch television, but her favorite show wasn't on. Then the games on Liz's phone didn't hold her attention, and the selection of books lacked as well. By the time Hannah started complaining that she was hungry and wanted something to drink, Liz realized that, depending on the diagnosis, it could still be hours before Matt was discharged.

Finally, the X-ray technician wheeled Matt back into the cubicle, with Ryan right behind them. Ryan looked grim as he helped transfer Matt to the bed. It must have been a rough time because Matt's eyes were reddened as if he'd been crying and could start again at any moment.

The X-ray technician said she'd let the doctor know they were back and then left the cubicle.

Liz swallowed hard. "Is it..."

Before he crossed over to join her, Ryan adjusted the bed so Matt could still see the television. "The tech wouldn't—and couldn't—say anything since the doctor will do the diagnosing. But I saw how he struggled to move his arm into position for the X-rays, so I snuck a peek over the tech's shoulder when she checked the images to make sure they were clear."

"And?"

He sighed. "And I'm pretty sure Cheryl will be taking time off from work."

"Ouch." She caught movement out of the corners of her eyes and snatched Hannah before she could finish climbing onto the bed with her brother. "Tell you what. Since you guys could be here awhile longer, what if we girls see about getting everyone some lunch and then setting up a comfy spot on the couch back home for Matt? Then you can focus on what needs to be done here without this distraction." She tilted her head toward Hannah.

Ryan looked relieved. "Thanks, but I don't want to completely wreck your free day."

"I don't mind at all." Lifting part of the burden from his shoulders made changing plans worth every bit of hassle. "Besides, I can just as easily rest up while watching a movie or two with Hannah."

Hannah immediately started a list of movie suggestions that kept growing and growing.

Ryan found a smile when Matt groaned. "Girl movies. Yuck."

"I'm sure we can find a guy movie for you when you get there." Liz located Hannah's coat and helped aim her wiggling arms into the sleeves, while Ryan worked a house key off his key ring so they could get into the house. She reached for her purse and caught a glimpse of her yoga pants and boots.

Of course, that reminded her that she'd left her apartment with no makeup on and—she reached up to check—her hair in a lopsided bun.

Too late now. She shrugged. "So now you know how I roll when I'm not at the theater or a fancy event. I might not look put together, but I promise you can trust me with your niece."

"You still look beautiful to me." Ryan's softly spoken words paired with the warmth of his hand as he slipped the house key into hers triggered fireworks in her heart. "Even more so because I know you put us first when you rushed over here."

With her face growing warm, she grabbed Hannah's hand and made a quick escape.

Liz tucked a blanket around Matt's legs, avoiding the pillow that cushioned his splinted and bandaged arm. "Is that better?"

"Yeah. I just got cold from the milkshake Uncle Ryan bought on the way home."

"I've heard that ice cream can cure a lot of problems."

"Does that mean I won't have to have surgery tomorrow?"

Ryan entered with a bottle of pain pills and a glass of water. "Sorry, little buddy, they still need to fix your arm—but the ice cream does put a little something in your stomach before you swallow these. I know you weren't hungry before, but does anything else sound good to eat now?"

"I've still got chicken nuggets from earlier ... canned corn ... a cookie... or I could try to find some celery or brussels sprouts," Liz offered.

Hannah giggled from her new movie-watching position on the floor near the other end of the couch, while Matt grinned.

"Maybe some chicken nuggets with ranch dressing."

"Coming right up."

Liz returned a few minutes later to find that Ryan had set up a TV tray with the remote and what was left of Matt's glass of water and milkshake cup. He squatted in front of the television, sorting through movies to find one that might entertain the boy.

She paused a moment to admire the fit of his jeans before rushing over to give Matt his very late lunch and settled in near Hannah to watch whatever movie Matt finally chose. She'd leave the recliner for Ryan.

Before the opening previews had finished, the garage door hummed and Cheryl arrived. She rushed into the living room and then surveyed the pampered setup. "Looks like you're being spoiled rotten."

Matt looked up from slurping his melting shake with a grin. "I don't mind."

"I don't mind either, then." Cheryl's voice cracked as she ran a hand through his hair and then trailed gentle fingers down his arm and over the bandaging. "If you're okay for a few minutes, I need to talk to your uncle."

Liz followed them into the kitchen in case Ryan needed moral support.

Ryan started the conversation with an apology. "I'm so sorry. I shouldn't have taken them sledding by myself."

"Nonsense." Cheryl propped her hands on her hips. "It was an accident. I know you'd never let Matt get hurt if you could have stopped it. Now tell me exactly what the doctor said."

Fifteen minutes later, Cheryl wound down her cross-examination of the details about the location of the injury, the necessary surgery in the morning, expected recovery time, and the long-term prognosis. It helped that Ryan had collected every piece of available paper, including a printout of the X-ray pictures, into a folder for her to read and reread.

Cheryl finally took a deep breath and blew it out. "I took tomorrow off from work. If Matt has to be there at eight, then we need to leave here by seven thirty to be safe. I'm glad you'll be here to make sure Hannah gets on the bus."

"But I was hoping to..." Ryan rubbed a hand over his chin.

Of course, Ryan wanted to go along.

Liz cleared her throat. "I can come over in the morning and get Hannah off to school. I can even be here when she gets home, so you don't have to worry about rushing home afterward. That is, if you trust me to watch her."

Ryan's smile was worth every bit of sacrifice she might have to make in getting up early or finding a way to entertain the small girl again.

"It's not that I don't trust you, but I can't ask you to take time away from your job." Cheryl turned her bossy-sister act toward Liz. "Ryan doesn't need to just sit around and wait at the hospital."

Ryan crossed his arms. "I'd really like to see this through and make sure he's okay."

"Don't worry about me. I don't have a shift in the box office until Wednesday, so I'm free all day tomorrow. Besides, if Ryan's there, then you aren't waiting and worrying alone. It might be nice to have someone to talk to instead of trying to distract yourself with an out-of-date magazine."

Cheryl frowned a bit, but then finally nodded. "Okay. Just be here around seven fifteen so I can go over the logistics with you." She glanced over her shoulder toward the living room and her children. "In the meantime, I need to call John with the news. This will kill him, to be so far away and not be able to do anything."

Ryan rested a hand on his sister's shoulder. "You can reassure him enough to keep him focused on his job over in Afghanistan. Tell him you've got plenty of help to take care of things here."

"Maybe he can even talk to Matt, too, and give him courage to face surgery tomorrow." Cheryl seemed to draw strength from Ryan's stability.

"While you call John and the kids are busy watching the movie, do you mind if Liz and I go for a walk?"

For the first time, it seemed that Cheryl finally saw what Liz was wearing. "Just don't stay out too long. I don't want Liz getting cold."

Yoga pants weren't made for being outside in cold weather, but just the thought of being alone with Ryan turned up the heat. She left the kitchen and grabbed her coat from the hook in the entryway before he could change his mind.

Hand in hand, they left the house, turned right at the end of the driveway, and headed west.

Ryan puffed out a frustrated breath as if he had been working hard to be strong for everyone else but was about to fall apart himself.

She knew the feeling. "Just start talking and get it all out. I'm a good listener."

He groaned. "I feel like an idiot. Not just because Matt is hurt and facing surgery and then weeks in a cast, or possibly even physical therapy. I came here to help out financially, and I'm not doing a very good job since the bills are piling up faster than my income here."

"Don't they have health insurance?"

"Yes, but I don't know how high the deductible is, and when you combine the emergency room visit with surgery and anesthesia, their part will still be huge." He kicked at a rock on the sidewalk.

Liz bit her lip. She wanted to be supportive, yet part of her was secretly glad to see the chinks in Ryan's armor.

He sighed and picked up the pace as they turned right again to round the block. "Since Cheryl's working some now, I'm more of a Mr. Mom instead of an income earner. Not very glamorous, but it helps. Still, I need to figure out how to earn more. The Christmas show pictures were a hassle, but they brought in a pretty decent amount while it lasted, especially with your idea to add the candids. I'd been using my savings to supplement the household budget before that got started, but unless I can figure out a way to make more money soon, I may regret turning down that job from *Traveler* magazine."

"A job?" Awe over his professional connections washed away in the reminder that he might leave.

"It was for a weeklong shoot in Yellowstone and would have paid enough to cover a month's worth of expenses or more. Except I can't leave Cheryl and the kids alone for that much time, especially now. I'm stuck between a rock and a hard place, and I'm the one who put myself there. Contracts keep passing me by, with no guarantee that I'll ever get to return to my freelance career. If I lose my contracts while waiting for John to return, I lose everything I've worked for all these years since I don't have a backup business plan."

Being stuck was hard enough without the internal "blame game" of guilt or fear. "I'll definitely pray for you to have wisdom when it comes to your career, but know this. You have very capable shoulders, but you don't have to carry this by yourself. I wish I could help more, but I promise to pray for God to meet your family's needs. Like I'm learning, He's got a plan for all of us. To give us hope and a future."

"Thanks. I think I just needed to get that off my chest and remember that God knows exactly what we need." He squeezed her hand. "Now give me some good news for a change. What were you doing before all this chaos?"

She told him about mailing the letter and a late Christmas present to her parents. "I'd collected a bunch of photos into a book—our sledding, some from the theater, and so on. I thought Mom would like to see what I've been up to, and Dad might…"

"Oh, he should love that!"

"I hope so." A twinge of internal doubt turned into a shiver.

Seeming to finally realize how cold it was outside, Ryan hustled them back toward Cheryl's house with the promise of hot chocolate to warm her up. But when he opened the front door, his teasing laughter faded away.

Past his slumped shoulders, Liz spied Cheryl huddled in the hallway, out of sight from the living room, clutching her phone to her chest with tears running down her face.

Chapter Fifteen

A week later Liz approached Cheryl's front door, only to have it open before she could knock.

Ryan grinned his familiar crinkly-eyed smile. "Thanks for coming. I could really use your help in getting this wedding order finished."

"I think you just wanted an excuse to see me." She winked as she passed by him into the entryway, very aware that they were here alone without the buffer of small children or his sister. "The bride can't have ordered that many prints."

He cleared his throat. "I might be guilty of the first, but just wait until you see the full order. The bride must have shared the disk of proof shots with the entire wedding party and all their relatives."

"So it's not just one order to fill?"

"Try eleven, including a photo book."

"Wow."

"And based on the numbers, I suspect they liked your candids more than the formal shots."

Her heart flooded with warmth at the thought that others liked her pictures, then sank at the inadvertent slight toward Ryan. "Maybe we should have switched assignments. After all, you're the famous photographer."

"No way. You've got a natural gift for capturing expressions, and that's going to make us a lot of money." He rested a hand on her shoulder before leading her back to the kitchen, where he'd set up his laptop and printer. With the Christmas photos done, he'd had to move his equipment back here, leaving no other options for public places in which to work.

They'd just have to keep today's time focused on the task and not on each other.

"How much are you charging for the prints, anyway?"

"Back when Cheryl asked me to do her friend a favor, I had no idea what to charge, so I cut a deal with the bride to do the shoot for a flat fee and then do her prints for the cost of materials plus ten percent."

"Sounds more than fair, especially since her husband is probably now deployed. But what about the rest of these?" Liz picked up the first of many handwritten lists intermingled with printed invoices. He wasn't kidding. They were going to be busy for hours, if not days.

"When she said others wanted prints, I called a couple of other photographers in town to get their prices before creating this list." He handed her a separate sheet of paper. "I'm still charging about twenty percent less than others in town."

She compared the lists in her hand. While math had never been her strength, the numbers added up quickly. "And knowing these prices, they're still ordering this much?"

He grinned. "And they all prepaid, which helped me afford to buy a giant box of paper and more ink cartridges. Not to mention, the timing is perfect because Matt's surgery bills will start to arrive any day now."

"So where do we start?" She shrugged out of her coat and draped it over a chairback.

"Well, that's another reason I wanted you here, because I'm sure you can come up with an idea or ten to help us work smarter." He stood behind her and looked over her shoulder at the lists.

Within a half hour, they had created a master list in order by print number, with notes about which person wanted which sizes. Liz cleaned off the kitchen counter and laid out each invoice in alphabetical order, while Ryan logged in and checked the printer settings.

"Okay, I'm ready for the first one." Ryan cradled his long fingers over the mouse.

Liz read the first line on their list. "File 002. One five-by-seven and three four-by-sixes."

"Hmm. We're going to waste paper if we're not careful. Can we come out almost even on sheets if we add in the next image we need to print?"

After a few calculations about how many prints were on each sheet and helpful notes on the master list about which pose each file number represented, the printer whirred into action. As the prints came out, Liz set them aside in a row on the table to dry, with a scrap of paper beside each noting the image number.

They soon settled into a rhythm of sending selected files to the printer, cutting apart the dried sheets, and then sorting the finished prints into stacks next to each invoice on the counter.

An hour later, Liz stretched her back. "Wow. I didn't remember photography being such backbreaking work. If the boss will let me, I could use a breather."

"I could be convinced." Ryan stood from his position in front of the computer. "Let's get a drink and…" He glanced around the cluttered kitchen. "Take it to the living room."

A few minutes later, she wiggled into the couch cushions and rested a can of pop on her denim-clad knee. Two and a half weeks ago, she and Ryan sat here when talking about God's love and opening presents. Then, just last week, Matt had used it during recovery from his surgery. Who knew a piece of furniture could hold so many memories?

Ryan flipped open the tab on his own can and settled in beside her, his shoulder rubbing against hers. "This probably isn't what you expected to do after a weekend at the theater."

"True, but it's a welcome change of pace." She could get used to this balance between the fast pace of the theater and spending time with Ryan, especially if photography was part of the mix.

Except, if they kept working here alone, they'd need to be careful not to cross into any compromising situations that would destroy Cheryl's trust. Liz was already tempted to lean into his side or turn her face up for a kiss.

Instead, she forced her thoughts back to the job at hand. "It's rewarding to see the finished product of the work we did."

"Usually when I see the finished work, it's on the pages of a magazine and not in a stack next to the coffeepot."

"Why don't you rub it in, Mr. Famous Guy?"

"Mr. Famous Guy? That's the best you can do?"

"I could have called you Mr. Montana or Wrangler Boy or Alligator Wrestler."

He laughed. "I didn't wrestle any alligators, just took pictures of them." He swiped his finger through the condensation on the side of his can. "No, my brother-in-law is the only one on an adventure right now. Or at least through sometime in April."

She caught her breath. After John's return, Ryan's sister would no longer need him close by to help out. He was a wanderer at heart and would be free to move on.

Unless there was a way to convince him to stay.

She cleared her throat. "Maybe I should you call you Mr. Wedding Photographer instead. I never dreamed there was this much money in weddings. If I didn't work weekends at the theater, I'd consider setting up a shop of my own. Maybe you could do that until April."

"No way. The last thing I want is to set up a business where I'd have to be there all the time. I just need to figure out how get a steady income for a few months."

"No one said you'd have to do weddings forever. Maybe just take it a month at a time. I bet you could find a few jobs between now and, say, the end of February. I'd think there might be more Valentine's Day weddings than available photographers."

He frowned. "Maybe."

"You don't have to schedule anything beyond February if you're afraid to be stuck here." Oops. Did that really slip out?

"I'm not afraid, and I don't think of this as being stuck." He swiped his free hand through his hair as if missing the security of his cowboy hat, then sighed. "Okay, so maybe I am a little afraid of being stuck and losing my freelance career completely, but I'm not sure weddings are the answer. The money is nice, but I don't want to shoot weddings for the rest of my life. Not to mention, there are plenty of other established photographers in this area as competition."

"True. But maybe while you're working a few jobs to make some extra money in the short-term, you could build an online business instead of a brick-and-mortar one."

"What part of 'I don't want to build a long-term business' don't you understand? I'm just filling time and need the quick money like we made before Christmas." He swallowed the last of the pop in his can and stood. "Like the job waiting in the kitchen, if you're done with your little break."

Liz stared at his back as he disappeared around the corner. Where had that come from? He'd asked for her help earlier but now didn't have the decency to listen?

It was said that a lasting relationship should be built on friendship and communication instead of romantic sparks. Except the only sparks flying here were hers. She chugged the rest of her drink and tried to calm her redheaded temper. Nope. It wasn't working.

A minute later she threw her can into the recycling bin with more force than necessary. "Excuse me while I point out the obvious, Mr. Big Shot. The extra money from the Christmas-picture reprints came from one of my ideas, not yours. And just last week you were moaning about not having a backup plan in case your freelance contracts disappeared. I thought I was being helpful by offering a few more ideas, but obviously, you know best. I know when I'm not needed." She crossed the kitchen and reached for her coat.

"Wait a minute." He sighed. "Just hold on."

"Why?" She folded her arms over her chest, her coat offering an extra layer of protection over her heart.

"Because you're right. It's just been a frustrating week around here, trying to take care of Matt as he came off the anesthesia and then managing his pain. Not to mention wondering what the surgeon's bill would be."

She relaxed her grip on her coat.

"I'm sorry I took my frustrations out on you." He gestured toward the chair where she'd hung her coat earlier. "I'm trying to help Cheryl, except I'm way out of my comfort zone. Please, forgive me?"

She returned her coat to its former spot, then pulled out the chair next to Ryan's. "You're forgiven."

"You said something about an online business?"

"Yes." Was he serious about listening or simply humoring her?

"But not some get-rich-quick or work-from-home scam."

"Definitely not. Whatever you do has to be photography-based because you could also build your brand while diversifying your streams of income."

"Diversifying my what?" He tugged on her ponytail. "That's kind of a big word for an actress, ain't it?"

"I'll slow it down for ya, cowboy." She propped her elbows on the table and winked.

"And a brand? Aren't those the marks they burn into the rear ends of horses and cows with a hot rod?" The lines around his eyes deepened along with his smile.

"A hot rod?" She fluttered her eyelashes. "You mean like a Porsche or a Lamborghini?"

Ryan's deep laughter erased any remaining tension in the room.

"Seriously, doing something online is perfect because you can run your business from anywhere in the world."

"That part sounds ideal."

"And customers from anywhere in the world can find you too."

"Even better. But what could I sell other than more pictures on my website? I do some of that already and don't make a lot."

Liz snagged a blank piece of regular paper from the bottom tray of the printer and started a list. "The first thing you'll need to tweak your marketing plan and add a few publicity campaigns to drive traffic to your existing online store."

"Tweak my... How do you know so much about business practices?"

"I started off studying business in college before I switched majors." She clicked her pen open and closed several times, then shrugged. "Rather than focus on a one-time sales offer—like a photograph—to a one-time customer, what else could you sell?"

"I could sell the rights to a few of my photos to some of those online stock-image companies. They'd do most of the publicity and advertising for me, but I don't know how much I'd make."

"It's worth checking into; every little bit would add up." Liz made a note.

"But besides taking pictures on assignment or speculation, what else do I have to offer?"

She eyed the strength in his hands and the character in his face. He had a lot to offer, especially to one lucky woman in the future. Reluctantly, she pulled her attention from his firm lips back to the topic at hand. "You do have years of wisdom and advice for beginners."

"Like a teacher? I guess I could see about teaching a class at the community college, but that's not online."

"They do have online classes using webinars or downloaded videos."

"As if I have time to learn the technology and then actually use it."

"What about writing about just one tip or equipment recommendation at a time like on a blog?" Liz's mind spun with possibilities.

"Except don't most blogs give away the information for free?"

"Honestly, I think they make most of their money from the ads in the sidebars, hoping people click through."

"And in the process, my website would start to look like Times Square in New York if it's plastered with advertisements. No one would know what to pay attention to first." He shuddered and frowned.

"I'm sure it could be done tastefully or even on a small scale."

"But then it wouldn't make as much money, and I'm back to doing the work for free. I'd much rather spend my time making money."

"Hmm." The seed of an idea began to take root. "What if you could charge someone to read each article you wrote? Like a subscription newsletter. Maybe charge people five dollars a month to receive an e-mail containing a super-helpful photography tip every Monday."

"Five dollars for a few articles?" The wrinkles in his forehead deepened.

"Ten people sign up and you get fifty bucks a month. They all spread the word to their photography clubs and soon you have one hundred people on your list. That's—"

"Five hundred a month, which would go a long way toward supplementing Cheryl's budget."

"And give you future stability, all for writing four or five little articles a month."

He reached over and squeezed her hand. "I think I could definitely do that, but how would we set it up?"

We? If only he meant that word in terms of her future as well.

But her future lay on the stage, not traveling the world.

She clicked her pen again. "First off, you'd need an e-mail subscription service to handle the collecting of e-mail addresses and delivery of articles. And then on your website, you'd need to add another page talking about the newsletter—maybe even offering a free sample tip so they know what kind of value they'd get if they signed up."

"Well, I know what kind of value I've found right here." He brushed a finger down the side of her cheek. "You're one in a million."

Chapter Sixteen

Liz spun her key ring around her index finger as she jogged along the second-story breezeway outside her apartment. Whistling had never been her thing, but she could imagine herself bursting into a cheery tune at the thought of seeing Ryan again in a few minutes.

Yesterday they'd taken the kids to a movie since schools were closed on Martin Luther King Junior Day. While the latest animated characters went on an adventure, Ryan had held her hand in the dark, his thumb tracing a lazy figure eight and sending tingles up her arm.

And today, they were getting together to work on the photography-tips newsletter business while Hannah had a playdate with a friend after kindergarten. They'd definitely get some work done in those few quiet hours, including brainstorming a catchy name, but since her weekends were so busy at the theater, she craved any excuse to spend time with Ryan during the week.

She skipped down the steps toward the ground level and the parking lot. Just the thought of spending time with the guy who was becoming more and more important in her life was enough to put a giddy smile on her face. Add in his family and her heart overflowed.

Speaking of family, she should check the mailbox. She detoured to the bank of collective boxes for the complex. While nothing would have been delivered yesterday due to the holiday, she'd been busy at the theater all weekend. What if a letter from home had sat there neglected for days?

She sorted through her keys, then opened the small door of their apartment's box. Inside the small space were a few bills and advertisements for her roommates, which she left behind for them to pick up later so they didn't get forgotten in her car. Not that she'd done that ... recently. But joy of joys, there was also a key to one of the larger sections reserved for packages.

Like a kid at Christmas, she snatched the key and soon held a flat box addressed to her in her father's handwriting with a return postage stamp from Wichita, Kansas.

It had been two weeks since she'd mailed her apology letter and gift. And now she held their reply in her hands.

She turned the package around to access the tape just in time for a gust of wind to send half of her hair into tangles across her face while triggering a shiver down her spine.

Better to open it inside her car. She swiped the hair from her face and hurried to her yellow Volkswagen Beetle. The bright color never failed to cheer her up and was the perfect symbol of hope on this glorious January day when she'd finally heard from home.

After sliding behind the steering wheel, she quickly started the engine so the heater could start thawing out the windshield and the rest of the interior. Of course, that made for an awkward maneuver in order to use one of the other keys on the ring to help tear through the packaging tape, but some things were worth it.

Inside the box she found an envelope addressed to her and a packet of folded papers atop her book of photos, nestled within wads of newspaper for cushioning. Pushing aside the papers, she focused on the book.

Why had they returned her gift? Had they even looked at it?

She flipped it open and then sucked in a breath at the sight of black writing over the top of several images. "Amateurish. Silly. A waste of time." And on another page, "I taught you better than this."

Except Dad had always brushed aside her questions, leaving online videos and experimentation as her teachers.

Her initial shock at the senseless destruction gave way to horror, then anger. How could her own father still think so little of her ability when Ryan, the Sheridans, and even Gloria complimented her work? What was wrong with him?

After turning the page, she spotted a different—but also familiar—handwriting with even more vicious things to say. Jerry the Jerk had once again lived down to his nickname.

She slammed the book shut.

To put her heart into her photography and then have it ridiculed was … the worst sort of betrayal. And to have her dad seemingly encourage an ex-boyfriend to add his opinions? Gasping for breath, she stared at the book in her hands. It couldn't get any worse, could it?

Tempted to hurl the ruined book against the passenger window, she instead set it beside her purse and picked up the sealed envelope with a shaking hand. Inside were two typed pages followed by her own handwritten letter with more comments slashed across it, this time in bleeding-red ink.

She turned back to the first page and began to read.

> Liz,
>
> I'd tell you to read this entire letter as you so arrogantly told me to do, but that would be pointless because you've rarely obeyed. Still, just in case there's a first time for everything, I'm hoping you finally acknowledge the truth and see the error of your ways.

So much for trying to rebuild their broken relationship. Tears stung her eyes and trickled down her cheeks as she continued reading.

> Did you think we would enjoy seeing evidence of your life of rebellion? While your grandmother talked us into dance lessons to improve your coordination, I never approved of the skimpy costumes. And with these pictures, were you trying to rub our noses in the fact that you chose a path of acting and dancing over your righteous upbringing? You say you love us but then ignore everything I've ever taught you. Shame on you.

Skimpy costumes? She glanced at the book containing just a few pictures from the theater. Only one costume even had a semi-short skirt. He must have meant something from a childhood recital before her dance lessons had ended. But still, no one could possibly consider the costumes from *Seven Brides* at all disgraceful or shame-worthy. Mr. Sheridan had a reputation for picking wholesome shows.

> You continually reject my offer of a legitimate business in favor of more frivolity on the stage. Am I supposed to be impressed because someone paid you to take pictures of actors ... people who flaunt immorality and kiss strangers simply because of a script? My business might not be exciting enough for you, but at least it's honorable. When the path you are on leads to ruin, don't come crawling back like the prodigal son, because I'd only have to say I told you so.

Dad might have a point about onstage kisses, but comparing her to the prodigal son? Really? In that story, the father came running with open arms and threw a welcome-home party to celebrate. His threat of an "I told you so" sounded more like the prodigal's judgmental brother than the loving God the parable was meant to illustrate.

> But worst of all is your blatant lie about going to church, because if you really were reading the Bible, you'd know what it says about children obeying their parents. As it says in Ephesians 6:1, "Children, obey your parents in the Lord: for this is right." In Colossians 3:20 it says, "Children, obey your parents in all things: for this is well pleasing unto the Lord."

As if she hadn't grown up having to say—or write out—those verses over and over.

> The Bible also says in 1 Timothy 5:8, "But if any provide not for his own, and specially for those of his own house, he hath denied the faith, and is worse than an infidel." By not returning home to help your mother and I, you are not helping to provide for our household. Therefore, you have denied the faith.

> We have tried to point out the error of your ways privately and discipline you accordingly, but since you refuse to acknowledge the truth of your responsibility or repent, we took it to the church for their wisdom.

She reread the last sentences. Had he presented her personal decision to stay with her job in Colorado to the church elders as a sin? What was next, an old-fashioned shunning? Could this day get any worse?

> Your mom hoped you would come to your senses, but Jerry helped me realize you were never coming back. If you won't listen to me or to the correction of the church, there is no chance of reconciliation. Therefore, like it says in Matthew 18:17, we are cutting off fellowship. "Let him be unto thee as an heathen man and a publican."

NO MORE PHONE CALLS. NO LETTERS. NO VISITS. YOU MIGHT STILL LEGALLY HAVE THE NAME FOSTER, BUT YOU ARE NOT ONE OF US AND WE HAVE WRITTEN YOU OUT OF OUR WILLS. MY BUSINESS PARTNER WILL NOW OFFICIALLY INHERIT IN YOUR PLACE BECAUSE HE DID WHAT WAS RIGHT IN THE EYES OF THE LORD AND—LIKE YOU SO NASTILY POINTED OUT—HAS TRULY BECOME THE SON WE NEVER HAD.

MAY GOD HAVE MERCY ON YOUR SOUL.

She stared at the spot where her father signed his full name as if the letter were a legal document. Below his signature was her mother's, along with a handwritten note.

GOODBYE, LIZ. I'M MOURNING THE LOSS OF MY DAUGHTER.

As if she were dead. Would her mom go so far as to wear black? Would her parents be celebrated among their church community for taking such a firm stand to separate themselves from their heathen child?

Unbearable pressure began to build in her chest as she opened the last packet of papers—notarized copies of her parents' new wills to rub salt in the finality of their rejection.

The cruel comments in the book might have rejected her talent, but to have her very existence erased from their hearts cut deep with the emptiness of a sudden loss. She'd been away from home for years, yet—at least until a few months ago—she still had an open connection with her mom.

She'd always believed she could go home if things got really bad. But now? Now she was essentially an orphan.

No safety net to fall back on. No inheritance. No family.

No one left who cared about her. Except Dani. And Ryan. And God, if her dad was wrong about that too.

She put her car into reverse and backed out of her parking spot as she fought the sobs shaking her body.

Parked alongside the curb outside Cheryl's house, Liz sucked in another shuddering breath and blew it out. If she concentrated on breathing, maybe she could then focus on Ryan's business once she got inside.

Another deep breath, this one steadier than before.

Good. She could do this.

She reached over to grab her purse and saw the contents of the unwelcome package.

Another wave of grief washed over her. When would it stop?

The driver's side door opened. "Hey, beautiful. What's taking you so—" Ryan leaned into the car. "What happened?"

"I … picked … up … mail." As if her crying wasn't embarrassing enough, her body decided to react with a case of the hiccups. She gave up trying to talk and just pointed to the papers.

"Come here." With a steady hand under her arm, Ryan helped pull her out of the car and then gave her a quick hug.

While she leaned against the side of the Beetle, he ducked back inside, emerging a moment later with the awful evidence. He flipped open the book long enough to see a few of the comments and then snapped it shut, a vein ticking along his jawline.

His reaction triggered more tears.

He slammed her car door. "Let's get you inside where it's warm." With a firm arm around her back, he almost carried her into the house and straight to the couch.

When he pulled her down onto his lap and wrapped strong arms around her, her fragile hold on her composure slipped even further, and she gave in to the overwhelming emotions.

Just to be held securely while her world fell apart … oh, this was what real love did. Love didn't abandon or shame or condemn or disinherit. Love rocked her, grieved with her, and then helped pick up the pieces.

The security of Ryan's embrace faded as she became more deeply aware of God holding her in His hands. She poured out the pain consuming her and let God's love fill the empty places left behind.

Gradually she became aware of a whispered prayer stirring the hair around her face. The beat of Ryan's heart beneath the soft-but-wet flannel shirt under her cheek. The strength of his arms around her.

She could stay here forever—but now that he'd endured her emotional train wreck, he deserved an explanation. She gently pushed away from his chest and, as his grip relaxed, lifted her head.

The letters and documents lay open on the couch beside them. "So you read it?"

"All of it." His voice broke. "I'm so sorry."

She blinked back fresh tears as she searched his face. "Why can't they just love me and accept me for who I am? Why do I have to fit into a mold that doesn't sound anything like what God would want?"

"Only God knows what's in their hearts. Sometimes people can try to do the right thing even for mostly right reasons but still end up far from the truth." Ryan eased her off his lap and shifted to face her. "All I can say is that your parents are the ones missing out on the real treasure. God will eventually make them answer for the way they've treated you."

She drew in a shaky breath. "Why does God let awful things like this happen in the first place?"

He sighed. "Ask the tough questions, why don't you? Philosophers and theologians have wrestled with the idea of evil in the world for centuries."

"What do you think?"

"I think the bad stuff is the unfortunate side effect of God giving us free will. Sin entered the world then."

"Huh?"

"He could have created us to be robotic slaves who do everything He says and never make mistakes. But, instead, he created mankind with the ability to choose whether to follow Him or not. By giving us the choice, it opened the door for an amazing relationship."

"Because we'd want to spend time with Him rather than be forced into it." Unfortunately, that thought reminded her of her mandatory church attendance while growing up.

"Exactly. Except that by giving us a choice, it also opened the door to lots of mistakes and even deliberate decisions to do really awful things, like the Holocaust or terrorist attacks. I truly believe that all the bad things resulting from our choices hurt God's heart too, but that was the price He was willing to pay—in the short-term—in order to have a genuine relationship with those who would choose Him."

"So bad things are only short-term because eventually He'll put a stop to it, return to earth, destroy evil, and we'll all live happily ever after."

"Something like that." He smiled. "The other problem is that many have said they want a relationship with God but then only see Him as a magic genie to solve their problems or give them a get-out-of-hell card. They don't seek God for the relationship's sake, and so they never truly experience the joy of just walking through life—good and bad—with God."

Just like she'd felt a few minutes ago by being held in God's loving hands. The earlier pain had truly brought her to a deeper joy and understanding of God.

Ryan brushed his fingers over her hand and then linked their fingers. "Know this. God knows exactly how you felt today. You chose to reach out to your dad, and he unfortunately chose to slam the door. Jesus reaches out to the world, but many still reject Him. He knows what it's like to be betrayed and rejected and more."

"Keep on reminding me of the truth, because I think I forgot for a bit."

"We all do from time to time." He kissed the back of her hand. "Do you mind if I pray for you? For them?"

Her eyes swept over his face. "Please."

He bowed his head, and soon their foreheads touched as his heartfelt words rose between them. "Father God, thank You for Your love and acceptance. Remind Liz how You have uniquely designed her and gifted her with incredible creativity. Remind her of the many people who have been blessed when she has used her talents. Help her to see that she did the right thing by reaching out to her family in grace and love. Then help her believe You have seen their response and will call on them to give an account. Give her an extra measure of grace and forgiveness whenever she remembers how they have wronged her. Continue to comfort and guide Liz in the days to come. May the richness of Your love continue to wash over her heart and heal any lingering hurt. Like it says in Zephaniah, quiet her with Your love."

Cleansing tears of gratitude dripped from her eyes to their clasped hands as Liz added her own prayer. "And God, help them to somehow to see the truth of Your amazing love. Set them free from their lists of harsh rules so they can learn to walk in the freedom of a true relationship with You. Give me the courage to keep on loving them well, just like You kept on loving me long before I listened. Amen."

"Amen." Ryan squeezed her hands and then released them, offering her a sleeve to wipe her eyes on.

"Thanks. I don't know what I'd do without you, especially since I've been shunned or excommunicated or whatever they'd call it."

"We'll keep praying for them, and maybe someday they'll relent enough to at least talk occasionally. Especially since they'll want to brag about their future grandchildren."

"Their what?" Liz choked on a laugh.

He grinned, then glanced over his shoulder at the letter. "While it helped my ego to read that you think I'm a special guy, I have to ask. Who's Jerry?"

Chapter Seventeen

"You're jealous of Jerry the Jerk?"

"That's quite a nickname." Ryan sat back against the couch cushions. "Remind me to be nice to you before I end up as Ryan the Ridiculous."

Her fresh burst of laughter caught her by surprise, especially after the emotional depths she'd experienced in the last hour. But while she was airing the skeletons in her family closet, it might be good to get the whole mess out into the open and put it behind her forever.

"It would take a lot to top Jerry as the biggest mistake of my life, especially since he ended up stealing my family and my inheritance."

He frowned at the reminder. "Go on."

"To set the stage, Grandpa O'Neill began the photography business, complete with a studio for taking family portraits. After my parents got married, Dad started helping out and added the school pictures and sports teams. Growing up, I spent many afternoons playing around the studio when I wasn't busy with dance lessons. By the time Grandpa gave me my first camera—when I was twelve—I was hooked."

"That explains both of your artistic talents."

"Thanks. But all that changed when Grandpa had a stroke and died. When Grandma died a couple of years later, Dad changed the name of the business to Foster's Fotos. The studio turned into more of a workstation where Mom and I helped print and package the growing number of school orders. About the same time, we started attending a different church than the one my grandparents had been a part of. That's when things got harder at home. Or maybe I only noticed because as a teenager I chafed against all the rules. Mom said that Dad had been raised in a strict household, but since I'd never met any other Fosters and he never talked about his childhood, I think I blamed the changes on the new church. And, by default, God."

"That's understandable. But I wonder what his childhood was really like."

"Guess I'll never know now." She shrugged. "Anyway, despite how tense things could get at home, I still dreamed of someday carrying on the family business. Except I didn't want to stay inside the walls of schools or even a studio like Grandpa's. I wanted to branch out and do weddings or senior pictures or family reunions, but I kept butting heads with my dad and his 'this is the way I've always done it' mentality.

"Since I wasn't completely sure how to make my ideas work, I decided to study business in college. I thought maybe then I could figure out how to grow the business enough to support both of us and even hire someone to do the busywork so Mom could be free to do the things she enjoyed instead."

"Sounds wise." Ryan smiled. "Let me guess. College is where you met the jerk."

"Close. I'd come home on breaks, full of ideas about marketing or a new website. And Dad would not so patiently shoot down every one of them even though the demand for his work grew along with the area's population. Until the summer after my sophomore year, I mentioned he could get cheap help by hiring an intern."

"Aha."

"Jerry was such a hottie, excuse the expression. Dark hair, brooding eyes, and surrounded in serious mystery that made a girl want to get to know him and uncover what made him tick. And somehow I caught his eye. Or rather, as it turned out, my dad's business caught his eye, and I was simply the means to an end—the doorway into a family and a partnership in a ready-made business."

"When did you figure it out?"

"Not until it was too late." Liz tugged at a loose string on the sleeve of her sweatshirt. "We actually went out a few times, but mostly we just spent time together at my parents' house because he claimed he didn't want to monopolize all my limited time with them. The rest of that fall semester after I went back to college was filled with long-distance calls and emails. I was so enamored with him that I naively dreamed of us working together in the business. I used to send him these long, rambling descriptions of my latest business ideas. I even came up with an idea for a cute logo using the vertical part of the F in our name as part of a tripod."

Ryan reached over to still her nervous hands under his. "And then what happened?"

"Christmas break came. I'd just finished taking pictures of the drama department's winter production for the college newspaper and was riding high on the buzz from the backstage action and dramatic expressions of the actors."

"And you caught the acting bug in addition to the dancing."

She nodded. "My childhood dance classes had a few little programs, but those were nothing like an actual play. The alternative was so alive and vibrant and creative, it just reinforced my desire to expand Dad's business into something bigger. I tried several times to start a conversation with him about it, but all I got were hints that he had a surprise planned that he thought would make me very happy. And when I tried to get Jerry alone to share my dreams with him, he hinted that I wouldn't need to head back to school in January because of something about on-the-job training."

"Which meant…"

"Something entirely different in my overactive imagination." She rolled her eyes. "I alternated between hoping the mysterious box under the tree contained the Leica camera I'd asked for and the frightfully nerve-racking idea Jerry might propose."

"Did he?"

Liz smoothed her hand over the ticking vein in Ryan's jaw. "Yes, but you can relax. It was so businesslike that it took me several minutes to figure out what he was asking. In fact, when I asked why he wasn't down on his knee, he said he didn't have time for any inconvenient romantic tripe. All he wanted was for me to quit school and come home to stay so they could add a second team out in the field."

"What was the catch?"

"How could you nail him so quickly?" She shook her head. "I immediately started in on all my ideas for booking other events in the future and how I was thinking he could take over the school jobs when Dad wanted to retire, but he just looked at me as if I'd sprouted another head. Then he patted my shoulder and said, 'You just leave that to us men. And you don't need a business degree to answer phones and stuff envelopes.' "

"That's ridiculous. Had he ever seen your pictures?"

"He had seen a few." She waved at the rejected gift book on the coffee table. "And evidently he still finds things to criticize."

"Some of those comments were his?"

She massaged his ticking vein again. "Hold on, this story gets better, er, worse. We return from our little very-unromantic walk on Christmas Eve and Dad is waiting inside the door, more excited than I'd seen him in years. Jerry tells him I'd said no."

"As you should have. Marrying that jerk would have destroyed your dreams. If he really loved you, he would have found a way for you to use your talents in a way that brought you joy."

"I know that now." And in the process she'd realized that Ryan's including her in his photography business was evidence that he might… She cleared her throat. "Anyway, Dad frowned and said maybe his gift would help me reconsider. Turns out the mysterious box under the tree contained a couple of monogrammed company shirts with this cute new logo *Jerry* had designed—the same logo I'd sketched out and e-mailed a picture of the month previous."

"Thief." Ryan clenched his hands in his lap.

"That's what I said. But Jerry just smirked and told my dad some lie that Dad totally believed, which made me wonder what other ideas he'd been stealing. I thought maybe I could undo some of the damage if I started to work alongside Dad because I had a few new ideas to run by him. Of course, that suggestion bombed too since he only wanted a receptionist, scheduler, and picture-printing-order-fulfiller. He'd leave the ideas to Jerry. So just because I'm a glutton for punishment, I flat-out asked whether I'd ever get the chance to step behind the camera."

"And?"

"He said I was being ridiculous. That it was too much for me to handle, and that as a woman—"

"He's a fool."

"Yeah. Well, I might have gotten a little heated in my response, but then so did Dad. He laid down an ultimatum, and before I knew it, I was packing my suitcase to move back to campus while Jerry settled in to enjoy Christmas dinner with his new family."

"The jerk."

Liz patted Ryan's arm. "I switched majors and spent my summer breaks working as a waitress rather than return home and submit to Dad's ultimatum. Other than Mom coming to see my graduation last May, I haven't seen either of them in three years, just had phone calls with Mom about once a month. So, after graduation, I got a one-show acting contract here and the rest is history." She snuggled in beside him on the couch. "The not-so-funny thing is that Dad was open to new ideas for his business after all, just not from me."

"Ouch. No wonder you got mad when I didn't listen to you." He pressed a kiss onto the top of her head. "I'm really glad I backed down and we were able to brainstorm together."

"For the project we're supposed to be working on right now?"

"That one. Except I'm enjoying just sitting here, talking with you. And I'm glad you didn't end up staying in Kansas after all because Jerry's loss is my gain."

"Thanks." Her mind drifted back to where this conversation had started, with Ryan feeling a bit jealous of her ex-boyfriend. As if he had anything to worry about.

But what about Ryan's ex-girlfriends? How many of them still lingered in his memories?

"Um, since now you know all about my messed-up family and my biggest mistake in the romance department, what about you?"

"What about me?"

"I've seen how you are with your niece and nephew, and you already told me about your parents' relationship. Why aren't you happily married already?"

He picked up her hand and brushed a thumb across the back of her knuckles. "Guess I was just waiting for the right girl to come along. However, since you asked, there once was a girl back in Montana who caught my attention. She had hair as yellow as the sun and eyes as blue as the sky."

"That's poetic."

"Yep, that gal sure had plenty of sugar to give, except she wouldn't give me what I wanted."

"Say what?" She hoped he wasn't saying what she thought.

His crooked smile grew. "I mean, who in their right mind would hold on to their delicious chocolate pudding when they could have a baggie full of crunchy carrot sticks guaranteed to improve their eyesight?"

And suddenly she realized he joked about a childhood incident. She laughed. "Seriously? That's the reason you're still single? Because a girl wouldn't trade you a pudding cup for your carrot sticks?"

"Haven't you heard? The way to a man's heart is through his stomach."

She playfully tried to slap his stomach, only to discover that it was hard as rock. If it wasn't covered in flannel thanks to the winter season, would he sport a six-pack of muscles?

"You're just so fun to tease, and I've missed seeing your smile." He settled her in beside him. "There actually *was* a girl back in Montana. Come to think of it, she was best friends with the pudding-cup hoarder."

"Oh, hush up and tell me the truth."

"We went together for a couple of years in high school. After graduation, she started dropping all these obvious hints about us living on my parents' ranch and sipping tea in the evenings on the porch—as if ranchers have time to sip tea."

"Yeah. Can't see you as the tea type when you obviously drink gallons of super-thick black coffee strong enough to grow hair on your chest."

"What do you know about my chest?"

"Just that it's all wet." She eyed the damp spot on his shirt. But below the muscular package beat a heart filled with selfless love and strong character. "And it makes a great pillow." Heat flooded her face.

"You're blushing."

"You would have to point that out. But you keep changing the subject. What happened with the pudding-cup-hoarder's best friend?"

"I already told you about working at my uncle's camera shop in town. Well, one day he hung up a flier about a photography contest where the main prize was a trip to a big city in another state and the chance to tag along with a famous photographer on a real live photo shoot. Of course, I agonized for a week over what pictures to enter."

"Which was more appealing? The chance to travel or the photographer?"

"Both. But don't tell Grant."

"Grant who?"

"Grant McHenry."

"As in the big-shot owner of the Bricker Communications empire with a gazillion magazines? Who you so casually name-drop as if he's no big deal?"

"He's the CEO—not the owner—but he was just a photographer back then."

"Just?"

"Shall I continue?" Ryan's lips twitched as if he tried to hide a smile. He knew he'd caught her attention.

"Please." Like it or not, she couldn't help but be impressed at his connections that high in the industry.

"So I won the contest and experienced my first-ever plane ride on the way to Boise. I was flying high even before being introduced to Grant at the main studio. Of course, he was both shocked and annoyed to find that the winner was some punk kid. He loaned me a camera for a few minutes to see what I'd do with a nearby setup for some food magazine shoot. I think it was a test to see if I'd really entered the contest with my own work, so that after proving I was a fraud, he could get out of the day's plans."

"Meanwhile, you were drooling over the camera more than the food."

"Absolutely. So I took a bunch of pictures, and something made him pay attention to the way I moved around. He then checked the images. I can still remember his raised eyebrows and then the half smile, as if he had a secret. He said, 'Not bad, kid,' and we got on with the day's plans. But on our way out, he handed the card of images I took to his boss."

Tingles ran up her arms at the implications. "And you got your big break."

"A week after I got home and two weeks before I was supposed to start taking classes at the community college—since I still didn't know what I wanted to study at the big university several hours away—I received a call from somebody at the food magazine asking me to confirm my address so they could send a licensing contract for the pictures I took. And then she named the fee and asked if it was acceptable."

"Well, duh."

His crooked grin grew. "Exactly. Then before the contract even arrived,

Grant's boss called with an internship offer. They said they'd pay me enough to cover my living expenses and I'd shadow Grant for six months."

"Amazing."

"And that open door changed the direction of my life." His grin faded. "Before the six months was up, I received a formal job offer to stay on as a staff photographer with the opportunity to take on freelance work in the future. And then my dad died in a four-wheeler accident while checking the fence line."

"Oh no." She squeezed his arm.

"I came home for the funeral and spent hours agonizing about my future—should I take the job offer doing what I loved or stay in Montana to help Mom take care of Dad's ranch? The night before I was supposed to return to Idaho to finish out the internship agreement, Mom made my dilemma easier by announcing that she was going to sell the land and move here to Colorado so she could be closer to Cheryl."

"But what about you?"

"In her own way, she was thinking about me too. She knew where my passion led and that I wasn't wired for ranching forever. Rather than chain me to Dad's dream out of some sort of implied obligation, she freely gave her blessing for me to leave the nest."

"By actually dismantling the nest?"

"Hey, when the Callahans do something, we go all in." He laughed. "But Mom's a wise lady. Just like I'm here right now because I love my family, I might have stayed then too and missed out on launching my career. But since I didn't have to make that choice after all, I poured my energy into my new job. Then Grant quickly moved up the ladder into management and I was in position to take over his prime assignments."

"Like those alligators in the Florida Everglades." She finally had a true sense of how much he'd given up to come here to help Cheryl … and why he feared his career might pass him by. "But you still haven't said what happened to the pudding-cup-hoarder's friend."

He reached over to take her hand again. "She actually cornered me at my dad's funeral. Asked if I was done playing and ready to come back and settle down where I belonged. She was completely clueless about what made me tick and never would have helped me achieve my dreams. And I wasn't willing to give up those dreams for a forever life with her either." He frowned. "Turns out she was only interested in the ranch anyway. Ironically, she's married to the fellow who bought Dad's place and has three rowdy boys who definitely leave her with no time to drink tea on the porch after all."

"Except maybe losing a little part of her dream was worth it in light of what she gained."

"True." His warm gaze drifted over her face. "I gave up a few assignments to come here, and look what I've gained in return."

He wasn't the only one who had found something special. Over the past few hours, her heart had been ripped open and then carefully pieced back together by the Creator of her soul and this man who was teaching her what it meant to love deeply.

His gaze lowered to her lips, followed by his mouth. First with a gentle exploration and then with more urgency, his kiss took as much as he gave, staking his claim and pulling her into a connection so powerful that the world around her faded.

When they came up for air, she discovered his heart beating a wild rhythm under the soft flannel she clutched in her hands. His hands trailed through and then smoothed the tangles from her hair.

He wasn't kidding when he said the Callahans went all in when they did something; his kisses had practically branded her for life.

Outside, a car door slammed, followed by the approach of childish voices and girlish squeals. Hannah was back from her playdate, and Matt wouldn't be far behind.

Good thing, too, because with chemistry this strong, they could use a chaperone.

Ryan cleared his throat. "Saved by the niece." His amazingly kissable lips curved into a crooked smile. "But I've got this sudden craving for chocolate pudding."

Chapter Eighteen

Liz hummed the melody to "Love Never Goes Away" as she slipped into the crowded dressing room after Sunday's matinee. Making her way to her usual spot, she reached behind her to unzip her costume.

"Hey, aren't you getting sick of that song by now?" Renee's voice carried across the room.

"Maybe not this song." Liz smiled before singing a few of the lyrics. " 'He holds me and I know where I belong.' "

Especially since those lines made her think of Ryan.

And God.

But mostly Ryan.

She quickly changed into a pair of jeans and a fuzzy green sweater before hanging up her costume on the community rack. Around her, the dressing-room chatter centered on their collective boredom.

With five weekends of shows behind them as January faded into February, another seven weekends loomed on the horizon. And while speculation about the cast list for the next play might provide future fuel for the gossip mill, another month remained before they would even start rehearsals.

Another month of singing the same songs over and over. Of dancing the same dances. Of saying the same lines and of kissing the same bad-breath actor every time he proposed.

Gloria's voice broke through the chatter. "I, for one, would love it if Mr. Sheridan shook up the casting a bit. Just for a little variety, you know."

Liz glanced toward the mirrors to find the former star—her current understudy—staring back with a half smile.

Or was she staring at Dani, busy hanging up her own costume beside Liz?

"Just what do you mean by that?" Dani tossed her dance shoes into her rehearsal bag, then propped her hands on her hips as she faced off with the diva.

Gloria's laugh sounded forced. "Well, I don't know about you, but I'm getting tired of kissing the same guy every day. Couldn't we brides swap brothers for a show?"

"How perfectly scandalous." Anna fluttered a hand under her chin as if about to swoon and then laughed. "But a switch would wreck the choreography in so many places. I'm not bored enough to ask for extra work if I don't have to."

"Me neither," Anna's housemate Sarah chimed in from near the door. "However, I might need to go get a part-time job just to fill my days. I've already read all the new releases at the library."

Liz turned back to cleaning up the rest of her area as the conversation shifted around her.

At least she had Ryan's photography business to occupy her time outside the theater. Yet it wasn't just the challenge of thinking outside the box and brainstorming ideas in order to get more jobs ... Ryan himself occupied more and more of her thoughts.

And her dreams.

"So do you have plans for tonight?" Dani asked beside her. She was running a brush through her hair, undoing the hair-sprayed collection of curls from the show.

"Not really." Liz shrugged. "I was going to get together with Ryan for dinner, but he left a message. He's doing something with Matt instead."

"You got ditched for time with his nephew?"

"Yeah. It seems he's having nightmares about his dad going missing or getting hurt. Ryan thought they needed some one-on-one man time."

"That's sweet."

"The kid's had a rough month already, without adding unnecessary worry on top of his itchy cast."

"How much longer with the cast?"

"It's been four weeks, so he might be getting it off this week. He has an appointment soon, and they'll know more then." Liz shoved her tights and dancing shoes into her bag before zipping the top closed and returning to Dani's earlier question. "Don't you have plans?"

"I was wondering if you were available to come to the Sheridans' tonight for dinner." Dani shouldered her bag and glanced around the area as if checking to make sure they hadn't forgotten anything.

"I couldn't intrude on family time."

"Well, it's also wedding-planning time, and since I'd like you to be my maid of honor…"

"What? Really?" Liz squealed and then smothered Dani in a hug. Over her roommate's shoulder, she caught a dirty look from Gloria and quickly let go. "Of course. Let's get out of here."

They ducked out of the dressing room and into the cooler backstage area. "If you can drive us over there, then Alex can bring me back here later for my car."

"Don't you usually ride together? I could always follow you." Liz led the way through the auditorium toward the lobby.

"It's okay. He'll understand."

"Understand what?" Alex met them in the lobby.

"I'm going to ride over to your house with Liz. You know, girl talk." Dani patted him on the arm.

Alex winked at Liz, then gathered his fiancée into his arms for a lingering kiss.

Liz cleared her throat. "Save it for the honeymoon, lovebirds."

Dani broke free of Alex's embrace with a giggle. "Save the rest of that thought for later."

"Just giving you something to talk about." Alex waggled his eyebrows, then jogged toward the door.

Liz smiled at Dani's sigh. "Come on. The sooner we get to my car, the sooner you can see him again."

"True. It's getting harder and harder to say goodbye."

"Have you decided where you're going to live after the wedding?" Liz held open the door for Dani as they exited the theater, then pointed to the left, where she'd parked.

"That's still under discussion. Blake and Theresa have offered to let us stay with them for a few months while we save up for a down payment on a house, but I think it could get really—"

"Awkward."

"Exactly. But I don't want to be rude, especially since we're not accepting their help with the wedding expenses."

Liz started her Beetle and followed Dani's pointed directions to turn north. "What about one of the company apartments for a few months? The cast will dwindle over the summer so there would be room temporarily while you decide what to do before fall."

"What a great idea. I'll ask Alex later."

"Before your good-night kiss?"

"You have no idea how hard it's getting. I mean, I want to spend time with just Alex, but it's easier to control the hormones when we're around other people. I can't imagine how we're going to wait another four months plus a week until June."

"Not that you're counting?" She'd laugh, except after kissing Ryan, she knew how quickly temptation could flare up. Waiting months to plan a wedding would be agony.

"I know that look. Spill it."

"Well, I sorta know how you feel, but without the ring and wedding date."

"Oh. Ryan?"

"Yes." Liz felt her face heating up.

"So you told me about how he comforted you after your dad's nasty letter."

"And then we ended up kissing on the couch until his niece got home."

"That was almost two weeks ago. What's been going on since then?"

"The days I'm not performing at the theater or working in the box office, I've been over at his sister's house helping him work on his business."

"Hmm." Dani pointed to the stoplight ahead. "Turn left at the light, then take your second right. So, other than kissing on the couch one time, this thing with Ryan is all work?"

"Not all work. There have been a few dinner dates and a movie too."

And the time last Thursday morning when she went into Cheryl's kitchen to get a drink and Ryan trapped her against the countertop, nibbling on her neck while she giggled and squirmed against his big body until his mouth moved to cover hers and—

Dani giggled. "You should see your face right now. I know the feeling, but … be careful. Emotions are powerful things, so make sure you've got strong boundaries in place. And accountability." She swallowed hard. "In fact—this is so embarrassing—but I'd like you to ask me the tough questions every day I spend time with Alex. Every. Single. Day."

"Okay." She swallowed hard just thinking about what those questions might involve but knew Dani's heart was to do things right and start her marriage on a strong foundation.

Dani pointed toward a duplex at the end of the street. "It would be easier if I could just spend more time with you, but you're not around much either."

"Sorry, but Ryan's much more fun. Plus, I get such a rush of energy from the photography side of things." She parked in front of the house.

"I don't think I asked what he's been up to since the Christmas-show pictures finished." Dani got out of Liz's car and then started up the driveway to the opposite side of the duplex from where Alex had just disappeared.

"Um, shouldn't we be…"

"Nope. We always have dinner at Margaret's."

Liz glanced from one half of the house to the other. The family spent time together both inside and outside the theater, the director and his wife and son on one side, with his mother—the theater's costume designer—on the other.

"Oh, and I should warn you… Jake and his adoptive parents live on this side too."

"Making me the"—Liz attempted the math in her head—"ninth wheel?"

"My guest and maid of honor." Dani opened the front door to Margaret's house and called out a hello.

"In the kitchen, Dani." Margaret's voice filtered down the hall.

Soon the older woman had put the two girls to work, tossing a fresh salad to go with her roast, and Dani repeated her earlier question about what was going on with Ryan's work.

"He approached a couple of bridal shops to see if they knew of any last-minute couples looking for a photographer in February. He has a wedding lined up Valentine's Day weekend and one for a couple of weeks afterward."

"I might have to ask him to be our photographer." Dani nudged Liz's side with her elbow. "Except he might be your plus-one instead."

"Or he might not be willing to make a commitment that far out. He's taking it a month at a time until his brother-in-law gets home from Afghanistan."

Dani frowned as other members of Alex's family drifted in and out of the kitchen, helping to set the table and fill water glasses. "So he might not be sticking around here?"

And that innocent question was enough to keep Liz up at night, dreaming of ways to persuade him to stay. "I'm helping him create an online business, but while that grows, he's still trying to fill in the gaps. He'll do those weddings, but he's also lined up some freelance work for the newspaper, covering college basketball games, and is pursuing a few other ideas as well."

"I can see how a guy would rather shoot pictures of sports than a wedding." Alex's cousin Jake reached around Liz for a stack of napkins.

"Especially when he's already ridden in an airboat while shooting pictures of alligators in the Everglades."

"Alligators? Then he should definitely be prepared to deal with bridezillas like Dani."

"I am not a bridezilla." Dani looked up as Alex entered the room. "Just the man to defend me."

"Did I hear somebody talking about alligators?"

Dani groaned. "Not you too."

Liz laughed. "Before he landed in Fort Collins, Ryan had quite a few freelance assignments. I was just telling Jake about the alligators in Florida, but Ryan's also traveled all over the United States and to places like Peru and the Panama Canal."

"Sounds exciting," Mr. Sheridan spoke up. "What also sounds exciting is eating this meal while it's hot. Is the salad ready?"

"Sure thing, boss." Liz added the salad tongs to the bowl and followed the rest of the family toward the dining room.

Soon they were gathered around the table and Mr. Sheridan led the group in prayer, adding a request for patience while they waited for a kidney transplant for his sister, Jake's mom. As the serving dishes passed around the table, the conversation turned toward the wedding; Liz soaked in the family atmosphere so unlike her own upbringing. Like her few meals with Cheryl and her kids, love and laughter were freely shared. But under it all was a strong foundation of faith. God was here.

The conversation shifted to wedding planning, and it became apparent that the Sheridan clan measured time theater-style. First up was the current show of *Seven Brides*, then *Anything Goes*, followed by the wedding right before the dress rehearsal for *Annie*. Leave it to Jake to point out the obvious parallels, as if Dani and Alex's wedding was just another show complete with costumes, meal planning, and stage decorations.

Dani slapped Jake's arm and then snuggled up against Alex's side as ideas flew around the table.

Anyone who saw the love between the happy couple couldn't help but get excited about planning their wedding. But when the conversation shifted back to the theater business, Liz's attention faltered.

She must be tired, with the long weekend of shows behind her, because why else would a discussion about reviews and increased revenue cause her eyes to glaze over? She blinked twice and regained her focus in time to see Mr. Sheridan watching her closely.

After dessert was served and cups of coffee sipped, the family began to drift away from the table. Mr. Sheridan stood too. "Liz, can you join me in the other room for a few minutes?"

"Sure." She exchanged confused glances with Dani, who then turned to Alex with a frown. Liz followed her boss into the living room and took a seat on the couch while Mr. Sheridan began to pace, his typical stance while thinking.

What had they been talking about earlier to make Mr. Sheridan seek her out? Did it have something to do with the wedding? Perhaps the budget?

That must be it. "Are you wanting my help to convince Dani to let you help pay for some of the wedding expenses?"

"What?" Mr. Sheridan stopped pacing. "Well, yes, but that's not what I..." He sat on the other end of the couch and faced her. "As the director, I've been very pleased with your level of work. I mean, you learned the Christmas show so quickly, and then the photography angle was an added boost to the holiday season and our website. Plus you've done a great job as Milly."

"But?" She braced herself for bad news. Why else would he have such a serious look on his face. "You're warning me that this is my last season?"

"Not really."

"Then what's the problem?"

"I couldn't quite put my finger on it until tonight when you were talking about your boyfriend's business and adventures. You had an extra energy about you that I haven't seen on the stage lately. I can tell your heart really isn't at the theater. At least not anymore."

"Isn't that what love does? Makes everything seem brighter? Or maybe I'm starting to get bored with singing the same songs." She scrambled for an excuse. "I'm not the only one feeling a little restless. Just ask Dani. Some of the girls were talking today about mixing up the couples for a little variety."

"Maybe. But I sense it's deeper than that with you." He stared deep into her eyes until she realized not only how much he cared for her heart, but also the truth and wisdom in his words. "All I'm asking is for you to pray about it. I would hate to see you go, but I would understand if God has a different direction for your life."

Chapter Nineteen

"Yuck, you put green beans in there." Hannah groaned.

"Minestrone has vegetables in it." Liz gave the pot of soup another stir, then glanced over her shoulder to where the little girl colored a picture at the kitchen table.

"I still want macaroni and cheese." She stuck out her bottom lip in the most adorable fashion.

"Well, I happen to like soup on a snowy day like today." Cheryl entered the kitchen, twisting her hair up into a messy bun after changing from her work clothes. "But I suppose we can expand the menu just this once."

"Goodie." Hannah jumped down from her chair and skipped over to the pantry to search for a box.

Cheryl stopped next to Liz. "Smells delicious. Thanks for babysitting this afternoon while Ryan finished up that photo shoot ... but when I invited you to stay for supper, I didn't mean for you to do the cooking."

"I didn't mind. Besides, I like spending time with your kids." Playing games together allowed her to spend time with Ryan while still being chaperoned.

"Even I know that Ryan's the main attraction. But still, homemade soup is a nice surprise. I wasn't sure my little brother could handle anything more complicated than ordering pizza."

"Hey, I heard that." Ryan's voice echoed down the hall from the living room. "I can make soup."

"From a can." Cheryl rolled her eyes, then moved to the sink to fill a small saucepan with water to cook Hannah's noodles.

Liz's kitchen experience wasn't much better than Ryan's, except she'd found an easy recipe online and improvised from the canned goods on the shelves.

"Good news, Liz." Ryan rounded the corner into the kitchen with Matt riding piggyback on his shoulders. "We've got three more sign-ups for the newsletter, for a total of thirty-five so far."

"In just a couple of hours?" Liz rested a hand over her heart. "And to think I was a little worried about the price of the ad."

"We're doing more than breaking even, for sure." He jostled Matt until the boy squealed, fake-dropping him toward the floor and gently setting him down.

"Boys, no roughhousing in my kitchen when there's food on the stove." Cheryl turned on the burner under the pan of water. "Why don't you make yourselves useful and whip us up some garlic bread?"

"Aye, aye, boss." Ryan sent Matt to the pantry for whatever bread he could find, while he set a cookie sheet on the counter beside Liz. Of course, he had to reach around her to get the garlic salt from the spice rack—and used the proximity to drop a quick kiss onto her cheek.

If only they were alone.

Then again, it was probably a good thing they were surrounded by others, knowing how fast this kitchen could heat up. Dani's accountability talk on Sunday made more sense every day.

"This is the last box, Mom." Hannah returned, shaking a blue-and-orange box, and set it on the counter next to Cheryl.

"I'll just put it on the grocery list for tomorrow." Cheryl crossed the kitchen to scribble a note on the magnetic pad attached to the refrigerator.

In her absence, Hannah grabbed a chair and slid it toward the vacated spot in front of the stove.

"Oh, no you don't, little miss." Cheryl stopped her progress mid-kitchen. "You know the rule. No hot stuff until you're tall enough to stand on your own two feet by the stove."

"You're a meanie."

"No, I'm a nice-y. The rules are there to protect you from getting hurt." Cheryl softened her reprimand with a sideways hug, then diverted her daughter toward getting out place mats for the table.

Liz glanced up at Ryan with a smile. "Did she learn that line from your mom?"

Cheryl laughed as she joined them at the stove. "I've heard it more times than I can count."

"Guilty as charged, sometimes. But I wasn't the only kid in the house." Ryan crossed to the fridge just as Matt brought up a variety of mostly empty bread bags. The boy then ditched the job in favor of helping his sister set the table.

"Just the last one." Cheryl opened the box of macaroni and poured the noodles into the now-boiling water. "So what's this you were saying about a newsletter ad?"

"We're experimenting with a pay-per-click advertisement to see if people searching for information about cameras would also be interested in signing up for Ryan's photography-tips newsletter." Liz untwisted the wire from one bag and removed two hot dog buns. They somewhat resembled breadsticks but would broil best if divided into halves.

"At five bucks a month, the more subscribers, the better for the bottom line." Ryan came over with a tub of spreadable butter in time to see Liz pull out an English muffin. He laughed, handed her the butter, and returned to the fridge. "I'd better add bread to the list."

"About that bottom line. How red is it?" Cheryl stirred the macaroni with a little more force than necessary, the spoon clanging against the sides of the pan.

"Just pink. Like a medium-rare steak."

Liz laid out a few more pieces from the ends of several loaves and then picked up a knife to spread the butter. It might be the most interesting assortment in garlic-bread history, but when surrounded by a loving family and lots of laughter, nothing would taste as good.

"Explain yourself, young man." Cheryl propped one hand on her hip and waved the spoon at her taller brother.

Ryan grinned at her antics, then batted the spoon away so he could give her a sideways hug. "The first few months, we used some of my savings and the Christmas-picture money to make up for John's pay cut while you searched for work. Your new job is just about covering the difference. So now my income is bridging a tiny gap, and I've got enough jobs lined up through the end of the month to pay for Matt's surgery bills."

"So this newsletter thing?" Cheryl returned to stirring. "It can go toward rebuilding your savings."

Ryan sprinkled garlic salt onto the crazy assortment of freshly buttered bread. "No, first, it will go toward Matt's physical therapy."

"And your savings." Cheryl glared at her brother when he nudged her aside and slid the pan of bread into the oven. "John told me to keep track of what bills you've paid so we can pay you back when he returns."

Ryan spun the dial for the broiler and pushed the timer button. "What if I refuse? I thought that was what family was for. Besides, I should pay something for room and board while camping out in your guest room."

"I can't put a price on your coming in so I wouldn't be alone with the kids while worrying about my husband overseas. Not to mention, you've been taking care of them while I'm at work, so I didn't have to hire a nanny. So listen up: rebuilding your savings is the least we can do to say thank-you."

He sighed. "I'll think about it."

Cheryl wrapped her arms around him. "Thank you."

"Group hug!" Matt shouted from across the kitchen, and before he and Hannah had latched onto the adults, Ryan reached out an arm to include Liz in the family circle.

The beautiful moment felt like coming home ... until it was rudely interrupted by a beeping from the oven timer.

"Uh-oh. Let's not burn supper." Liz pulled away. "That's the last of the bread."

A flurry of knocking on the front door interrupted them about halfway through their meal. Ryan was closest to the door and stood. "I'll go see who it is and what they need."

Cheryl rolled her eyes. "Probably some neighborhood kid needing us to buy a magazine before their quota is due tomorrow."

"If it is, I'll come get you. You're better at saying no." He winked at his sister and then disappeared down the hall. A moment later, the murmur of deep voices filtered through the house to them.

Cheryl groaned. "A grown-up salesman."

"The worst kind." Liz dipped her garlic-covered hot dog bun into her soup broth and took a bite. Actually, it wasn't half bad, all things considered.

Ryan returned a moment later and cleared his throat. "Um, Cheryl, can you come here for a minute?"

She tossed her napkin beside her soup bowl and stood. "Leave it to a woman. Just for that, you owe me a pan of brownies later."

"Deal." His voice sounded strangled as he watched her leave, and then he stared at Liz, the kids, and the food. Something about his expression set her nerves on end. As if memorizing the moment or bracing himself for...

"Oh, no!" Cheryl's cry cut through the tension in the room, sending Ryan scurrying back down the hall—leaving Liz behind with two very confused children who needed a distraction while their mother apparently learned something bad. Hopefully it was about a neighbor, not her husband.

Liz pasted a smile on her face. "So, Miss Hannah, are you going to eat all the macaroni and cheese, or will there be any left over for Matt and me?"

The little girl patted her stomach. "I'm full. You or Mommy can have it. Matt only likes it if there's hot dogs in it too."

Matt stared for a moment more at the doorway where his mom and uncle had gone, then swiveled back to face the table. His green eyes stood large in his ashen face as if he had a feeling about what was wrong.

"I used to like ham cut up in my mac-n-cheese. Ham is kinda like hot dogs." Liz caught Matt's attention and then tilted her head slightly toward his sister.

"Um, yeah. Those are good, but I'm not very hungry anymore." The little boy squared his shoulders as if trying to be the man of the house.

Had his fears about his dad been justified? *Lord, that's too much weight for such a tiny guy to try to carry.*

"So, I heard your mom say something about brownies. I hope you're not too full for dessert once we're done with dinner, because otherwise I might be tempted to eat the whole pan."

This time the change in topic worked, and soon the trio discussed their favorite desserts and how much they could eat.

A few minutes later, Ryan returned to the kitchen alone.

Matt rushed to his uncle's side. "Did Dad die?"

"Oh, no, kiddo. He didn't die." Ryan carried him back to his chair.

"Daddy?" Hannah started to cry.

Ryan glanced at Liz, then gathered his niece and nephew onto his lap. "He did get hurt, though. Really bad."

"Is he in the hospital?"

"Where's Mommy?"

"Your mom is packing a bag, because she's going to travel a long way to where your dad is so she can help him get better—and I'm going to stay here with you." He held the kids close while they cried, then caught Liz's eyes over their heads. Tears welled in his eyes too, and she hurried around behind him and rested her hands on his shoulders, her cheek alongside his.

This man, who had carried so much of this family's burdens so far, needed help. But so did Cheryl before she forgot to pack something important.

Liz pressed a gentle kiss onto Ryan's cheek before straightening. "I'm going to see if Cheryl needs any help packing since girls are better at such things." She patted his shoulders, then moved around the table to pick up Cheryl's abandoned bowl and spoon. "I'll see if I can get her to finish eating, too, since it could be a long trip. When you're done with your dinner, maybe you can help Hannah and Matt bake those brownies we were talking about."

Ryan frowned as if she'd lost her mind, but the children's crying eased.

She mouthed, "distraction," and he slowly nodded. With the kitchen trio taken care of for the moment, Liz hurried down the hall, past the two sober-faced uniformed military officers waiting in the living room, and up the stairs to the family's bedrooms.

She paused in the doorway to the first room where Cheryl hugged an armload of shirts and stared at a framed photograph on her dresser. Liz took a deep breath and then hurried over to face Ryan's distraught sister. After tugging the clothes out of Cheryl's hands, she replaced them with the soup bowl. "Eat this."

"I couldn't possibly … when…"

"It's going to be a long trip, and you need your strength, so eat."

Cheryl sank onto the side of the bed and lifted the spoon.

"Where is your suitcase?" Liz quickly inventoried the haphazard collection of clothes already on the bed. With this random collection, Cheryl would be stuck with two dozen summer shirts to go with a single pair of jeans and no clean underwear.

"Top shelf." Cheryl waved a hand in the general direction of the walk-in closet. "They just about scared me to death, showing up here. Said they tried to call me at work, but I was out of the office at an event and my phone was turned off so it wouldn't be a distraction."

"What happened?" Liz ducked into the closet and soon had her hands on a medium-sized suitcase along with a rolling carry-on bag and a travel toiletries kit.

Cheryl hiccuped. "A roadside incident. That part is classified. He was medevaced to a field hospital and is now on his way to the main hospital in Germany."

Liz set the bags on the other side of the bed and opened them. "And so you're going to Germany?" She detoured for a few warmer layers; after all, it was the first week of February.

By the time Cheryl was done sharing all she knew about being met in Washington, DC, that night for another briefing and how John's serious condition needed to stabilize before he could be transported back to the US, Liz had stacked a week's worth of complete outfits into the suitcase.

A minute later, she steered Cheryl into the bathroom to collect the right makeup and other necessities. Soon a robe and nightgown, extra shoes, a couple of novels, a laptop with cord, and a phone charger had also been added to the bags.

"Do you need your passport? And how are you on cash?" Liz paused beside the open bags and tried to think of anything else Cheryl might need to spend a night in a foreign country and occupy her time sitting at a hospital.

"Whew. Good call." Cheryl crossed the room and dug into her sock drawer, coming up with the familiar blue folder. "I've got some cash and my debit card for more."

Meanwhile, Liz spied a framed family photograph on the bedside table and carefully placed it in the middle of a stack of clothes.

"Thank you. John might appreciate seeing the rest of his family while he recovers." Cheryl paused beside Liz and took a shuddering breath.

"And he'll have you right there to hold his hand and tell him how much you love him." Liz squeezed her arm, then zipped the bags closed. "Let's get you downstairs and on the road."

A few minutes later, while Cheryl hugged her kids goodbye, Liz slipped the last few granola bars into Cheryl's carry-on for her to eat while on the plane.

Then Ryan wrapped his sister in his strong arms. "Don't worry about the kids. You just focus on John."

Cheryl blinked at him. "But what if something goes wrong here?"

Liz patted her on the shoulder. "We're just a phone call or text away. There will be lots of people there to help John, and I know Matt here is going to help Ryan." She winked at the boy, and he nodded back with a half smile.

Ryan caught on to her ploy to help Matt feel as if he were in control for a moment. "That's right, buddy. I'm going to need you, especially with packing lunches in the morning."

After another round of quick hugs, Cheryl left with the officers. Liz and Ryan tried their best to distract the kids with brownies and even a movie, but soon everyone resorted to a collective time of tears and prayer until finally the kids fell into an exhausted sleep in their beds.

Back in the kitchen, Liz loaded the last of the dishes into the dishwasher and wiped down the counter while Ryan sat at the kitchen table with his head in his hands.

"How on earth am I going to do this?"

"With God's help." She pulled a chair over beside him and rested her head on his shoulder. "And mine. And if the kids end up eating more pizza or hot dogs or mac-n-cheese in the next few weeks than they have all year, then so be it."

He swiped a hand over his face. "I'm worried about John. Not so much that he'll die and leave his family behind, but what if he's permanently disabled? Unable to work again and saddled with enormous medical bills?"

"Hold your horses, cowboy. Why don't we wait until she gets there and actually sees him before you start putting him into a chair or with prosthetics for life? In the meantime, I'm here to help you as you handle the home crew one day at a time."

"One day at a time. Right." He took a deep breath and nodded. "So this is Wednesday, February third. Making tomorrow…" He checked the cluttered family calendar on the fridge. "Tomorrow is Matt's post-surgery appointment at one o'clock. Hannah's going to a birthday party on Saturday, and next week there are school Valentine's Day parties with cards to address, boxes to decorate, and I hope no treats to bake."

"Ahem. One day. Just think about tomorrow." Liz squeezed his forearm. "I can come back to watch Hannah while you take Matt to the doctor to get his cast off, but I'll need to leave here at four o'clock to get to the theater for the evening show. Maybe I can do the grocery shopping in the morning while you meet with that couple to finalize their Valentine's Day wedding."

"I almost forgot about our meeting." He called up the calendar on his phone and quickly punched in a few notes while looking at the schedule on the fridge. "Speaking of groceries, I'll have to buy Matt a hot lunch tomorrow since we don't have any bread left for sandwiches. But I'll also need to get you the—uh-oh. Cheryl usually gives me the envelope of grocery money when I go shopping for her, but it's probably still in her purse."

How many other things had they forgotten in the packing rush?

Matt swiped a hand over his face as if collecting his thoughts. "Okay, the first question when we talk to Cheryl later has to do with money. I can float groceries and incidentals, but if she's going to be gone for several weeks, then I'll need to know about the big bills like the mortgage and utilities. If they're on auto-draw, then we only need to make sure there's money in the bank, but if we need to write a check..."

"Then we'll figure that out later." Liz started a handwritten list of things to ask Cheryl about. "Number one, bank-account access for online bill pay or deposits. And does she need to overnight you a limited power of attorney?"

"Speaking of bills, if Cheryl isn't working, then I'm really going to need to get some more work lined up. Except the kids..."

"One day at a time, right? But number two on the list is probably contacting Cheryl's boss. I'll bet she forgot to call him."

Ryan's phone rang and he glanced at it. "It's Cheryl." He put the call on speakerphone, then reached over and took Liz's hand. "Hi, sis."

"Hey. I made it to DC and will be staying here tonight before flying over to Germany in the morning. John's heading into surgery right now to have some shrapnel removed." She blew out a breath that whistled through the speaker. "They think he might be stable enough to fly to Walter Reed in about a week."

"That's good news, right?" Liz bit her lip.

"Especially if we can spend Valentine's Day together here in the good old US of A. Now in my scatterbrained rush out of there, I realized I forgot a lot of details. Not to mention, I just dumped a huge load on you."

"It's okay." Ryan squeezed Liz's hand and stared into her eyes. "We're in this together."

Chapter Twenty

"You seem distracted." Liz set aside the menu and studied Ryan across the table at her favorite Italian restaurant. So far, their delayed Valentine's lunch date was off to a slow start.

"It was a hard weekend." He frowned at his opened menu.

"Then I'm sorry I missed it." With her regular weekend marathon of shows at the theater, she hadn't seen or really even talked to Ryan since the middle of the day on Friday, making today's invitation for lunch that much more special.

Except that until he got whatever bothered him out of his system, she might not hold his full attention long enough to ask for his advice. As Mr. Sheridan had suggested, she'd spent the past two weeks praying for direction but still didn't know whether her future lay at the theater. The pros and cons were about equal since she seemed to thrive on the busyness of both, but if she could only walk one path...

"Catch me up on what happened."

Ryan closed his menu. "First, Matt came home upset on Friday because some boy kept making fun of how much his arm shrank while in the cast, so I got to call the teacher and talk about the bullying. But apparently the real trauma came when a girl in his class gave him a certain valentine, and he's afraid she really meant it."

"While we both know there's a limited variety in the package and even if the cards weren't picked randomly, a few somebodies still have to get the mushier ones." Liz grinned at the memory of helping little Hannah address her cards on Thursday afternoon while Ryan helped Matt.

"Unless you buy a big box on purpose and your uncle steals the mushy ones." Ryan reached into his shirt pocket and pulled out a tiny white envelope. "For my valentine."

"Oh, that's sweet." She reached out to take it just as their waiter arrived to take their food order.

Ryan held onto the card until the waiter left. "Now where was I? Ah, yes, this is for my valentine."

She practically snatched it from his hand before he could take it back. "How mushy can a superhero card get anyway?"

"You'll see."

Inside the envelope was a cartoon drawing of Superman. " 'I'd rescue you any day.' Aw, thanks." She glanced up to find Ryan's warm gaze focused on her and couldn't help but remember times he had already helped her, from negotiating a price for her first photos to inviting her to participate in several jobs in his business and holding her on the couch while her life fell apart.

"You certainly have a way with words." She reached across the table and squeezed his hand. "My hero."

In return, he intertwined their fingers on the tabletop as his gaze dipped to her lips. If only they weren't in the middle of a restaurant, taking advantage of the break while the kids were at school.

And yet, the more intense the pull toward him, the more relieved Liz was that they were out in public.

She coughed and latched onto another topic. "So, Friday was the day of the Valentine's Day parties. And Saturday you shot a wedding while Cheryl's neighbor watched the kids. How did that go?"

The fine lines around his eyes deepened with an extra layer of strain. "I really could have used your help ... and I don't say that to make you feel guilty about working. The bride went a little crazy with the list of pictures she wanted, while the groom kept complaining about how long it was taking to get to the reception. It was like watching a train wreck, and I kept wondering how I could get any good pictures when the happy couple was about to strangle each other."

"Ouch. I guess my being there would have helped divide up her list."

"It's more than that. Don't you know? You keep me centered when I'm about to lose my mind. You know what I'm thinking, and a single glance shared across the room is like a private joke. You might even be in another room, but I still know exactly where you are." He leaned forward and pressed a kiss to the back of her hand. "You make me smile with your honest humor yet make me want to be a better man. You make me dream impossible things."

Her breath caught in her lungs as his words kissed her soul. "Like I said, you certainly have a way with words." A lifetime with this man would beat any job at the theater.

"Here you are." Their waiter chose that moment to deliver their salads, and Ryan released her hand to make room for the basket of breadsticks. "Would you like any freshly grated Parmesan cheese on your salads?"

As if the man didn't know that his poorly timed interruption grated on her nerves, which didn't bode well in the tip department.

A minute later, the waiter finally left them in peace.

Ryan's eyes twinkled with humor. "Like I was saying, I know what you're thinking, and cheese wasn't the only thing about to get grated just now."

"True." Drat her redheaded Irish tendencies.

"So, without you, that wedding was just no fun at all. And now I need to load and edit the wedding pictures and get the proof disc ready to send. Most of the money comes from the picture order and not the booking fee, but I'd also like them to order the pictures before their marriage falls apart."

"That's bad."

"Maybe. But it was a frustrating day, and now I get to spend countless hours more staring at their faces, with another hopefully happy couple on the horizon in a couple of weeks." He broke a breadstick in half and used part of it to soak up the abundant dressing on his salad. "I'm glad for the money, but being a wedding photographer is almost as appealing as facing down the mountain of laundry at home."

Liz blinked at the abrupt change in subject. "Laundry can usually wait."

"Especially when I get to spend time with you instead." He took a long drink of iced tea from his glass. "I love those munchkins, but I don't know how moms do it every day. Never-ending laundry, cooking, and cleaning up messes, plus the emotional meltdowns... How do folks do it all, especially the working moms?"

Not that she knew. She'd only gotten a small taste of the necessary juggling in the past few weeks. But apparently her superhero had found his kryptonite.

"Do you need help?" If she could help sort through his issues first, then maybe he could help her resolve her dilemma too. A new cast list was coming out on Friday, and she still didn't know whether she should submit her resignation.

"Not really. You've done so much already. I guess I'm just tired."

"Maybe we shouldn't have come out to lunch." Liz frowned.

"No. I needed to get away. It's only been a week and a half since Cheryl left, and I'm about to lose my mind. "

"Speaking of Cheryl, have you heard any news about John?"

"They finally made it to Maryland and the Walter Reed Medical Center yesterday."

"On Valentine's Day like she hoped."

"True." Ryan nodded, then sat back as the waiter arrived with their meals. "After getting him settled in last night, Cheryl was eager to talk to the doctors today to see if she could find out how soon they may be able to return to

Colorado. She said she'd call me as soon as she knows something." He tapped his phone waiting on the table near the bread basket.

As Ryan shared more of the medical roller coaster his brother-in-law had been riding, Liz sensed an underlying excitement beyond a normal desire for healing. Ryan had been mostly content with his plan to stay around his sister's family until John was originally coming home in April. But now that the possibility of an earlier military discharge loomed, it was almost as if Ryan saw the light coming and couldn't wait to leave his Mr. Mom responsibilities behind.

As if he couldn't wait to fly back into his freelance work and leave his family behind.

To leave her behind.

Was this the answer to her prayers for direction? That she would see the truth now before she fell deeper in love with him?

The realization caused her heart to skip a beat and a few tears to well up in her eyes. She loved this man, and whatever choices he made affected her too, whether he knew it or not. But what was it they said about loving someone and setting them free?

Ryan's phone rang and he quickly smiled and answered it. "Hi, Grant. It's been a long time."

While she could see him taking a call from his sister or the kids' school, why would he talk to some guy in the middle of their belated Valentine's date? She tried to eat some of her baked ziti, but the rich cheese soured in her stomach.

Across the table, she caught a snippet of conversation. "I can see how you'd miss going out on location." With that, Liz assumed he was talking to somebody in the photography world.

Oh. Right. That Grant. His mentor and now a big shot in the industry. No wonder Ryan had taken the call, especially when he'd been worried about his freelance career slipping away.

As she watched, he twirled his fork in his fettuccine alfredo and glanced over at her with a grin. She hadn't seen that much joy in his eyes in a while. While she celebrated the fact he'd regained the spark, it hurt that she hadn't been the one to put it there.

She blinked back a few tears and set down her fork before excusing herself to use the restroom and regain control.

Her emotions were too close to the surface, probably because she was already tired herself after a long weekend on the stage. And tired of missing Ryan and his family while she was consumed in a different world. Who knew that she'd actually miss the hugs of a little girl and a marathon of Sorry games? How was Cheryl handling being away from her kids?

When she returned to their table, Ryan wore an even bigger smile on his face. "I'll know more in a few days. Can't wait to talk to you." He disconnected the call and met her eyes. "That was an unexpected pick-me-up."

Of course, the energy oozing from him served as further evidence to Liz that she needed to let him go. Despite her best efforts to build his business, she wasn't enough to hold him here.

A moment later, he seemed to realize she was only picking at her food. "Are you okay?"

"Just a little queasy."

"Oh, I'm sorry."

She might as well face the truth head-on. "What was that call about?"

"Just a huge freelance opportunity in Hawaii that would pay about three months' worth of bills with just two weeks of work."

"Wow." The tropics would be a welcome change to combat the lingering chill of winter. And the income would certainly lift the financial burden that had been weighing on his shoulders. Not to mention, it gave proof that once John was recovered and back to work, then Ryan would be free to choose his future path with his professional contacts still intact.

"I have to give them an answer by the end of the week." Ryan picked up his phone and scrolled, then frowned. "I'd have to cancel a couple of contracted jobs here."

"When does the job start? Maybe I could take them on for you."

He shook his head. "You can't handle—"

His phone rang in his hand, and he quickly answered it. "Hey, Cheryl. Are you calling with good news?"

Liz set down her fork and gave up on eating. Just what couldn't she handle? The technical skill involved as a photographer? The business side? Or wasn't she competent enough to handle a job by herself? Surely he knew her better than that.

"Is there any chance you could be back here sometime this weekend?" Ryan leaned against his chair with a frown as he questioned his sister.

The waiter chose that moment to return with their check and the offer of a to-go box for the remainder of her meal. As she scraped her food into the plastic container, Ryan's phone conversation scraped her battered heart.

"Doesn't he have doctors and therapists to help him for a week or so? Because this opportunity won't last."

As if he had to beg Cheryl to return home.

As if he couldn't get out of town fast enough.

She rubbed a hand over her churning stomach and shook her head when the waiter asked about dessert.

Ryan gave her a strange look, then told Cheryl he would have to call her back.

As if he didn't want Liz to hear how excited he was to leave.

Turned out she had gotten that answer about her future after all. Ryan was on his way out of town sooner rather than later.

At least the theater couldn't break her heart.

Chapter Twenty-One

The annoying buzz of her phone vibrating on the bedside table drew Liz out from under her pillow. Just the thought of Ryan's leaving sickened her, making it easy to convince him to take her home to rest after their botched lunch date.

She had then cried herself into exhaustion while alternatively asking God to help her be brave enough to let him go and for the courage to face at least one more season in the theater no matter how boring it got.

And now the sometimes-considerate Ryan probably called to see how she felt. Why couldn't he cut things off in one fell swoop instead of stringing her along until he packed up all his stuff and set foot onto a plane?

She pulled the phone close enough to spot Cheryl's name on the screen instead, then bolted upright as she answered the call with a flood of adrenaline rushing through her veins. What else could have happened to their family?

"Maybe *you* can explain to me why Ryan would turn down a huge job?"

"What? I thought he was taking it." Liz propped her pillow against the headboard and leaned back. "You should have seen how excited he was when he got the call today at lunch."

"Except he just texted that he has decided to pass on the opportunity."

"What's that supposed to mean? Pass as in skip it or pass as in give it to someone else?"

"That's what I thought, so I called him back to demand that he answer to his big sister."

"I'll bet that went over really well since he's still taller than you."

"Not to mention I'm half a country away." Cheryl's sigh echoed through the line. "All he said was that the timing wasn't right and that some things were more important than a paycheck."

"But the money would have—"

"I know. The amount he'd told me earlier would have paid the bills for months. Then John could focus on recovering completely without worrying about how soon he had to go back to work. And you can't put a price on that peace of mind. I hate to say it, but I really need him to agree to take this assignment."

"If it's the photo jobs here that are holding him back, I offered to cover them, but he said I couldn't handle it."

"That doesn't sound like him. He's always telling me how gifted you are when it comes to people's expressions."

"He's told me the same." Not to mention that a professional like Ryan would never have trusted her with parts of a job like that pre-Christmas wedding if she couldn't deliver the necessary quality of pictures.

" 'Couldn't handle it.' Hmm. Didn't he line up something with college basketball, like where you might not be allowed into the men's locker room?"

Liz frowned. "I babysat the kids one night last week while he did a game, but he didn't say anything about locker rooms—just zooming in for action shots. And how he wished he had my knack for faces. And teasing that maybe we should switch roles for the next game."

"So if he already suggested that…"

"Then my skill isn't the issue at all. What are we missing?" She rubbed a hand over her forehead. "Why can't I step into his shoes?"

"Maybe because you already have a job? Could you really juggle the theater schedule and his contracts at the same time? Isn't one of his things a weekend wedding or something?"

The truth started to dawn on her. They'd never finished that conversational train of thought since Cheryl's call interrupted them. He must have been thinking of the big picture and scheduling.

Liz groaned. "Not to mention that he's also taking care of your kids and already needing to find babysitters like me or your neighbor for photo jobs outside their school hours."

"No wonder he was pushing to know when I was coming home. But John's got another surgery scheduled in the morning, and I told Ryan I didn't know when I'd feel comfortable leaving Maryland."

"Totally understandable." So rather than make his sister leave her husband's side, Ryan would stand by his commitment to watch over her kids. Just as he would never ask Liz to give up the theater in order to help him.

He'd turn down a miracle job instead.

After all he'd already given up in order to be there for his family, he'd give up even more. He'd claim the timing wasn't right and that some things were more important.

Well, she'd seen the look in his eyes, and Ryan's dream was important too. "I won't let him do it. Two can play the limit-myself game."

"What are you talking about?"

Liz clambered out of bed and began to pace the small floor of her shared bedroom. "What if I *didn't* have a job that conflicted with his contracts and the kids?"

"But you do."

"For now." An amazing peace began to filter into her heart. "I've been praying a lot lately about what direction I should take, ever since my boss kindly pointed out a few weeks ago that my passion for the theater has faded."

"I don't want you to quit your job for us."

"But what if I was going to quit anyway?" After weeks of confusion, the truth finally clicked into place. "Hear me out. First, would you be okay with me taking care of your kids instead of Ryan?"

"While he takes that amazing assignment that will provide for all of us?" She could hear the smile in Cheryl's voice. "Of course. I trust you, and you've already spent a lot of time with my kids. After all, you've been dating my brother for almost two months and you worked together for weeks before that. If I had reason to worry, I'd have said something long before now."

"Good." One hurdle cleared. "Now, how soon would he need to leave? I don't remember him saying anything other than he needed to give them an answer by the end of the week."

"I think it's Monday morning because he wanted to know if I could be in Colorado by Sunday night."

That was quick but possible. She could do the shows over the coming weekend and still give the company plenty of time to move her understudy into position and choreograph any changes during the next two weeks. Gloria would be thrilled to take the spotlight again.

"I think I can make that work, but I would obviously need to talk to my boss to give proper notice." She glanced around the bedroom. "Then I'd need to move into your place temporarily." At least until Ryan returned from his assignment. At that point she'd need to find a cheap apartment of her own since this room was part of her salary at the theater.

"No problem. Take our room until we need it. Oh, and I can take care of another limited power of attorney and notify the school too."

"Before you do that, let me contact my boss and make sure Ryan is on board."

"Good luck with that. He's stubborn sometimes."

"Well, so am I."

Liz disconnected the call but continued to pace.

She was going to take over Ryan's local responsibilities and photography contracts whether he wanted her to or not. And in the process, she'd free him to pursue his passion and help his family at the same time.

Joy welled up from within her and spilled over into a growing smile and a few happy tears. She had never felt more alive and complete. She might be giving up her theater career, but that was what love did. It sacrificed for others.

Except this didn't feel like much of a sacrifice after all.

She'd lose a career in show business—as if that offered any long-term financial stability anyway—in exchange for pursuing her true passion behind the lens of a camera. And with a wealth of ideas and God on her side to guide her every step, pursuing this new dream wasn't that big of a risk.

Especially if Ryan ended up as part of the package.

Now she only had to convince him.

Maybe she should talk to the Sheridans first so it was official and not just a suggestion for him to shoot down.

Early on Wednesday morning, Liz called Ryan and he answered on the second ring.

"Hey, beautiful. Are you finally feeling okay?"

"Never better." Or at least she would be once she had convinced him to accept her gift. "Could I stop by after the kids leave for school?"

"Of course, but you don't have to ask. I'm always happy to see you."

Emotion clogged her throat as she recalled the heated look in his eyes at the restaurant on Monday. She coughed to clear it. "Then I'll see you soon, cowboy."

She eyed the Superman valentine beside her clock. This time it was her turn to do the rescuing. To help Ryan dream his impossible dreams. To bless him with freedom while she tackled Mount Laundry in his place.

And suddenly she knew exactly how to approach him.

After a quick stop on the way, she arrived on Cheryl's doorstep with a red gift bag in her hand.

Ryan let her in, then wrapped her in a warm hug. "I've missed you."

"It hasn't even been two days." And yet she squeezed him back, soaking up the memories to give her strength for the weeks ahead, before slipping out of his arms and handing him the bag. "I never got around to giving you a present on Monday."

"That's okay. You didn't need to give me anything. All I gave you was a mushy superhero card." He led her to the living room and sat on the couch.

"And lunch. And plenty to think about." She nudged the bag on his knee. "Open it already."

"All right." He first pulled out the gourmet-food magazine and eyed the cover with raised eyebrows. "Just because I got my break taking their pictures and Grant runs the company now, doesn't mean I need this ... unless you're implying that I need to learn how to cook more than pizza, hot dogs, or mac-n-cheese."

"Go on and open the rest; there's a theme."

He set the magazine on the coffee table, then pulled out a four-pack of chocolate pudding cups. "Umm?"

She took pity on his look of confusion. "I'm not hoarding the pudding. In fact, I'd like to trade you for some carrot sticks, if you have any."

"I think there might be some carrots in the refrigerator." He looked at her as if she'd lost her mind, then glanced at the magazine on the coffee table before reaching into the bag again.

The last item was a new memory card for his camera with a Wonder Woman valentine taped onto the front. " 'I'll let you ride in my invisible jet.' " He followed her handwritten arrow and turned the valentine over. "It's my turn to rescue you as I wish you hours of joy from behind the lens while you use your gifts to pursue your dreams." He looked up. "That sounds like what I—"

"Told me at Christmas. And like I said, now it's my turn."

He looked at the collection of gifts before him. "What's this really about?"

She took a deep breath. "It's my way of saying that I won't be continuing at the Wardrobe Dinner Theatre after this weekend."

"What? Oh, honey, I'm so sorry. I know that acting is your love. Maybe you can get a job at—"

"No." She smiled. "Acting has slipped quite far down my list of favorite things. Actually, they wanted me back for the next show too, but there's something I have to do instead."

He frowned. "Go home?"

"Nope. Home is here." She spread her arms wide.

"I'm confused."

"I'm not leaving. You are."

"Now I'm really confused."

She fought the urge to kiss the perplexed pout off his mouth. "I talked to your sister, and I'll be moving in here to stay with Matt and Hannah so you can jump on a real plane—not an invisible jet—to fly to Hawaii."

"Wait, no. I can't take that job."

"Do they already have someone else lined up?"

"No. They're hoping I'll change my mind."

"Well, you just did." She slid closer to him on the couch then tapped the magazine and memory card. "You have a gift and a dream." She pointed at the pudding cups. "And they are pretty sweet, but you gave up your dream for a season so you could be here for your family because you love them. But now it's time to let someone else help *you* for a change. You get the chocolate pudding, and I get the lunch-packing, laundry-washing, kid-corralling carrot sticks."

"But why?" His eyes searched hers for the truth.

She cradled his face between her hands and stared deeply into his eyes. "Because I love you and that's what love does."

His cheeks rose under her palms as his smile emerged. "You love me?"

"Yes. Now try to keep up." Her smile grew to match his, and she lowered her hands to rest on his shoulders. "I've already talked to the Sheridans, and after this weekend, my understudy will fill in for the last four weeks of the current show. And since I've come to the inevitable conclusion that I love photography—and other things and people—much more than acting, I'm charting a new path. So that leaves me with lots of free time to pack a few lunches during the week and weekends off to take pictures of a wedding and such while you go be your heroic self earning the big bacon."

"The big bacon?"

"You know what I mean." She tried to shove against his shoulders, but he didn't move. "Seriously. It's like we're a team. You take that amazing job doing what you love and earn the money your sister and brother-in-law need. While I help out here by doing what I love."

He trapped her hands against his chest. "Which is?"

"Photography ... and family."

"You're really letting me go? I might have hoped, but I didn't think I could have both the job and the girl."

"Well, you do now."

"I don't know what to say."

"Just say yes."

"Yes. Absolutely yes." He pulled her onto his lap. "And thank you." He dropped a quick kiss onto her lips before gazing into her eyes. "I promise, we'll be back together as soon as I can arrange it." His gaze dropped to her mouth again, and her lips tingled in anticipation. "By the way..."

"Yes?" she whispered, glimpsing his heart through his eyes.

"I love you too. So very much."

He sealed his declaration with a toe-curling kiss, then crushed her against his amazing chest until their heart rates slowed.

"If I'm really going to do this, we've got a lot to do." He lifted her gently off his lap and took a deep breath. "First, I need to call Grant. And then I need to get you up to speed with the kids and the handful of jobs here."

She missed him already, but all it took was a single glance at his face to capture the depth of his excitement and know that she'd made the right choice by letting him go.

And only God knew how soon he'd return.

"I'll call Cheryl to let her know that you agreed, and then I'll need help with moving my stuff over here. Are you free on Friday morning?"

"You need me for my truck or my muscles?"

"Both." And for so much more.

Chapter Twenty-Two

Friday morning found Liz stuffing her comforter—or at least trying to—back into the bag she had stored under her bed. The other linens would have to wait in a trash bag until she eventually found another apartment.

Assuming, of course, that her new place had a twin-sized bed. Otherwise, hello Craigslist for a little extra money.

Across the room, Dani wrestled with a precut sheet of cardboard, constructing a box according to the cryptic instructions printed on the side. "I'm going to miss you."

"I'll still be around at the shows this weekend even if I'm not sleeping here tonight."

"You know what I mean." Dani secured the base flaps of the box and set it upright on the now-bare mattress. "Promise you'll stay in town."

Liz squished the air out of the bag holding the comforter until the zipper easily closed. "I promise that I will be here for your wedding."

"You'd better." Dani gave her a quick hug. "You've become like my sister."

"I'm going to miss you too." Especially since she had found a family of a different sort within the theater cast.

Liz set the packed bedding next to the growing pile in the middle of the room. She had moved a few pictures and enough clothes for a few weeks into her large suitcase, collected her bathroom stuff into a smaller bag, then packed everything else into the boxes Dani had constructed, leaving the last box free for food from the kitchen.

There was a knock on the front door, and Liz glanced at Dani's alarm clock. "That must be Ryan, right on time." She smoothed the hair that had escaped her ponytail.

Dani smirked. "Maybe I'll get to be in your wedding."

Liz fanned her hot face before rushing to let Ryan in and lead him back to her room. "If you can get started by carrying these boxes down to your truck, I just need to finish packing my food in the kitchen."

"Okay." He eyed the large pile in the middle of the room with raised eyebrows, then shrugged before reaching for his first load.

By the time Liz had finished in the kitchen and carried that box down to his truck, Ryan had already made multiple trips. She followed him into her former bedroom and realized they could get the remainder in one last trip.

Ryan stopped beside the last couple of bags and eyed the emptied half of the room, where Dani had started to spread her things out. "Um, Liz... Why are we moving all your... Oh." He got a funny look in his eyes, like he had just realized that by quitting her job, she was now also homeless. Like he was thinking about canceling his trip.

"Sit down a minute." Liz patted a spot on the mattress and waited until Ryan sat beside her. "Remember how you told me that your mom knew your heart wasn't in running your father's ranch? Well, I bet you could have done it."

He looked confused at the change in topic. "I grew up there, so yeah. Maybe not as well as some people, but I could have operated a ranch."

"But would you have been happy there for life?"

"No. It would have grown less fun and eventually I would have dreaded another year and come to hate it, probably. Are you saying..."

"Well, the theater was becoming that way for me."

Dani protested from across the room. "How could you hate the theater?"

"It's not that I hate it. I just love something else more." Liz turned back to Ryan and rested a hand on his knee. "Remember when I told you about shooting the drama department's production for the campus newspaper? Well, as I headed back to college after that awful Christmas, I remembered the energy backstage and wanted to be a part of something that alive. To recapture some of the joy I'd felt as a child when I was dancing." She thought of the painting nestled once again inside her suitcase.

"So you changed majors on a whim of emotion?"

"That's probably true, but then again, I really loved the variety. The challenge of learning new dances."

"What changed?"

"Dani knows that I'd been taking pictures for fun here and there, but you came along and opened the door to a dream I thought I'd forgotten about. And I started getting pulled in two different directions, and my boss noticed."

"He what?" Dani stopped shifting hangers in the closet. "He didn't ask you to quit, did he?"

"No. But the night I was over at their house, helping plan your wedding, he said he could tell that my heart wasn't in the theater anymore. He told me to pray about it and said he'd understand if God had a different direction for my life."

"And you've prayed about this?" Ryan covered her hand with his.

"More than anything in a very long time." She took a deep breath and stared into his eyes. "*Seven Brides* would have been my last show with the company, so I would have had to move out in a month anyway. Your job opportunity just moved up the timeline a bit."

He slowly nodded. "So you've got a place to stay at Cheryl's for the next couple of weeks."

"And while you're gone, I'll be looking for a cheap apartment, just like I would have been doing anyway."

"Got it." He stood. "Let's get your stuff out of here so you can get settled in before the kids get home from school."

"And before I need to leave for the theater and tonight's show." She gathered up one last armload and followed Ryan out of the room and into the future.

Liz straightened the blanket covering the stack of unneeded boxes along the wall of John and Cheryl's room, then set her framed copy of her and Ryan and the snowman on top, beside her grandmother's painting that leaned against the wall. To her right, her suitcase stood propped open like a temporary closet, and she'd already claimed a corner of the master bathroom counter space.

While she might still need to rearrange a few things, she was as settled as she could be for the moment. Her purse, keys, and packed theater bag even waited on the chair beside the door.

Taking a deep breath, she studied the painting for another minute. In the chaotic planning of the last few days, the meaning of the twirling dancer amidst the seasons had changed. She didn't have to dance professionally anymore in order to express the joy found in her relationship with God. The Maker of all nature's beauty loved her and, in turn, let her love others.

Starting with Matt and Hannah and Cheryl ... and Ryan.

She stepped outside the master bedroom and eyed the kids' rooms across the hall before turning toward the stairs down to the main floor. Hopefully she would be able to hear them if they needed her in the middle of the night.

Focus on Love

Halfway down the stairs, she heard a chair scraping across the kitchen floor, and her stomach fluttered in response. She'd been alone in this house with Ryan before while Cheryl was at work and the kids were at school. She'd even slept on the couch on Christmas Eve and tried not to think about Ryan sleeping down the hall in the guest room.

What was it about moving in that brought an extra level of intimacy?

And awkwardness...

Pushing her nerves aside, she rounded the corner into the kitchen and ran right into Ryan.

"Hey, there." Warm hands on her upper arms kept her from falling. "All settled in?"

She nodded. Except she felt far from settled as she continued toward the cupboard for a glass. A warmth on her back followed her as she crossed toward the fridge, intending to get ice and water from the door.

Enough already. She turned to face Ryan, only to be captured by the intense hooded gaze that drew her toward him.

They met in the middle of the room, and he brushed a finger down her cheek. "I'm finding it very hard to concentrate, knowing you're upstairs." His voice grew husky. "That you'll be sleeping here."

"I know what you mean." She swallowed hard. "So I guess it's a good thing that the kids will be home soon and I won't be around much with all the shows this weekend ... and that you're leaving in a few days at the crack of dawn."

"What if I don't want to go?" His eyes dipped to her lips.

"You won't be gone forever."

"Even if it feels like it?" His attempt at a puppy-dog expression melted her heart.

She patted his chest. "I'll still be here when you get back."

"Promise?"

Fifteen minutes before the call to preshow, Liz avoided the chaos caused by the posted cast list outside the dressing rooms and instead stepped through the wings onto the dimly lit stage.

Beyond the closed curtain, several hundred people were finishing their meals and making their intermission dessert selections. Those cast members waiting tables tonight would be hustling to refill drinks while other castmates put the finishing touches on their stage makeup or double-checked their costumes. Somewhere above them in one of the rehearsal rooms, the band members would be getting out and tuning their instruments. And near the back of the auditorium, Mr. Sheridan and his nephew Jake would be testing the microphone batteries and handing out headsets.

She paced out to center stage and took a deep breath as she closed her eyes. Soon the bright lights would blind her to the audience and she'd be lost in a fictional world, singing and dancing … and soaking up her last memories of this glorious adventure.

But in a few days, she would officially move on to a new chapter in her life.

"Saying goodbye or regretting your decision?" Gloria entered from stage left and stopped a few feet away.

"No regrets." Liz turned to face the woman who would be finishing the season in her role. "I'm glad you've got the chance to take a lead role again, even if it's only for a few weeks."

Gloria quirked an eyebrow. "So you knew about that joke of a cast list?"

"No." Liz glanced back toward the dressing rooms. "I didn't look since I wouldn't be here, but I assume you're not happy."

"That's putting it mildly." Gloria huffed. "They put Renee and Sarah in the top two female roles, and I'm stuck in the ensemble again. While Evan's already flirting with his new costar. Ever since I hurt my knee, nothing's gone my way around here."

"Nothing?" Liz gestured to the stage around them. "You're about to be Milly."

"A lot of good that will do. The future isn't looking so bright."

"Some things are more important than the spotlight."

"Well, I guess I haven't found them yet." Gloria looked around the stage area as if she, too, were saying goodbye. "And I'm not sure I'll ever find them here."

Liz fought a yawn as she stumbled down the stairs early Monday morning. A tiny light and the smell of coffee drew her toward the kitchen.

Thank the Lord for caffeine, because after the crazy pace of the theater, she'd spent her off-time getting familiar with the kids' schedules, Ryan's business contracts, and soothing Hannah's tears as more of her family prepared to leave.

Except only the aroma of coffee remained in the empty pot sitting on a still-warm burner. What was that Cheryl said? That Ryan stole all the coffee?

Liz shook her head and started a new pot for herself.

A *thump* echoed down the hall, and soon Ryan appeared, rolling a massive hard-sided suitcase with an almost-as-massive camera bag strapped onto his back. A giant travel mug in his hand completed his ensemble. He had sorted through his equipment last night as they went over more photography-business items, and she had wondered then how many bags he planned to take. If everything he needed was in those two bags…

"Leave any room for clothes?"

He looked surprised and then pleased to see her. "A corner. And yes, I packed clean underwear."

Her face grew hot at the thought of…

Nope. Not going to go there with him in the room.

He laughed. "You are priceless."

"And you are incorrigible."

"That's a big word for this early in the day, especially before you've had any coffee." He raised his mug. "Sorry about that."

She glared at him and folded her arms over her rumpled sweatshirt. "What time does your shuttle get here?"

"In about ten minutes." He eyed her mouth. "Did you brush your teeth?"

"Yes. Did you pack your toothbrush? Chargers? Passport?"

"I'm only going to Hawaii, but yes. Did you pack yours?"

"Yes, yes, and yes, even though I still haven't had a chance to use it."

"So why get one?" He tilted his head to the right as if confused.

"A graduation present to myself. Like a down payment on a future dream." Behind her, the coffeepot began to sputter. Finally.

"Any last-minute questions?"

She eyed the handwritten schedule on the fridge next to the list of emergency phone numbers. And the grocery list, with Laundry soap written in capital letters.

The difference a week made.

Last Monday, Ryan was the one feeling overwhelmed and worn down by the home duties, and now it was her turn to carry that weight for him. And since she'd already been helping out some over the last few weeks, it shouldn't be too hard to handle. Hopefully.

"I think I've got it."

"Good." He motioned her closer. "Then I need to hold you for a few minutes and remember why I'm leaving."

She wrapped her arms around his waist and underneath his backpack, resting her cheek over his heart. "You're going out into the world to slay the dragons and find the gold that will keep your family's castle safe and secure."

"That's quite a story. Are you sure you're awake?" His breath stirred her hair moments before he kissed the top of her head.

She smiled, then lifted her face. "You took all the coffee."

He brushed a finger along her cheek. "I can share." His coffee-flavored kiss was cut short by the ringing of his cell phone.

He groaned, then talked briefly to the shuttle driver, who had just pulled up outside.

She followed him to the front door and, after a final quick kiss, watched while his bags were loaded. He waved goodbye and soon the taillights disappeared from sight.

As she shut the door, a small voice called down the stairs behind her. "Liz? I just threw up."

Chapter Twenty-Three

Midmorning on Saturday, Liz welcomed Mrs. Stewart from next door into the house.

"Thank you so much for coming over again."

"Nonsense." The older woman set her large purse on the entry table beside Liz's camera bag, then hung her wool coat on a hook in the entry. "I'm just doing my part to help thank John for his service to our country." She turned and wagged a finger at Liz. "And don't you dare tell Cheryl I refused payment. If she insists, tell her we worked out a deal."

Liz clamped her hands on her own silk-covered hips. "And just what kind of deal is that?"

The older woman's eyes twinkled. "Today, you've given me the perfect excuse to sit around and read some of this wonderful novel I picked up instead of being harassed into helping my husband clean out the garage. My engineer takes his pre-spring cleaning very seriously." She shuddered. "I should be thanking you for letting me come over today."

"Well, the kids are in the living room either watching a movie or working on their new puzzle. I was just about to start fixing their lunch, but there are several other options for you and for supper."

"Don't worry, dear. We'll be fine, especially now that everyone is healthy again."

The reminder of their bout with the flu was enough to make Liz's stomach churn.

She'd have felt bad for Ryan's having to deal with similar symptoms while on planes and in airports, except she'd been too busy juggling buckets and handing out 7-Up and saltines to think about it much. The house had been thoroughly disinfected and the laundry pile almost caught up before she went down.

She'd barely recovered in time to shoot the college basketball game on shaky legs.

Speaking of which... "I still owe you a batch of chocolate chip cookies for helping out on Thursday night." Liz led the way to the kitchen.

"If you've got the ingredients, maybe the kids and I could bake them ourselves this afternoon."

"Only if they want to help." Liz laid the bag of chocolate chips on the counter next to the box of mac-n-cheese and supper-idea list, then checked the flour canister. "But what will you take for Tuesday night? Ryan had one more basketball game lined up."

"We can deal with that later. Tell me what's new with the rest of the family." She picked up Liz's list off the counter and skimmed the ideas.

"John had a slight setback, but they've got him stabilized. Cheryl's not sure when he'll be transferred to this part of the country. Then it's still unclear whether he'll need to stay at a rehab hospital for a few more weeks or be able to come home with outpatient or in-home therapy instead."

"And the kids' handsome uncle?"

Liz smiled. "After island-hopping around Hawaii the past few days on a different assignment, he's taking pictures of a surfing competition today."

"And you're headed to a wedding."

Liz glanced at the clock over the stove. "Soon. Can you take over the lunch prep for me?"

"Sure." Mrs. Stewart set down the list and reached for the box of noodles.

"By the time the reception is done and I've taken pictures of the getaway, I should be home by seven. I hope. But my phone number and Cheryl's are on the bottom of the list."

"Relax, honey. Those haven't changed since Thursday night. Now you head off to work."

"Yes, ma'am. And thank you."

Liz hurried to the living room to give the kids quick hugs and a reminder to mind their manners with the babysitter before slipping her fancy coat over the same dress she'd worn to the last wedding she'd photographed.

Hopefully the clothes would help her keep her mind on the job, even if they also reminded her of Ryan's presence at that event ... and their first kiss later that night.

Focus.

She checked the equipment in her camera bag a third time for the charged batteries, spare memory cards, and the extra lens Ryan had said she could use since he wouldn't be taking it with him to Hawaii.

All set.

With a deep breath for courage, she grabbed her things and headed outside to her car. The drive to the small church on the outskirts of town wasn't long enough to complete her personal pep talk. Instead, she masked her nerves with a smile and sought out the wedding coordinator.

But as soon as she looped her camera strap around her neck, the familiar motions took over along with an extra dose of creativity and then confidence. With each passing minute, she moved further away from being a hobby photographer and substitute pinch hitter.

While juggling all the required shots on her own proved to be a challenge, there was an element of joy, too, in finding unique variations for the traditional group poses. And by the time the cake was cut, she fully embraced her new role as a professional photographer and future businesswoman.

Yet something was still missing from the experience. Or was it someone?

The following Thursday, Liz's phone rang while she was transferring a load of laundry into the dryer. Ryan's picture covered the screen, and thoughts of him filled her heart. It had been ten days since he'd left town.

Ten very long days.

"Hi there, cowboy."

"Hey there, beautiful." Something in his voice sent a quiver of apprehension up her spine.

"How soon until you're headed back?" She held her breath as she leaned against the wall.

"Um, that's why I'm calling. I've got another day or two to finish up my original assignment and get the right pictures for upcoming articles in three different magazines. But Grant just asked if I could extend my stay for another week or so since I'm already here. Seems they've added more photos to the list and would like to also have a range of high-quality stock photos for a new magazine launch. Then he mentioned a new project under development."

"Oh." She gripped the phone over her ear and clutched a hand over her aching heart.

"You're awfully quiet."

"Just missing you."

"I miss you too. Ten days, but it feels like forever."

She drew in a shuddering breath and tried to change the subject to something safer. Something less likely to make her cry. "I'm a bit jealous of your adventure. And honestly more than a little amazed at your boss. I can't imagine the amount of organization required to coordinate the artistic needs of so many publications in order to maximize your travel costs."

"He's got an amazing staff that handles a lot of that, and he pays them big bucks in return. Speaking of which…" He then named an additional freelance fee that made her head spin. And that was on top of his expenses.

"That's an insane amount of money that would pay a ton of bills."

"And restock my savings account." He sighed. "I know. And that's why I'm so torn. I want to be two places at once."

She swallowed her boredom and the selfish desire to see him. "I can't believe I'm saying this, because I really miss you, but it will only be another week. Since you're already there, of course you should stay."

"Are you sure?" Hesitation and hope warred in his voice.

"Absolutely. In fact, Cheryl called this morning to check on the kids and told me they might be coming home in another week themselves."

"Great news. So the end is in sight, and with this extra job, I'll have a great big welcome-home present for them."

"Exactly. You're doing your part over in Hawaii, and I'm doing my part here."

"Sounds good, partner."

Together they were making a difference.

But, God, please let this season end soon.

Liz slipped the disc containing all the watermarked wedding proofs into the plastic case and snapped it closed with a *click*. Once she delivered it and the small stack of ordering forms to the happy couple, she would be completely caught up with Ryan's photography contracts.

She closed her laptop and pushed it to the center of the kitchen table before standing to stretch. With the basketball-game invoices sent and several more photography-tips articles preloaded for the newsletter subscribers, she was in a waiting game.

Of course, she would still be waiting for the wedding orders to finalize so those pictures could be printed, but in the meantime, it was probably time to start looking seriously for an apartment and another job to help pay her rent.

Except she didn't want just any job. She wanted a photography job.

She could wait until Ryan returned, to bounce around a few ideas, but that meant more time with only laundry and cleaning and kids to keep her occupied.

Maybe it was time to visit the local library and stock up on a little reading material to get her through the week. Or jog around the block before the kids got home from school.

A few minutes later, she laced up her tennis shoes and headed outside. The weather was relatively mild for being a week into March, but spring was still weeks away. Turning the corner at the end of the street, she leaned into an icy breeze and wished for her warmer sweatshirt. About the time tears began to leak from her wind-chapped eyes, her phone rang.

The perfect excuse to stop and walk back to the warm house with the wind at her back for a change.

She tugged the phone out of her pocket and swiped the screen with a smile. "Hi, Cheryl."

"Guess what?" The woman's voice was higher-pitched than normal. "We're finally coming home."

"That's awesome." The kids would be so excited to see them again. Cheryl had left town a month ago, not to mention how long John had been away serving. "When?" She'd need to move out of their room, wash the bedding, deep-clean the house, and... "What did you just say?"

"Today. We should arrive around five, Colorado time."

Liz checked the time on her phone and returned it to her ear. "That was fast." Six and a half hours. She started to jog.

"That's the military for you. When they issue orders, they get executed." Cheryl laughed. "So I needed to make sure that you'll be home. There's a pharmacy delivering his medications this afternoon, and then a home-health agency will be bringing a hospital bed, a wheelchair, and a walker. Just have them set up the bed in the living room so John can rest while still being with the family."

"What about your room?"

"He should be fine to take the stairs once a day for now."

Liz began a mental list of her own. Moving her mountain of boxes downstairs to the guest room—Ryan's room—and washing both beddings topped her priorities. That would be followed by a quick grocery run, probably right after Hannah got home. "Is there anything special he's been craving that I can fix for supper?"

"Oh, boy. Yeah. Mexican food like enchiladas or chile rellenos. Hospital food is so bland, though. You'd better make sure we have some antacids on hand in case my warrior can't handle the jalapeños." Cheryl's laughter rippled through the phone line.

What indescribable joy she must be feeling, to know that her family would be reunited under one roof soon.

"And some of those canned cinnamon rolls for breakfast…" Her voice faded as she talked to someone in the background. "Make that a couple of tubes, including one with the orange-glaze frosting. I'll call you if we think of anything else before we get on the plane."

Liz reached the front door. "We'll see you soon."

Six frantic hours later, the house was spotless and the pantry restocked, two pans of enchiladas bubbled in the oven, the living room had been transformed into a medical oasis, and two eager children perched backward on the couch while keeping watch for the airport shuttle.

Never mind the gigantic mess she'd left in the guest bedroom after shoving her things inside and shutting the door. There would be plenty of time for sorting later while trying to ignore the scent of Ryan's spicy cologne that lingered.

After all he had done—and was currently doing—to help this family, he should be here to welcome his sister and brother-in-law home.

"They're here." Matt's cry drew her away from setting the kitchen table and toward the entryway, where the front door stood wide open. Cheryl appeared briefly for a round of quick hugs, then disappeared with the newly delivered walker.

Within minutes, the children chattered alongside their father as he slowly navigated the sidewalk with their mother's help. Liz helped the shuttle driver carry Cheryl's suitcase and John's military duffel bags into the house.

Over the next hour, Liz drifted farther and farther into the background as the family enjoyed a meal together and then moved into the living room. Once there, Matt swapped surgery stories with his dad while Hannah snuggled on his lap and Cheryl flitted around, making him comfortable.

As John gathered his family around him to pray together, Liz slipped away to clean up the kitchen. She didn't belong here anymore, especially without Ryan.

After loading the dishwasher and wiping down the counters, she pulled out her laptop. It was time to move on.

Fifteen minutes later, Cheryl entered the room and eyed the screen filled with temporary job listings. "What are you doing?"

"I've just about finished all Ryan's contracts, so I'm looking for a job before I put a deposit on the cheapest apartment I can find. It's time for me to get out of your hair since your family is all together again."

Cheryl rested a hand on Liz's shoulder. "Just wait a few more days until we know Ryan's plans."

Chapter Twenty-Four

Two days later, Ryan called. "I heard you're looking for something to do."

"And a place to live." Liz glanced down the hall to where Cheryl was helping John with some of his physical-therapy exercises, then slipped into her temporary bedroom for a little privacy. "Not to mention, I'm not really needed here anymore. You would not believe the number of casseroles the church ladies have brought over."

"I can imagine." He chuckled. "So, since you're looking for something to do, I have a suggestion that would take up a couple of weeks. How does taking pictures in the South Pacific sound?"

"The real place, not the musical, right?"

"Of course." His chuckle brought a smile to her face.

"It sounds amazing, but aren't you still in Hawaii?"

"For now. Until you get here."

She sucked in a quick breath. "And then?"

"If you'd like to put that passport of yours to use, I need your help with a new job that will bounce from Fiji to Tahiti to Samoa. We'd fly out on Saturday morning."

"To do what? All I've really done is the theater and that banquet and a couple of weddings. Oh, and the basketball games too."

"What you've done is take remarkable pictures of people's expressions. Not to mention, I've also seen a yummy salad and melting frost on a twig. And like I told Grant—"

"You told him about me?" She pressed a hand across her stomach to settle immediate butterflies.

"Several times. So when he called me on Monday about yet another assignment, he also mentioned sending out another photographer. I recommended you and then sent him a sample portfolio from my laptop. He was as impressed as I've been—and he agreed to hire you."

"He's giving me a job?" Her knees wobbled and she sank onto the side of the bed.

"Darling, he's giving you a dream. Without your having to start at the bottom and work your way up to the choice assignments."

"I don't deserve it."

"We don't deserve our next breath or forgiveness either, but God loves to give lavish blessings. And I'd love nothing more than for you to say yes, sign the extravagant contract that should be arriving in your e-mail any minute, and come take pictures with me."

"How extravagant?"

Ryan quoted a number with a travel allowance that made her dizzy—and then even dizzier to realize that he was sharing his opportunity with her. Did he really want her as a photography partner, or was he just trying to repay her for letting him take the original assignment?

"I bet you're speechless." She could hear the smile in his voice. "But know this. It's not as sudden as it might seem. I've been suggesting something similar ever since Grant called during our lunch date."

She blinked at the realization that Ryan had set this in motion weeks ago. While she was thinking he would leave her behind, he had been energized by the possibility of bringing her alongside him someday to fulfill her own dream.

How could she ever deserve these blessings? Ever deserve Ryan's love?

"Talk to me. Will you do it?"

"Absolutely, even if I still think I'm dreaming."

"Great." He sighed as if relieved at her answer.

"But more than the travel and the cameras, it's you I really want to see."

"Exactly. And..." His voice choked off. He coughed and tried again. "If you had said no, I would have come home."

Liz pinched her arm and took a deep breath. It was really happening. "Well, since I said yes to this adventure, how should I get my plane ticket? And what do I need to pack?"

Twenty-four hours later, Liz and a mob of tourists wound their way toward baggage claim. The adrenaline rush of packing and wrapping up details in Colorado had carried her through her own middle-of-the-night ride to the airport, but after nine hours on a plane with a short stop in California, she now needed an extra-large dose of caffeine.

Or simply the sight of a certain camera-toting cowboy.

And there he was. Wearing a deep-green T-shirt and khaki cargo shorts, Ryan leaned against the nearest pillar, scanning the approaching crowd.

For a brief moment, Liz contemplated ducking into the closest restroom to freshen up and tug the wrinkles from her summery clothes, but she plowed headlong through the masses and into his waiting arms instead.

As Ryan crushed her against his chest, his lips found hers and the past few weeks of separation faded away. Her hands wound up behind his neck, and his mouth shifted for another—deeper—exploration until she could hardly breathe.

Someone bumped into her from behind and then spoke in a foreign language. *Oh, yeah.* They were in the middle of the airport.

She pulled away as Ryan slowly lowered her sandal-clad feet to the ground, but her eyes never left his face.

A moment later, his smile emerged. "Let's get out of here."

After claiming her suitcase and stashing her bags beside Ryan's in the trunk, they piled into his rental car. Ryan leaned across the console for another kiss. "It is so good to have you here."

She kissed him back. "What's the plan for today? Besides kissing."

"Work." He punched an address into the car's GPS system, then pulled out of the parking lot. "I brought a picnic lunch so that we can eat on the road to the North Shore. Today's agenda starts with a pineapple plantation and a coffee-bean tour after that."

"I could use some of that coffee about now." And then a layer of the sunscreen in her bag to make sure her complexion didn't turn into one giant freckle—or worse—under the tropical sun.

"I know. I brought you some." He gestured toward the thermos in the car's cup holder.

"I could kiss you." She untwisted the stopper and poured the steaming liquid into the cuplike lid. *One down...*

"You already have." Ryan grinned as he merged into traffic. "After the fields of coffee, we'll end with a traditional luau and behind-the-scenes access to the whole operation at the Polynesian Cultural Center."

"What's with all the tourist treatment? I thought you said this was work."

He handed her a three-page printout from off the dashboard, and she scanned the sheets, noting a detailed list of requested photographs sorted by location, with a billing code beside each. The footnotes gave an overview of each code's corresponding article, covering topics like farming practices, coffee around the world, and how Hawaii's tourism industry worked to keep ancient customs current enough for the modern visitor.

She laid the list in her lap and took another sip of coffee. "Wow. That's a lot of pictures to take."

"You should have seen the original list when I started—or the new list when they asked to extend my time here. Together, we should be able to get most of this remaining list knocked out today."

"In one day. Or make that a half day since it's almost noon, local time?"

"Okay, so I might be overly ambitious, but I hoped we could relax a little tomorrow instead of cramming in more work before we fly out on Saturday."

The thought of sunning herself on a tropical beach with Ryan brought a liquid heat to her bones. Then again... "It's not work when I'm spending time with you."

He reached over to hold her free hand, trailing his thumb in figure eights across her skin. "True. But just wait until you have to name each individual picture file using those codes. That part alone can take hours."

"I think I can handle that torture if this reward comes first." She squeezed his hand and gestured with her coffee cup toward the window, where the city views had given way to a more tropical setting.

"I can't imagine getting tired of seeing this." She glanced over at Ryan after speaking in time to catch him staring at her face.

He cleared his throat. "Actually, about that... I wondered whether you thought it would be okay if I sent your dad a letter."

"Whatever for?"

"I thought I should at least attempt to bridge the gap, especially since I'm spending so much time with his daughter. Even though it's been a couple of months since that awful letter, it may be too soon to hope for a response or even for his blessing. But still, he might appreciate the chance to know who I am and what I do. And to know that you've quit acting and are now employed by Bricker Communications."

"If it comes from you, he might actually read it. Or better yet, address it to my mom, so she can see it first in case he decides to shred it." She took another sip of her coffee as the possibilities swirled in her mind. "Telling them about my new job might not change anything, but at least we'd have extended an olive branch."

"That's what I thought." He nodded as if the issue were settled. "If you're ready to put down the coffee, I could use a sandwich. Our lunch is on the back seat."

"Sure thing, boss." She drained the cup, then twisted around and retrieved the bag of food.

After eating one sandwich to Ryan's three, she nibbled on pieces of fresh pineapple and mango while rereading the list of assigned photos. "Most of these sound like things they'd show us on a normal tour anyway."

"Yep. I usually just take a lot of shots of whatever strikes my fancy with the story idea in mind and check the list every so often to see what I'm missing."

"And with two cameras…"

"Exactly." That familiar crinkled smile touched her heart. "And by ending tonight with the Polynesian culture, we'll actually get a head start on our next assignment."

"Besides island-hopping, how long is that list going to be?" She waved the papers in her hand.

"That one's different. Instead of an article for the travel magazine, it's for a new series of coffee-table books starting with one about the Polynesian Islands. The authors are still working on the main text, but we'll need to add detailed captions with each picture we shoot of the unique culture on each island. Grant said the more pictures, the better."

"So getting the tour and collecting a ton of brochures tonight or tomorrow will help us know what to expect and what kinds of pictures we will need to take once we get there." Her mind whirled with the possibilities … but first things first.

Today's list.

In Hawaii.

With Ryan.

She swallowed the giddy feeling inside and sat back to enjoy the ride.

And enjoy it she did, from acting like a tourist with a camera strapped around her neck to holding hands with a handsome man as they strolled along designated pathways. She pretended to be a seasoned professional when Ryan handed over his press credentials to their contact at each location, and they were welcomed behind-the-scenes and given access to the perfect places to capture the rest of the shots they needed.

Of course, pineapple-flavored kisses turned into coffee-flavored ones, and eventually they found themselves enjoying a private tour of the luau dinner preparations plus backstage passes as the cast prepared for the evening's show.

Hours later, with their cameras finally stowed underfoot, she settled in beside Ryan for a private dinner-for-two before the show. With each plumeria-scented breath of humid air, reality soaked in. After a few hours of working on laptops in the hotel lobby tomorrow morning, all of the first assignment's pictures would be sent off to the publisher. And then something she'd photographed would actually appear in a big-name magazine. By then, she would be on a plane to even more exotic locations, with a private room of her own and the love of her life staying down the hall.

There had been a day when she had dreamed of taking senior pictures back in Wichita, but God had blessed her with opportunities beyond her wildest imagination.

And blessed her with an even bigger dream sitting beside her.

God, thank You for such amazing love.

"Penny for your thoughts," a warm voice rumbled near her ear.

"I'm just not sure this is real. Part of me still thinks that maybe you're only being nice and letting me tag along as a way to say thanks for helping out with Cheryl's kids and those few jobs in Colorado."

"Nonsense." Ryan shook his head. "You're the one who spotted that truckload of plantation workers and made me pull over."

"I think those pictures are some of the best we got all day."

"Exactly. And you took them."

She bit back a smile. "So I'm here to make you look good to your boss?"

"You certainly give me something good to look at." Ryan wrapped a strong arm around her waist. "But I think we make a really good team—with or without the cameras."

"A team. I like the sound of that." She swiveled to face him.

"Between assignments like these and the online business you started, we'd have plenty of money to support us both. And we can even set up a home base in Fort Collins for between trips."

"We?" Her breath caught in her throat at the potential meaning of his words and the emotion in his eyes. Maybe she wouldn't have to resist temptation as long as she feared.

"I've been praying a lot over the past few weeks about what I want in my life. And like you said, that revolves around photography and family. But now that John is recovering and back home with Cheryl and the kids, my family…" He swallowed hard, then smiled. "My family is you. Will you marry me and make this partnership official?"

Was he seriously proposing in the middle of a tropical paradise? "I don't know what to say."

"Just say yes."

"Yes. Absolutely yes."

He met her halfway for a searing kiss, followed by another, bringing everything into focus even as the backdrop of Polynesian drumbeats called her to the future.

Dear Reader,

Thank you for allowing me to share Liz and Ryan's story with you. I hope you have enjoyed the journey as Liz learned to trust the One who gave her hope and a future. The One who quieted her restless, yearning heart with a love too amazing for mere words to describe.

When I was writing Dani's story (*Dance Over Me*), I found inspiration in an older worship song called "Amazed" by Phillips, Craig, and Dean that talked about God dancing, singing, and painting the morning sky for us…and our being amazed by the depth of God's love. That song had roots in Zephaniah 3:17 which says, "The Lord your God is with you, he is mighty to save. He will take great delight in you, he will quiet you with his love, he will rejoice over you with singing."

That same verse held the theme for this story as Liz learned to focus on the love of God through a personal relationship instead of a list of rules. The Christian life really does boil down to two simple things: love God with everything you've got and then love the people around you. Of course, because we're human, we make mistakes and can hurt those around us instead of letting our love point them to God. Offering forgiveness is one facet of love, but even when human relationships fail, there is still One who is mighty to save.

Dani discovered that God was working behind the scenes in her life, and Liz embraced the freedom found through God's sacrificial love. Soon it will be Gloria's turn to search for something more important than the spotlight as she learns to *Sing a New Song*.

If you have enjoyed this story, I would love it if you left a review and told a friend. You can also sign up at www.CandeeFick.com to receive email updates about future releases.